PRAISE FOR MU...
NAIRO...

"An engaging insider's view of the cultural divide between Americans and Africans." **—PUBLISHERS WEEKLY**

"Once [Ishmael] arrives in Africa, the entire scene bursts forth in riotous color; every detail, view, scent, and character leaps off the page." **—LOS ANGELES EXAMINER**

"A clever peek at life on both sides of the divide ... [Ngugi] makes great use of his considerable talents for description and plot." **—THE GLOBE AND MAIL** (TORONTO)

"Thrilling." **—MACLEAN'S MAGAZINE** (TORONTO)

"Ngugi's ability to weave a complex narrative, which connects crime and racial tensions in the U.S. to an in-depth knowledge of Kenya and its nuances, to Rwanda and its genocide past within this African crime thriller, is nothing but the work of a genius craftsman and wordsmith." **—NEW AFRICAN MAGAZINE**

"*Nairobi Heat*'s biggest triumph is the way it forces us to re-examine accepted narratives and received truths." **—MAIL & GUARDIAN** (SOUTH AFRICA)

"*Nairobi Heat* rises above being just great 'international noir' ... Ngugi took it one step further and explored that murky world and motives of international charities, foundations, and religious zealots, and how the rest of the world pays for their conscience." **—BLOGCRITICS.ORG**

BLACK STAR
NAIROBI

BLACK STAR NAIROBI

MUKOMA WA NGUGI

 MELVILLE HOUSE
BROOKLYN · LONDON

 MELVILLE
INTERNATIONAL
CRIME

For my wife, Maureen Burke, and my
daughter, Nyambura (for her eighteenth birthday)

MELVILLE INTERNATIONAL CRIME

BLACK STAR NAIROBI

Copyright © 2013 by Mukoma Wa Ngugi

First Melville House Printing: June 2013

Melville House Publishing   8 Blackstock Mews
    145 Plymouth Street   and   Islington
    Brooklyn, NY 11201   London N4 2BT

mhpbooks.com   facebook.com/mhpbooks   @melvillehouse

ISBN: 978-1-61219-210-9

Manufactured in the United States of America
1 3 5 7 9 10 8 6 4 2

Library of Congress Control Number: 2013939765

CHAPTER 1
GATHERING CLOUDS

A day before the explosion at the Norfolk Hotel, O and I stood in the middle of the infamous Ngong Forest, looking at the body of what had once been a suit-wearing tall black man. Devoured by the wild animals of Ngong, the man's corpse looked more like an animal carcass. This was the worst kind of death—the victim barely resembled a human being.

It was around midday but it might as well have been midnight, with us canvassing for clues in the light of a full moon—the canopy of the ancient trees let in an annoying in-between light, too low to see well in, yet too bright for flashlights.

O said it first.

"This man has many secrets to tell." He pointed at the man's face—the half smile left on it suggested to me triumph at being discovered.

That was the point of Ngong Forest—a corpse left there sent a message.

In the United States, there's the Nevada desert—and football stadiums, if you count Jimmy Hoffa. In Kenya, if someone with enough credibility told you that he or she was going to send you to Ngong, you had better back down unless you could get them there first.

I hadn't been in Kenya that long, but I could rattle off names: J. M. Kariuki, a radical of this or that, tortured to death, his body discovered by a herd boy. Robert Ouko, a well-groomed politician who had allegedly committed suicide in Ngong: first, he maimed himself, and then, when he didn't bleed to death, he set himself on fire before finally shooting himself in the head. Witnesses for the prosecution and defense all died mysteriously, including the herd boy who, again, had found the body.

It was always a herd boy, venturing into the depths of the forest, who found the dead body. In our instance, he happened to have a cell phone and so we were able to get to the body in a matter of hours.

O and I should have just walked away. Add the detail that the disciplined grouping of the two shots, one through where the heart should have been and the other in the head, suggested a trained and efficient killer, and we should have run.

Had it been any other day last year, we would have. Since O and I set up what we had cleverly named the Black Star Agency three years ago, we had been working the strangest of cases: from missing penises—easy to solve with a sharp knee to the groin— to cheating spouses to rigged local council elections.

We were barely breaking even. It was only because O had never quit working for the CID that we were able to pilfer a missing-persons case here and a murder there, so we managed to stay afloat. Therefore, when Yusuf Hassan, the CID chief, threw the body at us, it was a favor. The CID would pick up the tab as well as pay me a consultancy fee.

More than just being flat broke, you could say we were like boxers who, having slugged through predictable wins, were ready to finally fight a worthy opponent. We were ready for a case like the one that nearly broke us, our first case together—the case of the dead white girl found on the porch of an African professor back in Madison, Wisconsin. Now, I'm not saying finding a missing penis is a waste of time, but sometimes, you just want to do what you do at your best, at its most challenging—not for show, but just because you are that damn good. We were hungering for real work ... and some cash.

"Whoever killed him took the casings," O said, pointing at their absence around the body.

We carefully pulled open the shredded jacket that was still wet from bodily fluids and rainwater. There were some clawed-through American dollars, a few euros, and Kenyan shillings, but no identification. His pants pockets were empty. The suit had no label. He could have been anybody. This much I knew, though: to deserve the brutality of Ngong Forest, our guy had to be somebody.

"We might never figure out who he is," I said, pointing to the barely fleshed bones that had been his hands. DNA was useful only with a large criminal database—Kenya's was in its infancy, and unless we were extremely lucky, there would be no match. And dental records? Forget about it. We just had to hope that the body would yield some secrets.

There was nothing more to do but get the body to the pathologist. We didn't have any body bags and the Administrative Police, or APs as we called them for short, had to carefully roll him onto a woolen blanket.

"Ishmael, you cannot come to Ngong Forest and not smoke a joint," O announced, looking up at the sun filtering in like moonlight.

"We're here—might as well enjoy the solitude," he added and lit up.

O hadn't changed much over the years—he still wore the same leather jacket, even on the hottest of Nairobi days. Though he was now in his early forties, he hadn't put on weight. His thin frame made him look taller than he actually was. His eyes were always bloodshot from sleepless nights and too much weed.

Whenever we were in a dangerous situation, a smile that seemed to suggest he knew something the other guy did not played on his lips. It had taken me a while to figure it out—he had no limits, he could maim, torture, and kill if that was what the situation required. It was just work for him. He had seen and caused enough death to come to terms with his own mortality. Most criminals are ready to kill but not to die—when fuckers met O, he had the advantage.

It was this capacity for duality, almost like a split personality, that ultimately made him dangerous. The good guy worked in the world of nine-to-five; he was happily married and always came home at the earliest possible moment. However, when we entered the world of thieves and murderers, he fit right in and he followed their rules as often as he made and broke them. There were advantages to working with a man like O—he never lost perspective, so much so that he often seemed cold. As long as you were on the same side, you were safe. I had once admired that but lately I had begun to fear what would happen if one day whatever held his duality in place came unhinged—and I happened to be standing on the other side.

"This place, it reminds me how lucky I am—just to be alive, to be walking out of here," he said.

"Any excuse to smoke up?" I said, not believing a single word.

He laughed. "No, Ishmael, any excuse to celebrate life," and he blew the dark marijuana smoke into the forest.

It was a long mile or so to the road and, as O sank deeper into his joint, I sank deeper into my mind, listening to the forest. There are several kinds of quiet: one kind is where everything around you is quiet, another is where everything around you is in rhythm and you are not—like the quiet that comes with white noise. The quiet in Ngong Forest was the noisy kind. We were no more or less loud than the wind forcing its way through the trees, or the laughing hyenas, roaring leopards, and God knows what else; we humans just happened to be making a different sound. The sound of tearing clothes caught in the bushes, well-padded shoes rubbing and pulling against the forest undergrowth, the curse that followed bare skin catching on something thorny. It was as if we were singing out of tune in a loud band. That feeling of being all too human made me want to get the fuck out of Ngong Forest.

We finally reached the road that cut across the forest. The other two APs we had left behind to make sure ghosts and criminals didn't steal the police cars couldn't hide their relief at seeing us. They enthusiastically helped roll the body in another blanket, heaved it into the back of their pick-up, and left for the pathologist.

Naturally, O and I went to Broadway's Tavern to discuss the case over some Tusker beer and roast goat. It was how we did our best thinking.

Broadway's Tavern, located between the slum of Kangemi and rich Mountain View Estate, had become our favorite joint over the last few years. It was an odd bar even on the best of days. Here, thieves, politicians, prostitutes, and cops made peace for the sake of beer and roast goat. It was a place where all those involved in criminal enterprises, be they the good or the bad guys, met. It was an informal trading house for information, where police and robbers exchanged tips—useful transactions, but ultimately self-serving. In matters of life and death, it was good for enemies to keep at least one door open—cops' lives had been saved, as well as the lives of some criminals.

Civilians were not welcome—and I suppose no one without a connection to the underworld would have wanted to come in anyway. The bar was really just one huge room, with chairs made out of thin bamboo, and wooden tables, a jukebox, and a long counter. If you circled outside to the back of the building, you would find an open-air kitchen that made only *nyama choma* and *ugali*, the latter a dish I ate every now and then to remember grits back home.

There were standards to uphold, though: wife-beaters, rapists, murderers, and petty criminals knew to keep away from Broadway's. In fact, more than once, someone at the bar had informed on some petty crook who had mistakenly sought sympathy from the classier professional criminals.

The bar made sense in another way, too, because the difference between Kenyan police and Kenyan criminals is that they just happen to be on opposite sides of the law. O, for one, could have just as easily been a criminal as a cop—and the longer I stayed in Kenya, the more I suspected the same of myself. There was no begrudging the others for the road they'd chosen. In the end, Broadway's was a testament to the fact that we cops had accepted that crime would always exist. And we'd decided to make peace with the kind of criminal that had some professional decorum.

We walked into the bar just as the five o'clock news was coming on. It had taken me months to adjust to how seriously Kenyans take the news hour. All bar TVs change their channels to one of the news stations—regardless of whether there is a replay of a European cup football game on. It was like common prayer, only in this case it provided fodder for beer talk.

As in the U.S., news presenters in Kenya were household names—this evening, Catherine Kasavuli, the Katie Couric of Kenya, was on. MC Hammer immediately yelled that he wanted to marry her. Dressed in the real Hammer's signature golden yellow pants, and with graying but dyed-red punkish hair, this MC Hammer was the jester in this court of police and robbers. He knew everyone and a bit of everything. MC Hammer was like a clown wearing a mask.

Senator Obama dominated the news, as he had since he declared his candidacy back in February—this time, it was about allegations that he was a Kenyan citizen and not an American. "Like being Kenyan is a crime," MC Hammer scoffed.

O and I had been driving back to town from somewhere. I turned on the radio and there it was. Barack Hussein Obama had declared his candidacy. We'd gotten back to Nairobi to find everyone honking, some people waving Obama posters, others selling T-shirts and coffee mugs. Much later, an Obama beer called the Senator would be born, though the knowledgeable suggested it was more of the same—regular Tusker in an Obama beer can.

"Eh, Ishmael, how do you feel?" O had asked. "One of your own as the president of the U.S.A.?"

I had always thought of Obama as black like me. Black people in the U.S. had been at the center of it all—the building of the country, inventions, science, sports—yet somehow we had remained on the sidelines. To be in the White House, finally? And yet, there was something else I could not articulate: I didn't feel like he could truly speak for me. But I guess the moment was bigger than any of us. Bill Clinton as the first black president? It was time to get rid of blackface presidents. I wanted Obama to win.

"How the fuck does racism survive this?" I asked O.

"You'll be surprised—we have had only black presidents and look at Africa, look at how divided ..." he said, turning his head to see my reaction.

"But enjoy it, it is going to be quite something," O said more kindly, when I didn't say anything.

As if on cue, the Kenyan president had got on the radio to say that the following day would be a public holiday. That was a good move; the whole country was going to be hungover tomorrow anyway.

For a moment, I had felt homesick. The strong but tired rhythm of small Madison, Wisconsin, where I had grown up; my parents and their pretense to wealth; beautiful Mo, the Pulitzer-winning journalist I had loved, but who saw me only as a black cop; the United States and its racisms of class and color. In that moment, I missed the career I had left behind. I missed my other life, my parallel life, the life I was supposed to live, the one that didn't involve being in love with a woman like Muddy, or having a partner like O—the life with a pension ahead of me, and if I did not make it that far, at least my own would be taken care of. I even missed the euphemism "died in the line of duty." Only for a moment, though, because the life I had chosen was here, in this country.

News about the upcoming Kenyan presidential elections followed—the usual name-calling—so-and-so was corrupt, a tribalist, and worst of all, it seemed, a politician. There was one piece of news that piqued our interest: large caches of machetes—made in China, like everything else everywhere—had been found at the port in Mombasa. It was not clear for whom they were intended, or for what purposes—the customs police were investigating.

"I have something to say," MC Hammer said, standing up and fanning his bright gold pants as soon as the news went to commercials. "Kenyans taking over the world. Machetes from China. To those who might have bad intentions—just remember. You can't touch this," he said and started dancing. The whole bar shook with laughter.

"Nothing to worry about," a man holding on to a Tusker bottle drunkenly chimed in. "We like to kill a little during election time—but we don't have the stomach for Rwanda. This will pass. A little bloodletting to bless the democracy … A Chinese machete? My noggin is like a fortress—impenetrable." Encouraged by the laughter, he stood up, chugged the rest of the beer, and broke the Tusker bottle on his head.

"I wonder where our guy fits into all this mess," O said to himself.

"Which mess, O?" I asked.

"All this shit—he is somehow connected with everything—elections, U.S., Kenya," he explained his gut feeling.

O called Hammer to us and he glided over.

"What time is it?" he asked us.

"Hammer Time," I answered. He laughed and sat down.

"Have you heard any ghost stories about Ngong Forest lately?" O asked him.

Hammer paused.

"My throat is very dusty, full of cobwebs—the only cure is nectar from the gods," he said finally.

O ordered a Tusker for him. Hammer waited without saying another word until it came and he took a sip.

"This particular ghost was manufactured with a shot to the head and the heart—very clean," O explained.

"We don't do clean—a foreigner killed him … haven't heard

anything, but it sounds like the kind of business Hammer does not want here—when it comes to crime, I am a nationalist. Let Kenyans do other Kenyans." He took his beer and glided off. If he found out something, he would let us know—maybe.

"Our guy fits nowhere until we know more. We find out who he is, and we break this case open. For now, we don't know shit," I said to O.

"I need some fresh air," he said, and stepped outside to smoke a joint. This was a strictly no smoking bar, cigarettes, weed, or anything else.

I was tired. I needed to go home. I wasn't worried about leaving O here, high and drunk; someone, friend or foe, would make sure he got into his Land Rover okay. I took a cab home to Limuru and asked the driver to drop me off a few wooden gates from home. It was a useless precaution because in this small town, all someone had to do was ask where the American lived. Still, I thought it was better than leading someone who wished me ill straight home.

I woke up the following morning to find Muddy at her desk, writing, a joint and coffee in hand. I stared at her for a few moments, mesmerized by her dead-serious beautiful face appearing through the ebb and flow of smoke as she puffed and typed. At times like these, I fantasized about getting old with her—the world remaining this still beauty of streaming sunlight, the only change being Muddy and I getting older and older.

She was wearing a red, green, and black wrap, long beaded earrings, and, unlike during performances, she had her dreads up, so that they seemed to shower around her face. All things being equal, she should have died in Rwanda. Often she wished she had—surviving the death of everyone she loved in a body that no longer felt like hers, joining the resistance and killing over and over again; it was hard to make a life out of those memories.

Older now, her face had lost that innocence I had never known but imagined, and the hardness I had come to know now changed easily into a smile. She cared more about life, hers and the lives of those around her. When I'd first met her, she was trying to figure some things out and hence was more sure; now that she had figured them out she was less sure, like me and everyone else.

There was a knock on the door. It was O, who, after a few puffs from Muddy's joint, offered to make breakfast. We groaned, knowing it was going to be an omelette, the same one he had been making for years now, adjusting the ingredients to a degree only he knew. For years, he had been trying to perfect it. Still, it was food, and the seriousness with which he prepared his omelet made me feel better about my life.

"How is your long-lost wife? After the show we should all go out, no?" Muddy asked. She had a performance coming up at the Carnivore Hotel for the Kenyan elite and the tourists who liked to go there to sample Kenya's wildlife—crocodile, zebra, and, for the right price, a protected animal.

Why did Muddy and Mary get along? I had asked myself that question many times. Mary had done everything right, except for marrying O, Muddy and I joked. There was some truth to that. But eventually I had come to understand that O was just the man she happened to fall in love with—and she had less control over that than over the choice to go a teachers' college and dedicate her life to saving one pupil out of a hundred each year at Kangemi Primary School. I suppose, like Mary, I didn't have much choice either—Muddy was the woman I loved.

"Yeah, she's almost done teaching ... I can see the Promised Land—and Ishmael, we are going to paint it red," O said, and laughed between puffs.

"And Janet? Is she coming?" Muddy followed up. Janet was Mary's unofficially adopted daughter, now a first-year at Nairobi University. Her real parents still lived in Mathare, still drank copious amounts of the illegal *changaa*. Rwandan refugees, they had found their salvation in self-destruction. Years ago, O and I had rescued Janet from a rapist and a life that would have spiraled down to hell. Muddy had given her hope, but it was Mary who became her surrogate mother.

"She can't make it, exams ... so she says. I suspect she has other plans—your performance or having fun with her friends?" O answered.

"My piece, I want it to carry some righteous anger and hope. What do you think, O? Can hope and anger co-exist?" Muddy asked. Now I knew they were both high. This was what they enjoyed the most—philosophizing over a joint—and O stopped chopping the red onions.

"Yeah, they can. Hope in a time like this," he waved his hands around, "hope alone has nothing to hold it to the ground ... it has no anchor, and it has no action. You need some anger in there to keep hope burning. To give it some oomph ..." He forgot about the onion and starting chopping some garlic.

"This piece—I am angry that motherfuckers can't see that Chinese machetes are not for farming—and the rhetoric, I know it too well," Muddy was saying.

"Muddy, you see Rwanda in fucking everything. This is Kenya. We know violence—remember, when other Africans were begging for independence, we were out in the forests fighting," O responded.

"Well, Castro Mao Guevara, I know the rhetoric—people were saying similar things in Rwanda—'a little blood-letting,' you Kenyans call it? There is no such thing as a little blood-letting," she said, managing not to sound bitter.

O started to say something but Muddy raised her arms to interrupt him.

"Wait, wait … Each drop of blood is a flood," she yelled, clapping her hands together in delight and jotting the line down.

O was now cutting a tomato, the garlic left half-chopped.

"What is missing from my motherfucking omelette?" he asked.

I pointed to the mushrooms and the green and red peppers—all from Muddy's garden—that he had yet to chop up. His phone rang.

It was the pathologist on the line. He had something for us. We weren't expecting anything useful. In the U.S., we used to say, "no body, no conviction," but in Kenya finding a body in Ngong Forest meant that you had just another piece of evidence that was as important as the powerful wanted it to be.

"To be continued … We gotta go," O said to Muddy. When high he liked to sound cool, like a rapper. It no longer irritated me. After all, pop black America was everywhere in Kenya, from the hip-hop Kiswahili rappers to teenagers in the streets of Nairobi looking like poor gangsters straight from Camden, New Jersey.

I kissed Muddy goodbye and followed O out.

Peter Kamau reminded me a lot of Bill Quella, the Madison Police Department's coroner back home. BQ was Southern, from the eye of the South, he liked to say, and he loved Southern expressions—he had once described a victim as being as full of blood as a tick. Peter Kamau used a lot of proverbs and riddles and wise sayings that invariably made sense only in his workplace. "Better dead than never" was his favorite.

Kamau and BQ were both tall and thin, and they smoked noisily, smacking their lips as they moved cigarettes from one end of their mouths to the other. It was my guess that this line of work called for certain personality traits, one of them being a love for expressions. Kamau, though, unlike BQ, was a hardcore Christian who prayed for each body that found its way to his table.

When O and I walked in, Kamau was sitting in a corner on a bar stool, as if he were watching a performance. The lights were off, except for the one that shone on the remains of the dead man. Kamau hopped off the stool and turned on the lights, but he might as well have done us a favor and left them off. I thought BQ's lab was bad. In Kamau's lab, bags of ice were laid on top of the bodies to preserve them, and so the floors were covered in this murky mixture of lukewarm water and human fluids.

He called us into his office, which looked like a supervisor's at a manufacturing plant: on the same floor, the only thing that separated it from the lab was a few hurriedly assembled low white-painted pieces of wood with windows stuck into them. At least it was dry ground. He raised his hands up in the air like a priest about to bless both of us.

"The moment I saw that body, I knew it. I knew he was trying to tell me something. Speak and I will listen, I said to the man," he said. "But you, ask and you will receive," he added, pointing at O.

"What do you have?" O asked.

"Your man is black," he announced.

"Shit, Kamau, of course he's black," I said.

"Hold it, open your ears and you will hear—I did not say he is Kenyan or African. I said he was black." He was barely able to contain his excitement, but he waited until O asked him to explain.

"Height, six-two. His clothing, at least what is left of it, appears to be American. But all that is like saying water is wet. I found this in his mouth." He placed two small capsule halves on the desk and brought out a magnifying glass from his back pocket. We peered over his shoulder as he pointed out indentations on the capsule, using a toothpick.

"Some lettering is gone," he explained. "But this eventually spells hydroxyurea."

"Okay, what's that?" I asked.

Kamau straightened up.

"Hydroxyurea," he said, as if addressing a class of primary school students, "is a drug used to treat sickle cell disease. Sickle cell can be a trait or a disease—mostly, black people have it. This type of cell is good for malaria prevention—think of it as nature's immunization. But let's say you were kidnapped from the hottest malaria-infested interior of Africa and exported to non-malaria zones. It becomes a disease—not lethal, but in some cases painful enough to require a doctor's attention—I mean real pain— like you've been nailed to a cross."

"Sickle cell—never heard of it," O said.

"Why would you? If you think you are well, the disease doesn't matter," Kamau said.

I didn't know anything about hydroxyurea, but I knew about sickle cell. My ex-wife and I were tested for it before we got married. She wouldn't bring a child into this world with sickle cell, she had said. Had someone told me that the next time I'd hear about sickle cell, it would be from a crazy pathologist, as a clue in a Kenyan murder case, I would have had *them* tested, for drugs. But here I was, happily thinking that at least my ex-wife had taught me something useful.

"Sickle cell, one in ten black people are carriers. A carrier marries a carrier—they get a baby with the trait, chances are. Only problem with your theory, Kamau—our guy could be from anywhere two black people marry. He could be British—shit, man, we weren't all sold in America. Spain? Brazil? Cuba? How do you know he isn't Kenyan?" I asked, unable to mask my irritation.

"Come on, Ishmael, how many Kenyans do you know that take any kind of medication? And don't you think Haitians, Jamaicans, and what have you have enough on their plates without worrying about sickle cell?" Kamau responded.

He was right. Of all the diseases killing people in Kenya, sickle cell would be like a migraine: take a Panadol pill and go to bed.

"And you know what that means if I'm right?" Kamau said, pointing to O and me. "It means his death was a ..." he lowered his voice, "a surprise. Who stops to take medication when they know their life is in danger?"

"I think Kamau is on to something. Two clean shots—this is not murder Kenyan-style. Now that I think about it, the last clean political murder was in 1969—a trade unionist," O reasoned.

"Murder Kenyan-style? Remember what they did to Ouko? Tortured, burnt, and shot? My friends, this man is as American as apple pie," Kamau said with a silly laugh, poking me in the ribs.

"Okay. I can grant that he isn't Kenyan. Could even be African-American. But let's look at this the other way round. How

does a black American end up dead in the middle of Ngong Forest?" I asked, not expecting an answer.

"How did you come up with this hydroxyurea stuff anyway?"
O asked Kamau, genuinely intrigued.

"My second bible," he said, pointing at a thick yellowing
book on his desk. "That and Google. My friends, I know this
is thin, but sickle cell, an execution in Ngong, the clothes—but
hey, you are the detectives—you have a hypothesis, go forth and
produce."

We turned to leave.

"One last thing," he said, laughing hard. "Remember, the first
shall be last and the last shall be first."

"What else you got, Kamau?" O asked him.

"I found this in his stomach." Kamau took a shiny silver ball
bearing from his pocket.

"What is that?" I asked.

"This was his secret—this is what he wanted found. It's a
riddle I can't unravel," he said. "But I can tell you this, there is
someone out there with a plan, and he won't be too happy if you
mess it up."

He could not have timed it better. Right at that moment, we
heard a loud explosion. The floor beneath us shook. Then, a deep
silence.

"And that, my friends, that is the sound of the plan," Kamau
said into the silence. We rushed outside to see a huge fireball rise
up in the air.

A bomb had exploded somewhere in Nairobi.

I was certain about one thing—our guy had something to
do with the explosion. For someone to want our guy this dead, it
had to be for an important reason, and my gut told me we had
just heard it.

All the people we needed to see would be at the bomb site; we might as well go see what kind of clues we could pick up. That, and curiosity, had us driving toward the city center without saying goodbye to Kamau.

O called Hassan's cell. After several tries, he reached him. The Norfolk Hotel had just been bombed and he was on his way there.

I hadn't felt American for a long time. In fact, I hadn't wanted to. A black man from the U.S., I liked getting lost in the sea of blackness in Kenya, rather than standing out in a sea of whiteness in Madison, Wisconsin. But the idea that a fellow American, a black man like me, could be shot and his body left in the middle of Ngong Forest to be devoured by hyenas stirred up an anger in me that I knew was dangerous. In the U.S., we died in all sorts of ways, but never like this.

My phone rang as we drove toward the explosion. It was Muddy; someone had texted her to tell her that Nairobi was under attack. I told her what I knew—it was just the Norfolk, not the whole city.

O's phone rang—Mary had felt the explosion at the apartment and she wanted to make sure he was okay. It was the first time I had ever known her to call O to check on him and that gave me a bad feeling.

My mind went back to when we had first seen our guy, with his half-smile magnified by the dulled sunlight and the loud silence of the forest. The body in Ngong—it reminded me of English 101, *Antigone*—the king leaves a rebel's body to be devoured by wild beasts … it didn't end well for everyone involved. I just knew there was no coming back from this one—whatever it was.

CHAPTER 2

ANCHORING HOPE

Chaos. Barely two hours after the Norfolk Hotel bombing that had so far left ten Americans, five Europeans, and fifty-one Kenyans dead, the Kenyan Special Branch, CIA, and U.S. Embassy folk—ringed by onlookers and TV reporters with their bright lights—were milling about the bomb site. Car horns were going off randomly, and small fires puttered along until a gust of wind made them flare up, only to be put out by a solitary fire engine that, in true Kenyan fashion, had more men operating it than necessary. There was danger still.

The power company had shut the electricity off—there had been power cuts that morning anyway, though they never touched tourist locations. But a generator trapped somewhere in the rubble kept surging, powering still-attached air conditioners, hairdryers and—this I could not help thinking in spite of the seriousness of the situation—all sorts of sex toys.

The chaos was why we were there. There had to be a connection between the bombing and our man. And maybe we could talk to Hassan and the people from the U.S. Embassy while we were at it. We decided to take advantage of the situation and canvass the site for ourselves. No one had stopped us, anyway, not even to ask us for ID. I guess we looked like we belonged.

The wounded were being rushed to the hospital and the

dead to the city mortuary. There were pieces of flesh and bones here and there, some recognizably human, others so torn apart that they looked like something you would see at the back of a slaughterhouse. The scents of blood, oil, water, and dust mixed with the whispery tangy smell of whatever explosive had been used to make the bomb, a smell that stung the back of your throat. Seeing the destruction in the late morning light drove the cruelty of the terror home. There were aged police dogs, given to the Kenyans by the Americans after the last bombing, sniffing in the rubble, looking for survivors. There would be occasional yells of hope from the policemen guiding them, followed by the overmanned fire truck finally pouring water on the area. And then deflated sighs as it turned out to be nothing.

There were questions of jurisdiction, arguments back and forth. Americans had died, so the U.S. government had a right to conduct its investigations, but it had happened on Kenyan soil and the majority of the dead were Kenyans. Eventually it boiled down to the fact that the Kenyans didn't have the technology to deal with this kind of thing.

The final shots were going to be called by those controlling the purse strings. Back in Wisconsin, when I worked on the force, the Chief would bury some cases. Pursuing justice for one case would mean that there would be no funding to buy bullet-proof vests, or our union would suddenly find itself in the red. It was the same all over.

Hassan was arguing about jurisdiction with a short American man who I didn't know and Paul, the U.S. Embassy spokesperson. Paul looked like the stereotypical Aryan male—tall, blond, and square-jawed. Over the years we had had a few encounters, nothing major or memorable, Fourth of July celebrations at the embassy, someone needing a visa, and so on—but I had never grown to like him for reasons that, if I was honest, would amount to nothing more than the way he looked.

"Ishmael—I hope they won't take our body from us," O said, as we stared at the crater created by the bomb—it appeared to be about a hundred feet wide.

"The man was killed here—they need locals—they need people like us who know the back roads," I guessed.

"You mean the black roads?" O asked.

As I looked at the devastation, I was getting increasingly angry. There was something about the American dead that made the bombing feel personal. A part of me felt violated. I wanted to help with the bomb investigation and find the motherfuckers who were responsible. But O and I weren't bomb experts. We would follow the body. It was what we were good at. Eventually all the threads were bound to connect.

O was cool—like he had seen everything and very little surprised him. And perhaps in this case it was true.

"It was much worse in 1998," he was telling me as we worked our way around what could only be called a crime scene, for lack of a better word.

"In 1998, it was twelve Americans, all of them with names, against about two hundred nameless Kenyans—collateral damage," he said with a wave of his hand. "You know, when two elephants fight, it's the grass that suffers."

O rarely used proverbs unless he was high and feeling lazy, and I did a double take to make sure he wasn't still stoned.

"Hey! Hey! Look at this," O said, pointing at something in the rubble. I leaned in. It was a ball bearing. I saw many more strewn around the site, now that we were looking. I compared it with the one that Kamau had found in our guy's stomach. I didn't have to be a bomb expert to know they matched.

We had something we could use. Beyond Kamau's hypothesis—this was concrete. It was time to go look for Paul and Hassan.

Just when we were about to make our way past what had been the patio, I heard it. The look on my face stopped O, and we tried to make out a sound underneath the sirens and the bulldozers and the jackhammers tearing into debris. It was a faint tapping. O rushed away to get help and I started to tap back, walking toward the sound carefully so as not to upset the delicately balanced debris. The tapping got louder, louder, and more urgent until I was almost standing over it. I started digging madly with my bare hands.

A night watchman, a large man in his fifties still dressed in his heavy raincoat and hat in spite of the heat from the morning sun and the flaring fires, waddled over and started tearing away at the debris with me.

"I am Detective Ishmael. See anything suspicious? Late-night deliveries? Anything out of the ordinary?" I asked him between heaves of heavy debris.

"No, night like every night—everything goes smoothly—then—boom!" he answered. I really had to learn Kiswahili. I had been saying that for years now, but always working with O had made things easier. I understood everyday conversation—asking for directions, ordering food—just enough to borrow water, O always said. Before long, between us and the sound, we came to a large slab over what seemed to be a foundation wall.

"Were you the only one working tonight?" I asked him.

"Nothing happening at night—so, my friends, the other watchmen deciding to go inside—to kitchen to eat," he tried to answer but he could not continue. I gathered that they were all dead or seriously wounded.

"This bomb—I do not know how it get inside. We sweep cars—since five years ago, we sweep cars for bomb," he added. I didn't take that seriously—this was Kenya, where $200 bought you a murder and $20,000 a small massacre. At the right price and in the right hands a bomb could be placed anywhere.

The minutes before O rushed back with the firemen seemed like hours. They poured water over the area. I asked someone why—it was to make sure the people trapped below had some water to drink. By now, all work had stopped and, save for the din of the never-ending Nairobi rush hour traffic several blocks away, all was silent.

I tapped again on the slab. Someone tapped back once after a few seconds and we all cheered before hushing each other. After this day of death, just one life saved would validate our own lives as first responders to all sorts of bad situations. There was an interval of about a second, another tap, and another second before a final tap.

"Three survivors—what else could it mean? There must be three survivors," one of the firemen said excitedly. It hadn't occurred to us that more than one person could be trapped underneath there.

Nothing else mattered—we had to save them. The fireman tapped back three times in acknowledgment.

Just then, the night watchman started yelling something and the firemen pushed him back. From out of the crowd that had gathered around, the short white man, followed by Paul, edged closer to us, and signaled that we should listen to what the watchman had to say. The firemen let go of him and he spoke rapidly in Kiswahili.

"He says ... he says that we are standing above an underground parking lot. Down there they have space, but it is dark and dangerous—and standing up here, we are making it even more dangerous. Get light to them and move away—they will let us know where to dig."

I was surprised to see that it was Paul who was doing the translating for the short white man, and I once again vowed that I would intensify my efforts to learn Kiswahili.

There were no disagreements. We left the firemen to figure it out and we followed the watchman to stand at a distance.

Soon enough, one of the firemen found a crevice through the debris that looked promising. They didn't have tracking equipment, the kind with thermal and vibration sensors, speakers, and headphones. And their only rescue equipment was a bulldozer. It would require ingenuity and most of all luck. I doubted that the three survivors would make it through this "third worldish" rescue attempt.

The firemen tried yelling instructions, but their voices couldn't carry through to the survivors. They debated for a few minutes, and then one of them came over to where we were standing and asked if any of us had an ultra-thin cellphone. Paul happened to have an iPod, so he and one of the firemen taped a message in English and Kiswahili telling the survivors to tap the rescuers to the least debris-filled space in the parking lot.

Meanwhile another fireman had gone to the fire truck and came back with a snake—the kind used to unclog pipes. They tied the iPod a few feet from the tip, but it wasn't thin enough to be snaked through the debris and, after a few attempts, they gave up.

Then the fireman came back and asked Paul for his headphones. From the truck, he unwound a few meters' worth of wire. They cut the jack end of the headphones and rigged them to the wire, which they then gingerly worked down the crevice.

After a few minutes, someone tugged on the headphones and we let out hushed yells of relief, shaking hands with whomever we could. One of the firemen waved us into silence and slowly started to follow the tapping sounds, occasionally backtracking and zigzagging until he stopped where he heard three emphatic taps.

One of the firemen called to the watchman and asked him something in Kiswahili.

"That is the back end of the parking lot—away from the building. That is a good place to dig," the watchman answered as Paul translated for us.

A bulldozer worked its way in slowly from the side of the rescue point. I guessed that a direct approach was more dangerous. Finally, it got to a huge slab of stone. It lifted the slab up but it was too heavy and the dozer threatened to tip forward—something was needed to wedge the slab. There was some debate. Two of the firemen got into two police Land Rovers and, in fits and starts, drove them up the debris to where the dozer was.

"Jesus—these guys are good—you know what they're doing? Cribbing! Shit, it's a rescue technique—I've only seen it done with crates of wood—never with fucking cars," Paul exclaimed to the short white man.

When the dozer lifted the huge slab a second time, they drove the cars underneath it up to the windshields, jumped out, and ran to safety. The dozer now tipped dangerously to the front and dropped the slab down on the cars—flattening the hoods, windshields breaking into pieces, tires deflating—until it was stopped by the heavy engines. The survivors slipped out underneath. There were only two of them.

The fireman in the dozer waited until they had staggered past him before jumping out and yelling at them to run. They had hardly cleared the debris when the bulldozer tipped over completely. Gas and oil started to leak furiously out of the crashed engines. The two cars exploded into flames and the whole parking lot imploded to become a massive crater.

Just as we started to panic about the missing third person, we realized that the survivors were a young black couple, and the woman was holding an infant. Everyone was safe. The two or so blocks around the Norfolk once again exploded, but this time into applause, as it dawned on us that the dead were all dead and the last of the living, this beautiful family of three, were alive. We needed this small victory in these two blocks of uncertainty, of death and hell. The couple and the firemen were hugging and crying by the time we had rushed to them.

The watchman and the firemen had brought the ingenuity; the rest of it was pure luck.

I had never seen anything like it.

The terror the survivors must have felt was gone and in its place was elation. They kept touching each other as if to make sure they were alive.

We pieced their story together. Their Kenya Airways flight from South Africa had been delayed. Shortly before midnight, they had pulled into the second level of the garage in their car rental. They almost certainly would have died had they been fast getting out of the car because they would have been either directly above the bomb a level below them or in an elevator. But the five extra minutes it took to get the baby out of the infant seat and gather her toys and feeding bottle found them still at the farthest corner of the second level of the garage when the bomb went off. Those five or so minutes had saved their lives.

"Who was I talking to? Who heard us?" the man asked, looking around.

"I enjoyed our conversation," I said as I walked up to him. I thought he was going to cry, but his wife leaned into him and they both looked at their sleeping infant.

I introduced myself.

"And I am Jack Mpande—and this is my wife, Nomsa," he said.

"His name?" I asked, gesturing at the baby in her arms.

"Her name is Nothando—it's a South African name," his wife gently corrected me.

"She has been asleep this whole time?" It struck me that we were having a normal conversation at the most abnormal of times.

"Eleven hours a night—the blast, you should have seen her—she woke up, let out one cry, and then went back to sleep. Travel, exhaustion," Nomsa explained, looking down proudly at her baby.

Everyone around us started laughing.

"Quiet," O whispered. "You might wake up the baby."

There was more laughter—a heavy chorus from a rough motley of men wiping away tears. This was a once-in-a-lifetime feeling—to be surrounded by chaos and death, and at the same time, to be looking at a sleeping baby, her father and mother safe and sound, standing in front of us. This laughter, I thought, it was what the Devil and God would sound like if they ever shared a joke—terrifying and uplifting.

"Nothando—what does the word … say?" the night watchman asked as he wiped away happy tears.

"The man to thank," I said to Mpande, gesturing to the watchman. "He figured out how to get you out."

"It means Love," Nomsa answered.

"And hers, my wife's name means Faith—I am surrounded by Faith and Love," Mpande said as he hugged the watchman.

"The small one—in my language—her name is Nyawendo," the watchman said.

This man, and his wife, and his sleeping daughter—I wanted what they had, without even knowing I had been missing it. In their terror, a terror I could not imagine, they were still a family—I wanted to know that feeling. I wanted to have that much at stake in this life—for terror and love to have meaning beyond myself. Amid all this death, and this little glimmer of hope, I knew there and then that I was going to propose to Muddy.

But Muddy, would she want the same thing? I thought back to the first night I had seen her on stage, performing a piece about her grandmother to the expatriates and tourists at Club 680.

I thought of a photo of her holding an AK-47 in Rwanda, trying to stem a genocide, the horror stories of being gang-raped and left to die, the madness that came with revenge killings, with being surrounded by so much death and anger and hatred that she became as cold and numb as her AK-47, and finally, how words had found her and through poetry she had found life again. These thoughts were more of an emotion coursing through me in waves than something that came with words.

"I save love and faith," the watchman yelled to the crowd, to more laughter.

The three firemen were taking turns holding the sleeping baby, rubbing her cheeks with their rough gloves until finally, with a resounding yell, she woke up.

We didn't want the family to leave and we hovered around them until it became a little bit awkward. They needed to get to a hospital and to find a place to sleep—and the rest of us needed to get back to the hell around us.

"Listen—if you hadn't heard us …" Mpande said, and gave me his business card. "If you ever need anything …"

"A cold Tusker will do," I said. He didn't need to thank me. It was me, O, and the rest of the men working the graveyard shift, literally, that needed to thank him, his wife, and his daughter— they had given us a reason to carry on.

The three firemen guided them away from the crowd and into the waiting ambulance, and as they got in, the Norfolk once again resounded with life as we clapped and hugged each other.

O pulled me away from the crowd. We walked over to what had been a hedge and was now a smoldering skeleton.

"The Norfolk was bombed in the early 1980s—I don't re-member the year but it was on New Year's Eve. The Palestinians or friends of theirs claimed responsibility," O said.

"The same people?" I asked.

"That's not what I am thinking. The eighties? Shit, that might as well be another century. You know what I mean? What I am thinking is this—our guy was killed recently. We need records from the hotel, security, repair and guest logs—there has to be a trail of some sort. Whatever can be salvaged, whatever might lead us to the bomb, so we can find his killers," O said.

This was O, so many things happening around us, yet he was still thinking about our case.

"Time to put on my American hat, then," I said, gesturing at Paul and the short white man, and we started walking toward them. On seeing us approaching, they hurried over.

"Jason Lauer, the head of Africa Bureau—CIA. Ishmael Fo-fona. The legend. You, Detective Odhiambo. O, I should say. I'm glad we finally get to meet. In the right circumstances too—you are needed here. You have already saved some lives," he said as he enthusiastically handed us his business cards.

"Luck—we merely happened to be walking by, coming to look for you guys before heading out for a Tusker …" I said. He laughed and looked over at Paul, who was just smiling.

"You mean for a Tusker breakfast? Wait, wait, I'll do you one better, brewskyfast," he said, and broke into giggles, before looking around, realizing where he was, and trying to stop himself. Finally he pulled himself together enough to introduce Paul.

"I'm pretty sure you two know each other," he said, nodding at Paul. We shook hands.

"Good call with the watchman," I said. Paul, he had done good work today—I had to give him that. The group of firemen and policemen wouldn't have listened to the night watchman if Paul had not asked them to. This was one of the things I had yet to reconcile myself to about Kenya—white skin still trumped black skin. However, Paul hadn't kept quiet so that he wouldn't be seen as an interfering white man. In a weird roundabout way, I could respect that.

I explained what we had found, giving them the ball bearings. Paul and Jason didn't seem surprised. But then again, after the bombing of a major tourist hotel, there wasn't much room for surprises.

"We aren't bomb experts, we understand that—but a man was killed in Ngong Forest—that is the case we are going to work," I concluded, stating the obvious.

"If the man is an American, then we would like to have an American involved—that's you. I have learned to listen to the people who know the lay of the land. You two are our best chance. But make no mistake, this is ours, we're calling the shots," Paul said, using the kind of tone that comes with training.

"Come on, Paul—let's give it to them straight—shall we? White guys in Kenya will stick out like … I don't want to say a sore thumb … like a broken white piano key," Jason said, looking at us expectantly. I smiled.

"Ah, Ishmael gets it—black and white piano keys—Booker T. who?" he said, raising his voice, and he high-fived Paul.

"We will help you in any way we can," Paul cut him short.

"Your theory?" O asked curtly.

"Before you came along, we were pretty sure it was Al Qaeda—probably with the help of their friends in Somalia. But with your guy in the picture, it suggests that they had some help from black American Muslims. It was just a matter of time before they joined the party, I guess," Paul said.

"Wait a minute, we didn't say he was a black Muslim, or that he was a perpetrator and not a victim," I interjected.

"I don't see Al Shabaab in this, there are too many Kenyan Somalis—they cannot afford to lose their support in Kenya … You know what I mean? You don't want your support base to be afraid of you—seems kinda logical to me," O said.

"Possible, but terror is irrational. Best to start with the usual suspects and keep widening the net if need be," Paul said, trying to sound less sure than before.

Though I thought O was right, Paul's reasoning made sense—it was how we would approach a bank robbery—start with what you know. O let it go and Jason didn't say anything.

"We need access to any records that might have survived," I said.

"Anything you need," Paul assured us.

But they had nothing yet. Paul asked us to check back with him in a day or two. They would get our guy's fingerprints, or try at least, and his DNA. If they found something sooner he would give us a call.

"And what's your theory?" Jason asked, looking at O and me.

"We have to work our way back—if our man was part of the group that did this, there has to be a trace of him somewhere," O explained.

"Ah, naturally," Jason said. "What I meant was—why would an American bomb a hotel in Nairobi?"

"At this point, no idea—all we have are his balls," I said, and held up the two ball bearings to lighten the mood. We had what we came for—cooperation—it was time for O and me to move on.

Jason burst out laughing and the others turned to look at what we were doing. He laughed so hard that he had to be propped up by Paul, who smiled in irritation as he tried to shut him up. A photograph of them, and there, would easily sink a career—"Diplomat and CIA Section Chief Laugh at Bomb Site!"

"My friends, I'm all tied up here but you and I, we shall share a brewskyfast soon," Jason said, still convulsing with laughter as we walked away.

"That guy was as high as a kite—I can tell weed laughter from a mile away," O said. "I mean, he could have been smoking up at home before being called in."

The Norfolk bombing in 1981, the U.S. Embassy in 1997, and the second Norfolk bombing in 2007. That was only three bomb explosions in almost thirty years. It's not like Jason went to bed every night thinking he needed to be sober in case a bomb went off.

Americans like to think of their overseas operatives as serious people who are guided by their sacred duty to democracy, who, in imminent danger, take extreme precautions. In reality, they were getting high and trying to get laid like everybody else. I started laughing at the absurdity of it all.

Humor in Africa, laughter in Kenya—you just had to be able to laugh—because some things were just funny, like a high CIA bureau chief at a bomb site.

"I don't need to tell you this—this shit is way over our heads, terrorists, bombs, a black American in Ngong ..." O said more seriously.

I agreed. We had no business here. But we had been called in and shown a dead body. We had no choice but to work the case and try to keep our heads above water. We needed the money and a way out of the minutiae of wading through other people's dirt to solve the petty cases we'd been getting. We needed this case more than it needed us.

I was going to work the murder—everything else was going to be background music, no matter how loud it got.

Yusuf Hassan, O's half-time boss, as O started calling him after we set up our private practice, had gone back to his office before we could speak to him. So we drove to the Special Branch headquarters to see him.

Hassan was an ex-military man. Tall and in his sixties, with an ill-fitting suit on a body used to standing and sitting straight, Hassan had been called in from the military to combat crime. He didn't believe in "innocent until proven guilty." In fact, he didn't believe in ascertaining guilt. Suspicion, and only poor young men from the slums were suspicious, meant a bullet to the head.

Kenyans loved him for it—he was a man of action and that's what counted.

I didn't like him, but if it weren't for him throwing O and me cases every now and then, our agency would have gone belly-up. And he had never asked me about my immigration status. I didn't hate Hassan's methods because I was American—it was because I was a black American. Before I was a cop, I knew being black, poor, and urban meant you were the scapegoat that no one cared about. After I became a cop, the stink of racist policing rubbed off on me and some family members called me a sell-out to my face. To see so many killed in Kenya without even the semblance of a court of law reminded me of what middle-class America, white or black, wished upon on the poor black male.

Everyone was happy with Hassan, the tough man from the coast—that's how a newspaper headline had described him. Or as a popular comedian put it: *If you don't wanna float, stay away from the man from the coast.*

O liked to point out that that I, too, had done some questionable things in the course of trying to survive in the Kenyan underbelly.

It was true, I had done some things in order to stay alive that would not stand up in front of an overpaid "Jesus is my savior but I am rich" human rights commission, but I didn't have innocent blood on my hands. For me it was always in self-defense or in the defense of someone else. I had come to know I was good with violence the same way a boxer realizes he is good with his hands—in and outside the ring I was aware of the rules, and whenever possible I followed them.

"This Hassan of yours," I said to O, trying to sound Kenyan. "He has already shown a love for the gun. When the election results are announced and his guy doesn't win, what do you think he will do?"

"He walks away—Hassan is a believer in hierarchy and order. He walks away unless asked to stay on. He is old-school," O replied.

"And between the people and government—who will he choose?" I asked, knowing the answer.

"Hassan will always choose the government. Look, man, elections are not our business—our business is this fucking case, and Hassan will give us what we want. We better find out who killed our guy before the elections—all this other shit will just get in the way," O said.

He was right—all these side questions had nothing to do with our dead guy. We had taken the case, we had to work with Hassan. It didn't mean we had to trust or even like him.

We walked into his office on the top floor of the six-story CID building. His office was always dark except for his desk lamp. He emerged from its light to guide us to leather seats that faced his desk. The office was already big, but its emptiness made it look even larger. I briefed him on where we were.

"The truth is we have nothing. We have an American who has been dead for a number of days. We believe he was involved with the Norfolk bombers, who are most probably foreigners ... but he just might as well be a guy who stumbled onto something he shouldn't have ..." I concluded.

"Talk to the Americans. They like to think they know more than the natives. I suspect that this once they might actually be right," Hassan suggested.

"The Americans seem pretty sure it's Al Qaeda, with a little help from your neighbors," I said. I wanted his response.

"Two things. The terrorists are not Al Qaeda, Al Shabaab, or Somali," he said emphatically.

"How can you be so sure?" I asked. O glanced at me.

"Because we are always one step behind these dogs ... always one step behind. We know the time they are going to strike, but not the day. Sometimes we know the day but not the place. There is always something—a noise. But this ... we had no clue we were dancing. You see? Nothing, not a sound ... in an economy of handshakes, we would have heard something. The people behind this are new, very good, and using different channels. We should be afraid of them—no one should be able to do such a bad thing so quietly. That is why I am inclined to go with your theory," Hassan answered.

He leaned back, then forward, and started looking at his files, which I was sure contained nothing useful. I almost felt sad for him—here was a man who at any moment could be a hero or a criminal depending on who took office after the elections.

"Follow the dead man. Just work your case," he advised. Or warned. It was hard to tell.

"I like having the truth, I like answers. Not for their own sake, or for a greater truth, but because then I can do my job better," he added. "I need to know who the man is, and why he was killed."

"What was the second thing?" O asked him.

"What?" Hassan echoed back.

"You said there were two things, what was the second thing?" O asked again.

Hassan looked irritated for a moment—like he had changed his mind about telling us. Perhaps we had said something we shouldn't have.

"Be very careful—if we could not see these people coming,

neither will you. This is an enemy without a face, a name, and a history," Hassan warned us. "There is no way of knowing where this will take us."

"Mzee, what is going on? These rumors about machetes, are they true?" O asked plainly. *Mzee* means many things. It means "an elder," but colloquially it was used to show temporary deference to someone with more authority than you, regardless of age—like when we used to say "Boss" in the U.S. But "Boss" wasn't the same thing as "Sir," and "Mzee" wasn't the same thing as "Bwana." You could say "Mzee" to a bartender or a bus driver.

"You know, we picked up two shipments … some might have slipped through," he answered, waiting for the obvious follow-up question.

"Where were they going?" I asked.

"The guy who came to pick them up—he knew nothing. He was just supposed to drop them off at this empty hut in the Rift Valley," Hassan said. "We just have to keep watching. This is Kenya—a little blood to bless the winner. But, hey, we have nothing to worry about, we have the guns," he added with a smile.

There were just too many things going on. The Kenyan police were already spread thin by crime and corruption. Now the bomb explosion, with presidential elections just round the corner. Something had to give.

Someone drops a cigarette butt in a California forest and it fizzles out. But sometimes the rains are late, and the ground is dry. And it happens to be windy. That cigarette butt might as well have been thrown into a powder keg. What people like Hassan were refusing to consider was that a little blood-letting, with all these other things going on, could turn into a flood, as Muddy put it.

Hassan stood up and walked us to the door.

"Mzee, who really called us in? And why?" O asked. Maybe that was the second thing.

"I did, O, I thought you said your agency needed a bone to chew on," Hassan answered.

"We need meat, not bones," I said, to their laughter.

"It worked out, didn't it? It makes our government happy that a Kenyan is involved, and it gives the U.S. investigators eyes and ears on the ground," he said, echoing Jason and Paul. "Besides, you can work quietly, especially if that body is American—a lot of people will not want what you find out to be known. Be safe."

I had never understood this side of Hassan—he seemed genuinely concerned about us, yet he was a murderer.

"So we can count on you," O said to him, but it was more of a question.

"To a point—you can count on me to a point—my hands—see the strings?" Hassan lifted up his hands and laughed. At least he was honest.

"Let's close this case. Bring it on home to me," he said, looking directly at me.

CHAPTER 3

FISSURES AND BREAKTHROUGHS

O and I drove to the American Embassy pretty much in silence. We always drove in silence. It was one of those things that would make a stranger doubt our friendship. When we were in a bar, in his house, or at Muddy's, we always had plenty to talk about. There was something about being in a car that called for silence. It had taken me a long time to figure it out, and then I had realized that we never drove to happy places, to weddings, for example. Like men going to war, our silence, at least mine, was meditation.

He slipped in a Kenny Rogers cassette. The rest of the country had moved on to music that sounded like it was being piped through tubes and sung by singers with stuffed noses, but O loved his country music and he loved his cassettes—and the whole process of it getting chewed up and him having to carefully rewind the loose tape.

I, who had grown up in the not-so-mean streets of Madison, Wisconsin, had come to appreciate Kenny Rogers—the storyteller, O called him. So with Kenny Rogers blaring in the old squeaky speakers of O's Land Rover, we drove to the U.S. Embassy out in the suburbs of Nairobi. It made sense that they would move the embassy to a suburb, easier to protect and, for terrorists, too boring to bomb.

We zigzagged around huge cement barriers meant to slow down a speeding truck bomb before getting to the gate. Once inside and past the security station where we disarmed we were led up the stairs and into Jason's office. It was like an executive's—large, with dark mahogany furniture—and in the corner, some leather sofas and a coffee table. Like something from a catalogue, complete with a quill pen laid out next to an ink pen.

"In Kenya, here we are, in the midst of elections—and what happens—a fucking bomb—but the elections go on. And in the States—a Kenyan is president ... almost president. All roads lead to Nairobi," he said cheerfully, as we shook hands with him and with Paul.

"Glad you decided to stop by—as you can imagine we are very busy, so let's make this snappy," he added, as we sat down on the leather couches.

"Have you found anything?" O asked them.

"Just so we are clear. The bombing is ours, we have the re-sources. And the body in Ngong is yours ... as long as we want it that way," Paul threatened.

"So you said," O replied.

"We followed the body, it led us here," I said to Paul.

"I want to hear you say it," Paul said, looking at me.

"Say what?"

"That you understand, that you will report directly to Jason and me," Paul said.

"I understand," I said, looking Paul in the eyes, and when he seemed relieved, I added, "I understand that you need us just as much as we need you."

"Everyone take a chill pill, okay? We can share the smoking gun, at least the smoke," Jason said to ease the tension.

"The partial fingerprints, DNA, dental records ... any hits?" I asked.

"Nothing yet, it will take some time, especially if your man knew what he was doing. We have nothing—the hotel guests, nothing special about them, nothing from the security tapes, and we have gone back six months," Jason explained.

"And our bomb guys have nothing conclusive but it looks like Al Qaeda. They have claimed responsibility. We are working that angle, unless we learn otherwise. We are going after them in Somalia. We are at war with them. We are going to take them out once and for all," Paul added angrily.

"It doesn't matter to you whether it was them or not?" I asked him.

"Guys, does it matter to you whether a bank robber robbed a particular bank or not? A bank robber is a bank robber even when not robbing banks, the same as you are always cops," Paul argued.

"They are trying to kill us—so we go after them. If they aren't guilty of this, they are guilty of other things. But we are working on the theory that there is a second group out there, sympathetic, maybe independent or working closely," Jason said. Paul started to say something but decided against it.

Jason excused himself to make a call. Soon after, a suit in dark glasses brought in a box and Jason took us through its contents. There were DVDs with zipped files from the last four years, a logbook listing entering and departing cars and their reason for visiting. And there was another disc with the Norfolk's financial transactions on it. It was going to take us a long time to go through everything. It was all about the details.

"What time is it?" Jason asked Paul.

"Four-ten p.m.," Paul answered.

"Wrong, Paul. You are dead wrong. Tusker time," Jason said as he tapped a wooden panel on the wall, reached in, and came out with four cold Tuskers.

"I am curious, Ishmael, Obama—do you think he can win?" Jason asked me.

"I'm not sure—but he has my vote," I answered.

"What is it that the Kenyans liked to say? That the United States will see a Luo president before Kenya does?" Jason asked O. This was a constant joke—there had yet to be a Luo president in spite of them being the second-largest ethnic group.

O smiled.

"I guess we'll find out," he said.

"I don't think he'll win. Race matters more than anything else … like tribe here, only without the machetes …" Jason said, bringing his hand to the table and laughing as he stopped his Tusker from toppling over.

"I have my money on Obama. You just needed to look at where his money is from, old white ladies sending in crumpled five-dollar bills," Paul said. "What we should be worried about is what's going to happen here. Things are going to get pretty hot."

"That I agree with," Jason pronounced, placing his hand on O's shoulder.

I picked up the box full of potential evidence.

"You know, a fellow cop back in the United States, he used to say that the only difference between an accountant and a detective is that one wears a gun. The search for details, that will be us crunching numbers," I said, thinking about the mind-numbing work ahead.

"There is another difference," O interjected. "The accountant gets paid more."

We left Jason almost dying with laughter and went to the security office to retrieve our weapons and phones. As soon as I turned mine on it buzzed with a text from Jason. He wanted to meet at Broadway's the following evening—8:00 p.m. That the

CIA chief in Kenya was sure he could have a confidential meeting in a public space added another detail to the bar. I showed O the text.

"Jason and Paul have two different agendas—for now, we trust neither, until we know more," O said, and I agreed.

Usually we took work to the bar instead of home. But we needed a computer and Internet access so we did the next best thing and stopped at a gas station, bought some beer, and went to O's. O and Mary had moved from the chaotic and sometimes dangerous Eastleigh to a high-rise apartment in the more peaceful Parklands. It was a high-rise apartment in name only—often there was no running water and they had to pay the night watchman, who doubled as the handyman, to carry gallons of water from the communal tap up the five flights. Just as often, there was no electricity. While Mary would have preferred that they buy a house, the apartment was close enough to Kangemi Primary School, where she taught, to make its temporariness well worth it.

Mary was correcting—or rather "marking," I had come to learn it was called—exams. She said a quick hello and informed O that dinner was in the fridge, then moved from the sitting room into her office.

"When you're done, I need help ... with my afro," she called from her office before locking the door.

Her afro, only an inch or so last year, now rivaled that of Angela Davis when she topped the FBI's most wanted list back in the 1960s. Mary liked O to braid it into knots before going to bed, and it was always worth a laugh or two to sit and watch one of the toughest detectives in this part of the continent braiding his wife's hair as he chatted away about nothing.

We hadn't eaten and we ploughed through the *ugali* and *matumbo* collard greens as we went through the security discs.

"How would I get a bomb into the Norfolk?" O asked himself. "What would be the perfect cover? One that would allow you to go in and out without any questions asked?"

"Construction ... anything that gives you access to the hotel for a long period of time ... Anything that makes it necessary for you to bring heavy equipment in and out," I said, seeing where O was going.

There were a few vans going through the gate in the videos but they left within a few minutes. In the logbook, their reasons for visiting were listed as food and beer deliveries. Finally, we found something: a week before the explosion one of the logbooks revealed a repairman whose reason for visiting was listed as "Fixing Hotel Boiler"—the company's name was Ngotho Repair-It-All. We found the number, and a sleepy guard, thinking we were customers, gave us directions to follow in the morning.

It was close to midnight by the time we made it to the shop down on River Road. O showed the guard his badge and asked him where the owner, Ngotho, lived. Clearly, the guard was bored and needed a break, because he hopped into the Land Rover with us. It didn't take us long to get to Banana Town and, after weaving in and out of poorly paved roads, we came to a wooden gate secured with heavy-duty chains and padlocks.

"You could just burn the gate," I said to O.

"Or saw through it," O said in turn.

We rapped on the chains, and big Alsatian dogs leaped up and down—we could see their flashing teeth in the glare of the Land Rover headlights. Someone called to them from inside, asking what we wanted. O explained that we were detectives and the owner laughed.

"I've heard that one before," he yelled in English through the grated doorframe. We held up our badges above the gate, but he couldn't make them out from that distance.

The watchman yelled something at his boss in Kikuyu.

"But you could be holding a gun to his head," he yelled back.

"And I could burn down your gate, shoot your dogs, and come in," O shouted back at him.

"The phone number of your station—the desk number, give it to me."

O gave him the number and looked at me as if to say it was a good thing he was still working for Hassan and moonlighting for our agency.

"What are your names?" he yelled after a few seconds. O gave him his name and, after a few seconds, he emerged and locked his dogs up.

"You can't be careful enough these days," he said as he opened the gate and revealed a short, stocky old man. By this time, it was obvious to me that he had nothing to hide. For one, were he involved in something as heavy as the bombing he would not be home, and if he were home, he would not have answered, and if he did—it would be to try to bribe us.

"We are investigating the Norfolk bombing … an aspect of it, anyway. Have you been there lately?" I asked him.

"Well, I was there a few days ago, the manager is a good friend and throws work my way, otherwise a job at the Norfolk would never come to a man like me. But I didn't do any work on the boiler—I ran some diagnostics … oh God!" he exclaimed as the possibility came to him.

"Are you telling me, all that damage, all those deaths—a boiler did that?" he said with his hand over his mouth. "No, that's not possible—that level of damage …"

"What was wrong with the boiler?" O asked him.

"Old ... it needed a new pressure valve. I told them that they needed a new boiler immediately. They said they would order one from the United States and get it shipped in. I guess it's still on its way," he said, trying not to smile at his joke.

"Did you see anything suspicious?" I asked.

"No, nothing around the boiler," he answered.

"Has anyone else come to see you? Americans?" I asked. He looked alarmed. The stories about the U.S.'s extraordinary renditions, when told with a Kenyan flair for lurid details, would alarm even the bravest of us.

"No, no one else has come to see me," he answered.

"You have nothing to worry about," I reassured him.

Ngotho really was a working stiff and he looked genuinely unhappy that he wouldn't be completing the job—he needed the cash, something I understood. We had to go back and continue looking. We left the guard with Ngotho for what we were sure was going to be a long conversation about abandoning his post.

This was detective work—detail after detail, some leading somewhere, others nowhere, but I had come to learn that there were no wasted details. At least you ruled out something when you were wrong. We had ruled out Ngotho—and without it costing us anything. Because, in Kenya, the truth costs. A Kenyan reporter for CNN had been fired because he was bribing witnesses. But how else was he going to get the truth?

"It's a little bit odd that no one else has visited Ngotho," I said to O.

"And we're all looking at the same evidence ... someone knew it was a waste of time," O agreed.

We needed to dig deeper and more carefully into the records—tedious—but it was what it was.

"Shit—I forgot my wife's hair," O said suddenly.

Before I could start laughing, I remembered I hadn't called Muddy.

We went back to O's and continued sifting through the records. Besides Ngotho, no one had done any work in the basement for at least a year, unless there was deleted or missing footage—but the days and hours were in sequence. There were no suspicious-looking deliveries, or any that ended up with a truck in the basement.

Soon, Mary woke up and started getting ready to go to work. We had worked through the night.

"No laughing," she said sleepily as she walked by us to go to the bathroom. Her huge afro had been matted into a huge mohawk.

"Razor sharp," I said to her, now that I was high with fatigue.

Mary made herself a scrambled egg and a cup of coffee, kissed O goodbye, and then she was off to teach. This much I had come to know—love and deserving love do not go together, love has nothing to do with being worthy. At least not in my case, and certainly not in O's.

"Let's keep digging back. You go through the security discs, and I'll go through the logbooks," I said.

The farther we went back, the more it seemed like our strategy wasn't working. No one plants a bomb months before its due date—it was against all logic. But we had nothing else to do and so we kept at it.

Finally, after a whole fucking day, something at last. Five men getting out of a van in the basement of the hotel. I couldn't make out their faces but clearly four of them were white and one was black. The date was September 14, 2006, about a year before the bombing.

O flipped through the logbook to the same date. There. We finally had it: "Reason for Visit. Fix crack in basement." The company name listed was Golden Bears Co.

"What kind of a name is that?" O asked.

It sounded familiar. I knew it from somewhere. Then it hit me.

"It's the name of a university football team—Berkeley ... California," I said.

"Someone has a sense of humor," O said with an excited laugh. "I can bet you there isn't a single company by that name in Kenya. That alone ... the guys at the gate should have been suspicious."

"Not surprising they were let through—four white men," I answered.

O knew what I meant—there was a high premium on whiteness in Kenya. Even criminals who were busy terrorizing their black brethren left the *wazungu* free to roam the country— one could argue it was a service to Kenya, the tourist money benefited everyone. The four white men would have had the run of the place just because they were white.

I rewound the video to the moment where we could see the van pulling in and one of the guards walking around it with a mirror, looking for explosives underneath.

In the video, he walks to the back, looks at what is presumably equipment, and then waves them on through. The van goes into the underground parking lot. The men get out and the driver reverses and parks facing the ramp. One can see the men appearing and disappearing in the outer edges without actually being able to see what is going on. So simple: rather than mess with the security camera by pulling complicated stunts, they give the guards in the security room a full view of nothing important.

They worked out of sight for six hours before leaving. When they pulled out, we saw a space covered over with a plastic sheet. They came back a second day. When they left again, the floor appeared freshly cemented.

We had something, but not quite. Why plant the bomb a year in advance? We went through Kenyan history looking for why October 28 might be important—nothing. Searched through the major American holidays, still nothing. There was nothing special about that day. There was nothing special about the guests. It had to be a planned random attack, I said to O.

"A planned random attack? Have you been smoking?" was his response. I couldn't have agreed more.

But still, we finally had something to work with. It was nothing in the world of lawyers and judges, but in our world, it was something.

It was time to go meet Jason.

We arrived at Broadway's just in time for the seven o'clock news. Wanuna Sophia was reporting that Al Qaeda had claimed responsibility for the Norfolk bombing. She showed a clip of a masked man promising all sorts of hell to come. Then the commercials came on—and the bar came alive with conversation. Even for criminals, love of Kenya had no moral borders. The outrage in the bar was sincere.

I had once asked O how Broadway's had come about. He couldn't say for sure. It had opened sometime in the 1950s at the height of the Mau Mau guerrilla war for independence. It was rumored that the bar owner was a nationalist who knew both

Dedan Kimathi and the man in charge of tracking him down, Ian Henderson. He got them to meet to discuss how to stop the killing of civilians by both sides—the Mau Mau kept their end of the bargain, while the British continued with their mass detentions and killings. *It is the lion and not the hunter telling its story*, O had said with a laugh. Henderson couldn't change British policy after all. But they had also talked about many other things—the toll of warfare on them and on their families—and fantasized about world peace.

Eventually they started meeting for the sake of meeting—you know—they became each other's shrink. At parting, each would go their way. Henderson eventually captured Kimathi but he never used the information he gathered from their meetings against him. In fact, O said, Henderson, sensing British defeat and Kenya's coming independence, had pleaded with the British not to hang Kimathi. I knew that the bare facts of the story were true but the substance—there was no way of telling. What I did know was that throughout history principled enemies had created safe spaces to meet—their destinies were shared, after all.

"Who better to understand you than the motherfucker trying to kill you?" O had reasoned, by that time nicely high.

On the news, the Kenyan presidential candidates were calling for justice and blaming the government for the security lapse. Bush, after promising help to the Kenyan government, made tough statements about defeating terror.

The miracle at the Norfolk was the last item. As the story unfolded, the whole bar stood up, the beers on the tables orphaned for the moment. KBC had pulled out all the stops—a two-minute background story about me, the American with the sharp hearing of a wolf, who only a few years ago had solved a major mystery. There was O, the local principled cop who made things happen. There were shots in slow motion of the survivors coming out of the debris and the exploding cars shown from different angles. There was a shot of Mpande, Nomsa, and Nothando—a camera zooming in to show the still sleeping baby, and the firemen hugging the rescued family. There I was again, the American who called Kenya home, shaking hands with Mpande before he hopped onto the ambulance. There was a final shot of the night watchman yelling "I save love and faith" and the wild applause in the bar joined the pandemonium breaking out on the TV.

Shit, even I, in spite of having been there, clapped along. Cases of beer were ordered, *nyama choma* on cutting boards was passed around, and the night turned into a celebration. O walked back in to find a party—cops and robbers eating and drinking to the lives saved.

Jason walked in just as the news ended. There was a bit of silence when he came through the door—his whiteness had broken the magic spell, and we all returned to our tables and continued with whatever we had been doing before the news.

I waited for him to get a beer.

"Straight up! Why are we here?" I asked him.

"Because only you can do what needs to be done. This is your city—I've been told you have an extensive network—you can use it," Jason answered.

"What I mean is, why the secrecy? Where is Paul?" I asked. We needed to get the most glaring question out of the way.

"It's simple, really, in a complicated kinda way. I don't think this was an Al Qaeda job. The official line is that it is Al Qaeda … but just because they claimed the bomb was theirs doesn't make it so. They take credit for shit they haven't done all the time. Think about it—you are a terrorist organization; you explode a bomb in the middle of Nairobi, killing ten Americans ..." Jason was saying.

"It's funny how you Americans never count the African dead ..." O interrupted.

"Okay, and fifty Kenyans, but it's not you they want to kill ..." Jason said, trying to correct himself.

"Death is death ..." O said plainly.

"Let's not get sidetracked," I intervened, trying to get the conversation going. O looked at me but kept his peace.

"What I'm saying is, if you're Al Qaeda you would try and maximize casualties, you would do it when the hotel is packed. We have spoken to dozens of witnesses, contacted all past hotel guests from the last month—and we have turned up nothing. This is not them—bombing a hotel after bringing down the Twin Towers? These fuckers don't know how to downgrade. I know these guys, you have to see their rationality—like good businessmen, they want to build on past successes—and now they go back to bombing hotels in third world countries after striking at the very heart of the empire? And there was no chatter. This is too much outside our radar to be Al Qaeda," Jason said, echoing Hassan earlier. "And then there is your guy ... I think an American crew pulled the job."

"You said that we would work the body and you'd work the bomb," O reminded him.

"That hasn't changed ... You stay with the dead American. If he leads you to the bomb, and I believe he will, then you come to me and we bust this thing wide open," Jason answered.

"That still doesn't answer the question of why Paul isn't here," I said.

"We are on the same side—you and I. We need facts—that is how we stay safe and keep people safe. We need the facts before the spin, otherwise people, my people, die. I need the truth before it gets to the politicians and ambassadors. This is what makes us who we are—no illusions, we want the truth first. If you manipulate a lie, the truth will come back to bite you in the ass. Paul's job is to spin the lie if the facts are as ugly as he is," Jason explained, almost breaking into laughter.

"Mine is to find the facts about who is doing what, and how and why, so that we are protected from the blindness that comes with spinning. Paul and I, we're on the same side, but our jobs are very different. I need to know the truth in order to do my job. He needs a good media day," he continued, after holding himself together. Maybe Jason laughed to mask tension. I had seen it before.

He had a point. You have the people on the ground looking into something and you have the spinners. The spinners want things to look neat and categorical, and therefore they must have answers. The people on the ground want facts. As cops, if we are to solve the case, we can't spin things—yes, we assume, we follow our gut, but when a fact contradicts that feeling, you follow the fact. I could see Jason and Paul having different priorities—one wanted facts, the other wanted what would sell well.

"So you're saying we get to the truth of what happened, make sure you know it all, and then you do as you please?" O asked. "That would mean I'd be working for you guys. That will never happen."

The CIA was not well liked here: the secret renditions, Guantánamo—it was no longer the schoolboys' fantasy job from back in the day.

"This is a case about Kenya as much as it is about the United

States. You keep what is useful to you, to your country—and I do the same," Jason replied.

He started to say something else, but O raised his hand to keep him quiet. We waited for a tense moment as O thought it through.

"When the time comes, just remember I said my piece," O finally said, and shrugged. He wasn't threatening Jason; he was just telling him where he stood. It was up to Jason to do as he pleased with that knowledge.

"This is what we know so far—our guy is most probably a black American. His death is somehow related to the bomb. We know there are another four white men involved," I said, to start us off on our new partnership. Jason looked puzzled and so I explained what we had found in the security videos.

"I can't believe our guys missed that," he said, seeming genuinely surprised.

"No one would have thought of going back that far into the records. It's like 9/11 and the planes, now we know it happens, but on September tenth it would have seemed crazy," O said. "But you missed something else—the boiler repairman. Why?" O looked directly at Jason.

"Was he involved?" Jason asked.

"No, but still …" O said.

"This is what I am telling you," Jason said. "This is something we have never seen before. And I have seen many things."

He ordered another round of Tuskers.

O handed him printout images of the five men, explaining the sequence of events as we understood them.

"I can't put any of my guys on this. Not yet. To get past Paul and my bosses back in Washington, we need to find out who these men are—we need something concrete," Jason said as he looked at them.

We agreed—we would start rattling the bushes and see what leaped out.

"You know, I remember you guys from the case of the dead white girl," Jason said, as some *nyama choma* arrived with his round of Tuskers. "That case, it should be in every training manual. I'm glad we're going to work together."

"Can I ask you something, Jason?" I said.

"Shoot ... I mean ask," he said, laughing and pointing at my Glock. At last we were relaxing.

"Is Paul really convinced that it's Al Qaeda and affiliates?"

"Paul—I have worked with him now for a number of years ... his heart is in the right place. We both want the same thing for our country. Like two lovers fighting over a woman, you don't want to cut her in half," he answered, laughing.

We all knew I was asking whether Paul could be trusted, whether Jason thought he might be involved, and he had answered. He was saying we should stay away from him. Jason stood up to go smoke with O, and I sat around drinking my beer, wondering what was coming next—knowing whatever it was, I was going to be unprepared. There was one thing I could do, though, propose to Muddy. No matter what happened afterward, I would have that one moment to hold on to.

"What brings us to fucking Africa?" Jason was asking. They were back from their session. It was a continuation of a conversation they had been having outside.

"I was an undergrad—somewhere in there, study abroad in Tanzania—some remote village, teaching English for a summer in return for Kiswahili lessons—don't ask me why now, I didn't learn shit. Most of my time was spent explaining America. I wasn't just a U.S. student, I was an ambassador. There were so many misunderstandings. And I thought, this is what I want to do—I want to be of service—I was doing it anyway, I was good at it, and I loved it, so why not make a career out of it. The bomb, the deaths, this fucking bar, all this shit takes me back to that moment when I believed," Jason said and looked at us expectantly.

"A religious moment? Saul becomes Paul becomes CIA?" O half-asked, laughing at his own high joke.

"Hell, yeah, it was a moment, all right. And you, O, why become a sheriff in the Wild West? For the pay?" Jason asked.

"You really want to know?" O responded, leaning forward. "Coz of a motherfucking tree . . . that's what I've boiled it down to. The worst storm in the history of Kisumu—and I decide to step outside. I'm about nine years old, and I decide to step outside and play, go up to my tree house and see how it's doing. I'm doing well, no one misses me in the house—so I keep going and I'm up in the tree house, which really is just a few boards and cloth for a window—something I had seen in a Famous Five or some shit like that." He reached for his Tusker and, holding up one hand in the air, chugged what was left of it before continuing.

"And then the storm worsens. Clotheslines are snapping and I can see the telephone and electric posts that pass close to our house coming down, trees snapping, debris flying—but the tree I was holding on to—a gust of wind would come and it would sway with it, get this close to the ground, its branches would ebb and flow, harder and harder until I thought they were going to break and take me down with them—but the tree would always sway and pull back up straight. Then there'd be a gust and it would dip so close to the ground again and there is me hanging on, knowing that my life was this tree. Anyway, no matter how close to the ground it came, it never gave me up or its other branches. That's why I became a cop—I think anyway," he finished, sounding almost sad. O was still high but it was a beautiful story that had Jason whistling in amazement. Now it was my turn to share.

"You're going to laugh at this—I became a cop to do good. Simple and naïve, but that's it," I said, under the influence of the by now numerous beers. "You know, I used to be a Boy Scout and I would think, if only I had a gun. So there you have it."

"There's gotta be more ..." Jason said as he and O laughed to the point of tears. There *was* more, like wanting to serve my people, but I didn't feel like getting into it.

We'd run out of things to talk about and Jason, well toasted, decided to drive home.

"His was a good story—but we can't trust him," O said to me, after Jason had left.

"Yeah, I know. I figure for now we are fellow travelers but at some point he will want to take a different road ... and it might not be very good for us. We just need to know when," I answered.

Suddenly I felt tired and wanted to go home. Long days were ahead. But I didn't stand up to leave. I sat there peeling the wet Tusker label from the bottle with the word "home" playing over and over again in my head.

Home—was I home here? Home, was home where I had come from? But if I went back far enough, wouldn't home be here? Where was here? Kenya, Senegal, Nigeria? Home! Home was Mpande, his wife and daughter surviving a bomb blast in a strange country, home was them tapping away, arguing back and forth in a dark and chaotic basement, trying not to wake their baby up. Home was us standing out there trying to find a way of bringing them home aboveground. Home was the chorus of barely equipped firemen using everything they had, even their own bodies, to make sure that Mpande and his family made it home.

I was going to propose tonight. It suddenly seemed silly that I had waited this long. I stood up.

"Tonight, I will ask Muddy to marry me," I said to O.

"About time—man, you guys ..." He stopped and laughed. "Do you even have a ring?" he asked.

"No," I answered, and sat back down. "Muddy—you know her, she won't care—she'll actually think I'm being frivolous if I have a ring."

"So you tell yourself," O said, sobering me up. He called to MC Hammer, who back-slid over to us.

"This man here, he needs a ring—he wants to ask his woman to marry him," O said to him.

"Two minutes," Hammer said and dashed off.

Soon he was back. He asked me for my hand, laughing at his own joke, and placed a bunch of beaded rings into my palm.

"Ten, one for each finger," he said with a smile. They were cheap beaded Maasai rings, but right about then, they were the most beautiful things I had ever seen.

I went for my wallet, but he stopped me.

"On me, my friend—for your work today," he said.

"You have some more work to do," O said to me. We stepped outside and he called to one of the taxi guys. "Go home!" he said.

I walked over to the taxi gliding on air, like MC Hammer.

But when I got home, I remembered that Muddy had a performance the following evening and so I slipped in next to her, leaving the rings in my shirt pocket. There was no way I was going to wake her up to propose now. Her response would be simple. "What the fuck? If I was going to marry you tonight, I would marry you tomorrow too."

I passed out.

The following day, O and I started rattling the bushes. We went from tourist hotel to tourist hotel, from one cold trail to another, until at last we made our way to Limuru Country Club. It was a golf club that pretty much functioned like an upper-class Broadway's. Under the guise of playing golf and protected by the privacy of a clubhouse, everything from land grabs to hostile takeovers was discussed here. The potbellied black and white men in white polo shirts and golf gloves went back to their businesses a little bit richer every day.

As we were about to sit down, a burly Kenyan man approached us, feigned a jab and a right hook in my direction, and I pretended to be knocked out and slunk into my seat.

The man's name was Nyiks, short for Wanyika. A former boxer, he had almost held the national title back in the day. He and I had fought for real once, when he had called me a *mzungu* and I had just lost it. I won, but only because he was out of shape then—a victim of too much *nyama choma*. With some persuasion from O, he had helped us with the case of the missing white girl, and we had done each other a few solids, as we called favors. We had slowly become friends before we lost contact. After the fight he started hitting the gym again, and now he resembled George Foreman: big, a bit comical but strong and fit enough for anyone not to want to mess with him, unless they were in it for the long haul.

He was at the club to buy and sell American dollars to

tourists and wealthy Kenyans. It was illegal, of course, but legality could be easily bought—and so he operated freely, so freely that he had set up shop in one of spa rooms. He even had regular business hours, 6:00 p.m. to 10:00 p.m.

After we explained what we were looking for and made it clear that there was enough cash to go around, he agreed to ask around the club and call us as soon as he knew something. It was past seven when we left him to go see Muddy's performance.

The crowd at the Carnivore was an odd mixture of people. There were tourists tearing into crocodile meat and God knows what else—someone had once told me that for $500 a plate you got lion meat. The Kenyan elite in evening gowns and three-piece suits were dutifully sticking to the *nyama choma* and cocktails. The urban youth, trying to be hip in baseball caps and 49ers jackets, but broke as hell, were slowly sipping their Tuskers, trying to make a single beer last the night.

They were all here to see Muddy. As she walked onto the expansive stage, the lights came on, revealing a shirtless muscled conga player. Muddy was dressed casually, a sleeveless white shirt, jeans, and sandals. She had let her dreads let down—set them free, she would say—so that they came to the small of her back. The drummer did a solo, eliciting thunderous sounds from the congas before cascading into a low constant trickle of beats.

Muddy started.

"Here is the problem of being a witness, it never happens to your confessor, a witness is to be pitied, to be patted on her shoulder, warnings become post-traumatic stress disorders, a cry of pain, remembrances of the past. So, I stand here to warn, but you will pity me, pat me on my shoulder, share in my tears but you will believe they are not yours, and you are not me. Deep down you will believe that I deserved it, it was because of something I might have done, or not done, and where I didn't, you will and where I did, you will show restraint. Listen! There is no such thing as a trickle of blood, each drop today is a flood to-morrow ..." and she went on and on until I thought she was los-ing the crowd. No one wanted to be told that tomorrow floods would come, especially when it had never happened. But she bravely continued until murmurs of open disapproval became grunts and yells of *Kenya Juu! Kenya Juu!*

"You can yell 'Kenya Up' standing on top of God knows what all you want. But someday soon, please remember my words," she said and silence reigned once again. She let the silence sit there as the drummer increased his tempo until the sound be-came terror—and then they both left the stage. There was polite applause, and then the conversations and the eating of exotic meat continued.

Muddy didn't want to stay at the Carnivore and make a night of it, and so a slightly tipsy Mary invited us over. We liked to dissect, or rather listen to Muddy dissect, her performance the following morning over a long, lazy late breakfast.

O and I had had too many Tuskers and Mary wouldn't let either of us drive. She hiked up her long teacher's skirt, hopped into the driver's seat, and sped us home through the Nairobi night. We stopped at a gas station, got a case of Tuskers, and drank late into the night, discussing Muddy's performance, lis-tening to music, and talking about things that had nothing to do with politics or the case. Just like in the old days when we were getting to know each other, we talked about past loves, hopes for the future, told funny stories, and just enjoyed being with each other.

CHAPTER 4

COMING UNHINGED

They had found us and I was pleading with Jamal. I was praying to him, in the name of our past friendship and all we had been through together, to let Muddy and Mary live.

I could tell that whether they lived or died was not on him. It depended on the four white men who had quietly and methodically handcuffed our hands to the chairs at the dining table using those humane cuffs that I too had often used back in Madison. Both Muddy and Mary were gagged. Muddy was looking around her, calmly and dangerously, while Mary was screaming and struggling against her cuffs.

Tall, dignified, charismatic, and violent when I first met him, Jamal was now fat enough to appear short—he resembled a mid-level Kenyan politician. He had saved Muddy, O, and me from certain death sometime back. En route to Jomo Kenyatta Airport on what we later called the Highway of Death, he had warned us of an ambush. Without him risking his life to engage one of the cars, we would have been outgunned, outnumbered, and dead.

But to a man like Jamal the past had no business being in the present. We might as well have been strangers. Blood to him was like water, neutral. To his credit, he never pretended to be anything he wasn't.

The four white men were casually dressed in various shades

of khaki so that they looked every bit the tourist. They had that American carelessness of dress that suggests casual power. Their T-shirts were an amalgamation of African tourist stops—Mount Kilimanjaro, Serengeti National Park, Sahara Desert, and Tsavo National Park.

Tall, with his hair cropped to hide the fact that he was balding in the front and back, Sahara had the kind of fitness that middle age ravages—but even though he was losing the battle of the bulge, it wasn't for lack of going to the gym. His glasses magnified his small, intelligent eyes. He looked more like a hip anthropologist on vacation, or an Episcopalian priest trying to dress down.

Serengeti and Tsavo were the musclemen, tall, hard, with a military look. Kilimanjaro was huge, with the appearance of a lazy football player. His snow-capped head, from which long, stringy hair ran, cast a shadow over his eyes. It was clear that he was the go-to guy for all things painful—he did the heavy lifting. In contrast to Jamal, they all had a certain kindness to them that I could not describe—like they did things out of necessity, as opposed to Jamal, who did them by choice. They were much younger than him, probably in their late thirties.

The one wearing the Sahara T-shirt was in charge. Not that he was shouting orders; he asked for and suggested everything politely.

"Can you please handcuff him?" "The door needs some attention." "And Mary, stop struggling so much, it only makes the cuffs tighter." "Could someone please make sure that there is nothing on the stove?"

The other three men didn't jump at his suggestions as if their lives depended on it, they listened first, and sometimes they even asked a follow-up question—like it was a learning moment.

"The stove—why?" Kilimanjaro had asked, for example.

"A very good question—the principle of an operation like this is the appearance of normality. Something burns, the fire alarm goes off, or neighbors smell smoke and come knocking. What was a contained situation becomes ..." Sahara explained.

"I see," Kilimanjaro said, interrupting him and nodding in agreement.

"Contain the situation, control all you can, and the rest ..." Sahara said, his voice trailing off.

"The rest is out of your hands," Kilimanjaro finished.

The white men had semi-automatics I had never seen before—the latest offerings from our fine American firearms industry, I could tell. Only Jamal had an AK-47—the African cigarette—an apt name because in some parts of the continent, the AK, like cigarettes, functioned as money, a medium of exchange.

Jamal had caught us off-guard. We were used to bad things being done only at night—daylight, at least the morning, was supposed to be the time when the good and bad guys got some sleep, or caught up with their loved ones, or prepared for war later, at night. In "Nairobbery," we woke up, unlocked the heavily barred doors and windows to let some fresh air in, and tried to remember a time when night did not turn your home into a prison. Morning was life itself, a reminder that you had survived the night.

How could we have expected four white men and a former friend to walk in unannounced and take us hostage in the fucking morning? It was well known that O was a cop. The neighbors who might have seen them coming through the single entrance to the building would have thought they were friends of O. So the men had literally walked right in to find Muddy and Mary sitting at the dining table, drinking chai and eating bread.

The men must have been monitoring our movements. They would have seen O leave to go see his sick mother in the hospital, followed by me on my way to Westland Gym to run on their worn-down treadmills. I never went running in Nairobi; it was just plain dangerous, with the dust, the fumes, and the driving. Whenever too much beer found me crashed at O's, I preferred to sweat out the Tuskers at the gym.

Coming back, the closed curtains only gave me slight pause—I knew Mary never slept past eight, and she liked her apartment sunny and bright. I figured she might have decided to sleep in this once. Blindly, I walked into the trap Sahara and his men had carefully laid for us. I didn't even have time to draw my weapon.

Jamal wanted to find out when O was coming back and so he untied Mary's gag. He didn't need to tell her not to scream.

"He went to the hospital. To see his mother, she has been ill," Mary answered truthfully.

It wasn't going to be a long visit. I didn't know why, but things were always tense between O and his mother. He'd be back any minute now, but Mary cleverly said that she didn't know how long he would be.

"Guestimate, as the Americans like to say. When can we expect his esteemed company?" Jamal asked.

"Midday, he said he would be back to make lunch," Mary answered. Jamal put the gag back on her.

"Could be later ... much later. O loves his African Time, or for the benefit of Ishmael, Colored People Time?" Jamal laughed, but the white men smiled politely.

"If you can give us what we want, we'll be out of your hair

in a jiffy," he added. Jamal and his Americanisms were amusing sometimes, but when he was pointing a gun at you, they were just plain cruel.

"You know O will come after you for this," I said to him.

"All the more reason for us to have a friendly and bloodless chat. No?" Jamal said in return.

The white men hadn't spoken a word to us. They were busy securing the room—disconnecting telephone and Internet lines, making sure the door was locked, and turning on the hallway lights. In the semidarkness of the dining room, O would be seen easily, without him being able to see us or his attackers in the shadows.

They pointed two reading lamps at us as Jamal dragged his gout-ridden body over to where I was seated.

"What the fuck do you want?" I asked him.

Jamal looked at the older white man, who stepped out of the shadows into the light.

"I guess that's my cue. Please, call me Sahara. That over there is Tsavo, Kilimanjaro to his right, and to his left, Serengeti," he said. Their tourist T-shirts; they were like masks, extensions of the wearer's identity.

"Forgive the names—we know Africa is more than its wildlife. Africa is not a country—as CNN might have you believe. Also, do excuse our mutual friend here for being so dramatic. What Jamal is trying to explain is that there are two options. We walk out and everyone lives. Or all of you die. I am quite afraid that this is indeed one of those situations where there are no in-between solutions," Sahara explained kindly. He paused for a few seconds before continuing.

"In the interest of efficiency and time, allow me to explain how we plan to proceed. We want some information. If we don't get it, we shall kill Mary first. And if we kill her, then we might as well kill both of you and O because if we let you live, you and the fellows at the CID will come after us … call it the domino effect, for lack of a better word. However, if you save Mary by telling me what I want to know, all that will have been lost is a bit of information. Surely, that cannot make us mortal enemies," Sahara said, placing his hand gently on my shoulder.

"Ishmael, I abhor the idea of torture. I tell you this because you are a man who has seen enough to understand what I'm saying here … what the options are. I would rather we came to an intellectual understanding of just how total and unforgiving the consequences will be," he added.

His reasoning, as odd as it was, made sense. A few years back, Jamal had seen Muddy shoot an unarmed man in cold blood for betraying her, and he knew her history with the Rwandan Patriotic Front. There was no threatening her, unless Sahara and his men could conjure up more terror than the genocide had. Jamal would have shared this with Sahara. They could threaten to kill Muddy with the hope that I would talk—except for one thing. If they killed Muddy, then I would have no incentive to talk.

And if they tortured Muddy to get me to talk? If they made the first cut they would have to kill her, and me as well, because we would come after them. They could torture me but the little Jamal knew of me would have told him that the chances of getting me to talk were not very high. Not because I am stronger or can withstand pain better than most. I would hold out as long as I could simply because the woman I loved was in the room—good, old-fashioned, useless male pride.

That left Mary for the opening gambit. Mary was just a schoolteacher; her innocence was their leverage. It would be harder for me to justify her death against whatever it was Sahara thought I was protecting.

It didn't make Sahara any more or less moral. He was simply speaking a language of pure violence, shorn of hate or love—he was laying out the most efficient way to get information from me. Had it been the other way round, had I been the one holding the gun, he would have seen the logic of all or nothing. Perverse, yes, but it helped move along the circuitous nature of torture. It was the perfect opening gambit. It was as intelligent as it was cold and rational.

Except for one thing. These sorts of transactions always had a cost.

"Why should I believe you will let us go if I tell you what I know?" I asked him.

"It is what you don't know that we are interested in," he answered with a condescending smile. "But that is a fair question. We do not want you back on our trail. So we have made it impossible for you to continue with the case … in fact, you could say that we have made it impossible for you to continue with your life as you know it."

He signaled to Tsavo.

"Can you please hand me my bag?" he said.

I was seized by fear and I looked over at Muddy, who was also eyeing the bag while Mary shook her head from side to side. Sahara pulled out a white Mac, patiently hooked up a Safaricom Wireless device, and after several tries managed to connect to the Internet. He placed it in front of me and opened two pages, one after the other: the U.S. Transportation Security Administration and U.S. Homeland Security. He pointed at the addresses so I could make sure they were authentic.

He typed something that took him to a secured page where

he entered a password. The page opened on to the U.S. Terrorist Watch List. He pointed to three names: Madeline Muteteli, Ishmael Fofona, and Tom Odhiambo. There were photographs of us, armed and looking dangerous, followed by short descriptions. Muddy was a Rwandan ex–guerrilla fighter who had fallen under the sway of Ishmael, a disgruntled black American Muslim who had in turn become radicalized in Kenya. O was the Kenyan cop who provided cover for both of us.

Where had I heard black Muslims mentioned before? Paul, on the night of the bombing—he had made that connection.

"Of course, there is more," Sahara said as he opened another page.

It was like watching a parallel life unfold. I was under investigation for being an enemy combatant and O was suspected of using his "good offices" to help me train Kenya-based Somali terrorists. There was a photograph of O and me in northern Kenya surrounded by Somali men. I remembered that trip; we had gone to report a death to the relatives of a Somali man killed by thieves in Nairobi.

There was a trophy photograph of O and me, both of us armed, standing by two dead men. But the reality was that we had ambushed some bank robbers and managed to kill two of them. A reporter had rushed to the scene and taken the photograph. Then there was one of Muddy with an AK-47 in what appeared to be a death camp. Out of context, the photograph made it seem like she was the one doing the killing. I knew the photo too well. The RPF had marched into this particular camp only to find they were too late. She was a victim of that war.

These photographs weren't speaking a thousand words, only one—terrorists.

"I'm not even Muslim … never been to a fucking mosque,"

I protested in spite of myself. "Who is going to believe this shit anyway?"

"Come on now, Ishmael. Isn't that the point? That you are so good at what you do, even Muslims don't think you are a Muslim? In my narrative, your cover is that of a black detective who because of identity issues moved to Kenya to recover his blackness, but in reality you are here to work with your extremist brothers and sisters. Your real life is really your cover. Beautiful! Context is meaning," he explained.

"But let's not get lost in the details. For you to believe me, I had to make sure there were consequences. I will let you go free, but into the hell of looking over your shoulders," Sahara said patiently, like a doctor explaining different treatment options.

"What Sahara is telling you, my friends, is that the truth shall somewhat free," Jamal said. I laughed but he ignored me.

Given his level of clearance, I guessed that Sahara and his men worked for or with an American intelligence service—one of the many with a presence in Kenya since 9/11. I was sure of one thing, though—these were the men who had planted the bomb and killed our guy—and they had the coldness, intelligence, and calculation to plant the bomb the year before it was due to go off.

I believed that Sahara was going to let us go—they didn't have to go to all that trouble so that we would appear to be terrorists after they had killed us. They could have just shot us and walked away—the mystery of our deaths would find an explanation—home invasion gone bad, drunken dispute over women, revenge killings.

Rattling the bushes had worked. Nyiks must have a hit a nerve, because right in front of me stood the men we had been looking for. There was one problem, though: I had nothing. That was the whole point of rattling the fucking bushes—it gives the

illusion of knowing more. They would not know how many hotels and bars we had gone to before arriving at Limuru Country
Club. It would appear to them that we were on to them because
we had something solid.

"What do you want to know?" I asked, trying to think fast.
My job, I kept telling myself, was to keep us all alive for as long
as I could.

"You have been looking for us," Sahara said as he pulled out
a chair so that he was facing us across the table. "Well, here we
are—all of us. I want to know everything you know."

"You have to listen to me. We were at the beginning of our
investigation, shit, if you hadn't come after us, we wouldn't have
found you. We walked around yelling fire and you are the only
ones who ran," I said desperately.

Sahara didn't believe a word I said. He stood up and rapped
my forehead with his gun.

"I know you well enough to know how good you are. Surely,
you must know that our understanding is predicated on your giving me the information I need. I feel slighted that my sincerity is
being treated with such pedestrian disregard," he said, sounding
genuinely pained, and that worried me.

"Rattling the bushes ... it's the oldest trick in the book ..." I
tried to explain.

"Let's get out of here. He knows nothing. Kill them all," Jamal said. He knew I was telling the truth.

"Let me have five minutes with the ..." Tsavo started to say
but Sahara interrupted him.

"We are not going to debase ourselves by torturing women,"
he explained to Tsavo patiently. "If we do, where do we draw the
line between us and them? Have I not explained to you that once
we start down that road the journey only ends when they are all

dead? You have to leave people a way back into the conversation. Do you understand what I mean?"

"Yes," Tsavo replied.

"Ishmael, I feel you are not telling me the truth, not even a little bit of it. I will count to three. Mary dies … remember what I said …" Sahara counseled.

"All for one, one for all," Jamal said.

He started the countdown.

"One!"

I started rattling off names—motherfuckers I didn't care for, who wouldn't be missed by anyone—my parting gift to Kenya.

"John Maina."

"Which one?"

Maina was a popular name, as was John.

"Minister of Home Affairs."

I kept rattling off names until Sahara stopped me.

"You are still lying. Let me give you an example so you don't think I am a liar as well. Some of the people you mentioned, they are in with us. They are not the enemy," Sahara said, sounding disappointed.

"Ishmael, you are an American just like us. It looks like a black man will be sworn into office soon. Now, some people say that this will be the death of racism. We can argue about that all day. But out here," he gestured as if pointing to the wilderness, "we are Americans. You and I should be having a beer. Yet here we are. You tied to a chair and I holding a gun. Stop your lies, my friend, and you can retire into your new existence as a wanted terrorist. In a few years, that too will pass and you will go back to your life."

I wasn't going to live long enough to see a black man in office.

"Two, Ishmael, two," Sahara whispered into my ear urgently.

"I know some things—I know you are from Berkeley …" I said slowly, thinking of what to say next. "And one of you went to UC," I said, looking at the men. "I know Al Qaeda and Al Shabaab did not plant the bomb—you did. I know you killed one of your men because he tried to stop you."

"Quit stalling with useless details, Ishmael. I sense the truth in there somewhere …" he said, searching my eyes. "Do something right, something good here and now. Save this woman's life," he implored, pointing at Mary, then banging the table.

I would have told them anything they wanted to know—the thought of Mary dead had broken me but I knew nothing. I had nothing.

"Enough, Ishmael. I have given you enough chances. I hate torture because it gives a pretense of certainty to the torturer: that truth is truth because it was exchanged for pain. I, on other hand, prefer the certainty of logic and conversation. Our conversation, Ishmael, did not establish any certainty—far from it, I cannot be sure if you know more or less. I just don't feel that," Sahara explained patiently.

I looked up at him.

"I have nothing more to say to you. Do what you must," I said as I looked at Mary, whose eyes widened, then closed as she let out a sigh.

"Shoot Mary in the head, kill them all!" Sahara instructed Serengeti and the rest of his men.

A soft sound coming from the door that freezes us in place—like someone is running a feather along it, followed by silence. As if on cue, Serengeti takes the safety off his gun and continues holding it to Mary's temple. Tsavo stands behind Muddy, his hand slightly over his gun, like he's in some sort of Western shoot-out. Jamal stands by me, while Sahara points his gun at the door. Somewhere farther away in the complex we can hear running water, and music playing. We hear curses as keys drop to the ground and then the lock turns and all the guns except the one pointed at Mary's head are pointed at the door. O doesn't stand a chance.

The tension fades to reveal panic, my heart beats faster, and I am desperately trying to meet Muddy's eyes. Mary's looking intently but calmly at the door. I want to say it's going to be okay but I can't. Then the sound of breaking glass, a blinding light as curtains and patio door fly open, I see a red spray, and I know someone has been shot. I am screaming in fear and anger. I push the heavy dining table, keep pushing until I crash a stunned Sahara into the wall. He screams in pain as his gun drops onto the table and he slowly slips to the floor.

As Kilimanjaro sidesteps away from the moving table to shoot Muddy, I see Jamal's hands snap back twice and the mountain falls. O comes in through the curtains and breaking glass, Serengeti fires and misses. O shoots and takes him down. Tsavo, blinded by the light, tries to make it to the door. He stumbles to the floor as blood sputters from his right thigh. O continues shooting at him until he falls to the ground. He tries to tell O something. O shoots him in the head.

I look under the table but Sahara is gone. I rush over to Muddy, dragging the chair along—she is a bit dazed, bleeding from a cut in her forehead, but she is all right. Jamal walks over to us; with a pocketknife he snaps the handcuffs away. I hold Muddy and we start touching each other as if to make sure we are not ghosts.

Then I see Mary's body on the floor. I take Sahara's gun and go after him. I'm going to kill him.

I ran out after him, down the stairs and past the now-abandoned gate into the main road, knowing he couldn't have gone very far. A limping white man would be easy to spot—he'd be reflected in the eyes of a curious crowd. The pedestrians and the traffic caught in a jam moved on indifferently. I saw nothing, no sign of him anywhere. So I turned to go back up to the apartment.

But just before I reached O's door, I saw little droplets of blood. They trailed to the apartment next to O's. I had missed them in my rush. I kicked in the door and followed the trail of blood though the sitting room, into the kitchen, and onto the balcony. A long rope was still attached to the rail guards. I looked down. There was Sahara, briefcase in hand, disappearing through a hole cut in the wire fence. I aimed and fired, he stumbled and fell, stood up, looked around wildly, and then dove through the hole.

I slid down the rope, welcoming the sensation as my hands burned. There was a wider trail of blood down here. He wasn't going to get far but I followed fast and cautiously. Just as I made it to the street, I saw him getting into a beige-colored Range Rover—a bad choice for a fast getaway in Nairobi—even the curbs that should have doubled as emergency lanes were jam-packed with *matatus* and buses.

I ran in and out of the traffic, following the slow-moving Range Rover. I could see Sahara in the backseat trying to steady an AK-47 with one hand. I must have hit him in the shoulder. He let out a wild burst of gunfire—a mistake, because drivers then abandoned their cars, leaving the Range Rover trying to force its way through. I shot back, he dived onto the seat, and I edged closer to take out one of the back tires. Driving away was now out of the question. I ran over and took cover two cars behind. Sahara's driver tried to get out, I let out a warning shot, and he scuttled back into his seat and tried the passenger door. That side of the car was blocked by an abandoned *matatu*. I sent another shot into the back of the Range Rover to let them know I had them covered. I had to make things happen fast—otherwise they would think of a way out of the mess.

Sahara was too bled out to try and make an escape on foot. He was sitting in the back, facing forward, shaking his head from side to side. Without the driver, I could wait him out.

"Walk away—leave. I only want him," I shouted to the driver. He hesitated—I fired once more. He stepped out and stood facing me, hands up in the air.

Mary's face, still looking alive except for the blood soaking into her afro, flashed through my mind and I wanted to shoot him. O would have shot him—but that wasn't me. I wanted Sahara.

"Your shirt," I shouted.

He pulled up his shirt.

"Take it off," I ordered. "Your pants and shoes, everything, and walk away."

He hesitated. I knew he knew I did not have to let him live. He got undressed. Soon, a nude white body was streaking, weaving in and out of the traffic as people threw whatever garbage they could find at him.

I ordered Sahara to come out of the vehicle with his hands raised. Instead, he let out a wild burst of AK fire. I didn't take his bait and fire back. What I held in my hand was a semi-auto Glock, a newer model than my usual, which gave me confidence that there had to be at least ten rounds left. I could wait him out. I could hear police sirens but it might as well have been a practical joke—in this traffic, they weren't going to get to me in anything less than thirty minutes.

"Do you want to die?" I shouted at him. "You will bleed out!"

He didn't answer but I saw the Rover shift from side to side. He was getting ready to come at me again.

Then I heard it—the slow whine of a scooter. It came into view to reveal a naked white guy riding it, whizzing his way through the traffic. Sahara knelt, facing me, so that he was resting the AK on top of the backseat. I should have killed the fucking driver. The scooter stopped in front of the Range Rover. The driver kept a steady barrage of AK fire coming my way and within seconds, a weak, bleeding Sahara had dragged himself onto the scooter. Sitting facing backwards and leaning into the driver, he kept firing wildly in my direction.

I emptied out the Glock after them, as they buzzed and zigzagged through the traffic. Then they were gone. I should have shot the driver in cold blood. But I couldn't help thinking that the spectacle of a naked white guy on a scooter in thick Nairobi traffic was worth keeping him alive.

I walked over to the Rover. The good news was that they hadn't been able to carry anything with them. I took the pants the guy had left behind and tied the legs into knots—there was a money belt and I stuffed it in there, after I took out a nice wad of clean $500 bills. There had to be at least $10,000 in there but there was no time to count. There were a bunch of things in the glove box and I took them all: maps, pencils, penlights, and finally, Sahara's briefcase.

Back home there are crime scenes. This is not to say they aren't tampered with and evidence isn't planted, but at least there is such a thing as a crime scene with clear perimeters. But here, anything I left behind or missed, there would be no second chances to recover. In the time it would take the cops to get here, the car would be stripped, if not altogether stolen. That reminded me to tear the pocket from the man's shirt and dip it into the small pools of blood on the backseat. If nothing else, I would have Sahara's DNA.

With the danger gone, the crowd had surged closer, some getting into their cars and others into the *matatus*. The sirens weaved in and out of the traffic, and when they were just a few cars away, they turned into another street. We weren't the only ones in crisis. I rushed back to O's.

I found O holding his old .45 to Jamal's head. Jamal must have understood that the moment O burst in, he was as good as dead and no redemptive act was going to save him. To kill a man like O, one needed a well-calibrated plot where nothing went wrong. The moment they lost the element of surprise, the advantage was no longer theirs. Perhaps if he had saved Mary, then O might have spared him.

I shouted to O to stop. I shouted that he had helped, that Muddy would be dead without him. He looked at me; tears were welling in his bright red eyes. He looked back at Mary, and then at Muddy, who was now holding her. He turned away, walked to one of the windows, and looked out. Jamal sighed in relief.

"Jamal, can you tell us anything useful?" I asked him.

"They were very secretive, I was on a need-to-know basis, as you Americans say." He smiled sadly. "I did once hear Sahara saying over the phone that in a game of chess you capture the king and kill the queen."

In Kenya, who were the king and the queen? In the U.S., could Obama be the king and Michelle the queen? Or George and Laura? It didn't make sense at all and I told Jamal as much. The tables had turned—his knowing too little to appear to be hiding something was going to condemn him to death.

"Why, Jamal? Why help them, then turn against them?" Muddy asked him.

He looked over at Mary.

"Nothing I say now can save my life. Nothing matters," he said.

"Try me," Muddy said.

"If they had killed all of you, it would have been me next—I was not one of them," Jamal answered. At least he didn't try to bullshit us by saying he had felt a change of heart—it was self-preservation.

"If you know something more, this is the time to give it up. You are not the 'worthy cause' type. Don't start now," O said to him quietly.

"I want to pray. Let me pray—let me pray something not all jumbled up," he said as he took off his black leather jacket and hung it on the only dining room chair still standing.

Maybe if I had brought Sahara back with me, dead or alive, I could have argued for Jamal's life.

"How did you connect with them?" I asked him.

"A money launderer—he was looking for them—he came to me," Jamal answered. Nyiks, as he promised, had asked around, and word gotten to Jamal. Jamal then sold us out for a fee. It was that simple.

"Do you even know their real names?" I followed up.

"No." He paused.

"But I know how to die," he said to the silence. "Who no

know, go know." He took a deep breath. It was a popular quote from a Fela Kuti song.

O asked Jamal to stand up and he placed his gun over Jamal's heart. Jamal's eyes went vacant. O pulled the trigger. His gun clicked—it was empty. Jamal stood there waiting as O reloaded while Muddy and I watched, transfixed.

"Jamal, just go—walk out now," O whispered. Jamal was shaking and crying. He grabbed his jacket, put it on, and, out of habit, straightened it out and left.

I could tell Muddy was as confused as I was by the way she was looking at O, who was now kneeling beside Mary, cradling her body in his arms.

He let out a wail. Muddy knelt down and held him. They rocked back and forth. O's wailing was getting quieter and quieter, as if he were calling back the rage into him. Then he was still, very quiet, the kind of quiet between a lightning strike and thunder. He stood up and pulled Muddy to her feet.

"We have to bury my wife," he said to us.

Sahara and his handlers, whoever they were, didn't know what had just happened. They had unhinged O. The duality in which evil and good were compartmentalized in him was over. O had once told me that we were good men who did bad things. Mary had been all that kept him in our side of the world.

I didn't know why O had let Jamal live, but this much I knew, O was going to kill Sahara or die trying. I held on to my secret, knowing there was no way of telling it—that if I'd shot the driver, we would have captured Sahara, and if we had him, we would have some answers and O could have his vengeance. I had made the wrong call trying to define myself against my friend. Then again, don't we work with who we are? I wrestled back and forth … silently.

Mary, even though she was dead, was still bleeding from her head wound. O went to the bathroom, returned with some bandages, and carefully wrapped them around Mary's head. I remembered him weaving her hair as he chatted away. I felt a dull knife tear into my chest and I knew that I too would go to places I had never been, to bring Sahara to justice.

Some people completely break down in a crisis while others take command of the situation. O was the latter—from the moment he pulled Muddy to her feet, he took charge. It was his way of coping, and, whether it was good or bad for him, or for us, it made things easier. In any case, had Muddy or I taken charge, we would still have been coming to him for instructions—we had never lost a loved one in Kenya.

I looked on as Muddy drew open the curtains, letting in the afternoon light and air, which took some sting out of the gunpowder, death, and pain in the room. O had called Hassan, and he was on his way with more cops and ambulances. I called Jason—three of the four white men from the security tapes were dead—we needed him here.

O motioned to the trousers filled with stuff and I piled everything on the table. He pointed at the laptop. I turned it on and as we waited, I zipped open the moneybelt—there was nothing in it but money. The laptop naturally asked for a password—we knew enough not to mess with it. I took out the battery and, when O asked me why, I said it was so that no one else could access it remotely.

We agreed to keep the laptop to ourselves, and I went into Mary's office and left it on her worktable—best hidden in plain sight. I told O that Sahara had escaped through the next-door apartment and we both went in to look, hoping for some clues. We heard some muffled sounds coming from the bedroom and found O's neighbor gagged and handcuffed to the bedframe.

We set him free and he explained what had happened. He was drinking at a bar close to where O lived when the African and the four white men came in. They started talking to him and buying rounds. When they stepped outside for a cigarette at about 10:00 p.m., one of the men jammed a gun into his belly and told him they needed his place for a few hours. They gave him a hundred dollars and then forced him to let them in.

We hadn't heard anything because we had been at Muddy's performance. He pointed at the dresser. I opened the top drawer to find the hundred dollars. If he had known what was going to happen, his asking price would have been much higher—enough to get out of town.

He asked what was going on; he had heard the gunfire and commotion. O told him to stay indoors and handed him back the hundred dollars.

When we got back to O's apartment, we found Muddy looking at the maps I'd taken from Sahara's Range Rover—she pointed to one of them, where tourist landmarks had been circled. The Jomo Kenyatta Conference Center, Nairobi National Museum, Fort Jesus in Mombasa, built by the Portuguese in the 1500s, Tree Tops Hotel, where in 1952 the then–Princess Elizabeth had learned that her father had died and she would be queen, and many others. We would have to visit all these places and figure out why they were of interest to Sahara and Company—and more importantly, what they had planted in them.

"Janet!" Muddy suddenly yelled. Janet, could they go after

her too? Jamal knew about her, but I suspected he would have
kept her hidden from Sahara and his crew. His pride and fucked-
up code would not have allowed him to drag a promising young
student, a survivor, an innocent girl whose only crime was being
saved by O and me, into this mess. Also, Sahara didn't appear
to me to be the kind of a man who would go after Janet for
revenge—he was too calculating for that.

All the same, there was no harm in checking to make sure
she was okay. Nothing was predictable anymore—not with Mary
lying dead on the floor.

What would become of Janet without her surrogate mother,
the person she trusted, feared, and loved the most? She had
found herself a home—now it would be as if its warmth was
gone and just the shell remained. She was doing well, finally she
had managed to put her life back on track—and the law degree
she had decided to pursue was within grasp—but sometimes all
it takes is one traumatic experience to bring others rushing back
in. O simply had to find a way of stepping up and becoming the
father that, by default, Mary had made him.

Muddy asked O for the keys to the Land Rover, tucked one
of the Glocks from the dead men into the small of her back, and
stuffed extra clips into her pockets. As she rushed out, Hassan
walked in, flanked by plainclothesmen dressed in tweed jackets
and other forms of ill-fitting and hot-weather-unfriendly attire.

He looked around, whistling after each dead white man. A
bomb explosion a few days before and now three dead white
Americans—his job was on the line, with Nairobi not only looking ungovernable but outright unlivable.

He knelt by Mary's body and, for just a second, he was no
longer the calm, dangerous manager of violence; this was just too
close to home. He turned to O.

"Whatever you need … we'll do whatever needs to be done," was all he said. All of us, including the tweed jackets in the room, knew what he meant. It was one thing if I had died, or O—but this was just too much. The balance, the divide, the pretense that our work would not come home with us—call it what you like—it had to be protected. Otherwise, why should the good guys care? If it became open season on spouses, it would be children, relatives, friends next—a civil war, with cops on one side and robbers on the other, and those that we cared for in the middle. This line had to be protected at all costs.

Paramedics, armed with first-responder equipment so archaic that it looked downright dangerous, rushed in to triage. Hassan waved them away and they lined up against the walls as if mounting an honor guard.

There were some American dead—no one was going to get bagged before the Americans said so. Mercifully, Jason and Paul arrived.

"I am very sorry," Jason said to O, as he went and held Mary's hand for a second.

"Are these the guys?" Paul asked.

"What do you think, Paul?" I said angrily. He called out to someone in the hallway and the suit from the embassy came and fingerprinted the dead. The rest, the DNA samples and dental impressions, would be taken at Kamau's. The suit picked up the two remaining Glocks still on the floor.

"That's all?" he asked. I just shrugged, thinking to myself, *Welcome to a Kenyan crime scene, motherfucker.*

Hassan pointed at the paramedics.

"Can they?" he asked O, who nodded yes. They picked up Mary first, then the rest of the bodies, and filed out the door.

"Hassan, can I talk to your men?" Jason asked. Hassan agreed, and O and I stepped outside with Jason and Paul.

"I understand this is a bad time … a very bad time. We," Jason drew a circle to include O and me, "must always stop to take care of our dead and protect our own, but I have to insist, and I implore you, to tell me what happened. I want each word, each detail that comes to mind—accents, scents, anything. Our friendship works to the extent that I know everything." Jason reached up to place his hand on O's shoulder.

"Listen, Jason—one of the guys, the main guy, showed me a terrorist watch list and O, Muddy, and I were on it. How about we talk about that?" I said.

O looked at me—we hadn't had time to talk about what had gone down before Jason arrived.

Paul indicated that we should walk down the courtyard, away from other ears. He left us standing next to the tree in the middle of the courtyard, walked to a Pajero with embassy license plates, and came back with a briefcase.

He opened it and handed a file to O and me. We flipped through it in amazement. Sahara had shown us the very same parallel lives.

This much I knew, we were only a few steps away from having drones firing missiles at our cars, or even worse, some might say, ending up in a torture chamber in Kenya, Yemen, or the U.S. Guilt or innocence didn't matter—only being on the list mattered.

"How did you get that?" I asked Paul.

"An alert was sent to us this morning," he answered.

"Can we get off the list?" I asked.

"The short answer is no. Even if I called in your innocence, the response would be 'better safe than sorry.' It will take hard evidence to get you off that list, if it's even possible. The only way out is to get the people behind this and bring them to justice," Paul said. "O, I'm sorry you have to hear this after your loss."

"Who is powerful enough to get our names on that list?" O asked, looking at Jason.

"Any mid-level government employee. Suspicion alone— neighbor calling in neighbor—we had some people in Guantánamo because some motherfucker wanted their piece of land. The question is, who is powerful enough to whip up this sort of evidence in a short time and get it noticed enough to land you prominent spots on the list? I don't know, but I'll find out," he answered.

It worked for us that they should not try to clear our names at this point. If we played along, then at least any action to be taken against us would go through them. Innocence at this stage was no defense. We would make a good news story—Muddy, the beautiful but wounded cold bitch; O, a disgruntled marijuana addict who loved violence for its own sake; and me, the American who never really felt at home in the U.S. and who had betrayed all those who loved him for the warm bosom of jihadists. Sahara had done well for himself and his handlers.

I looked at O. He was smiling. O leaned in closer to Jason, looked him in the eye, and then looked down into his jacket. I followed his gaze and saw his old rusty .45 pointed at Jason's gut. Jason's eyes widened for a second and then slowly wound down. I looked around, looked again, and, in the late afternoon sun, high up on the rooftops, I could make out the snipers in position. Some of the windows above O's apartment were opening slowly.

"Jason, mark my words. I am not dying until I kill them all. If you and Paul are involved in my wife's death ..." His voice trailed off.

"The guys who killed your wife, I want them as bad as you," Jason said, trying to be still.

"Hey, look, O, I know you are not a fucking terrorist," Paul said. "We have to work together—we have no choice. We have to work the different angles."

"You haven't given up on the Al Qaeda shit?" O asked him as he poked his gun harder into Jason's gut, making him gasp for air.

"No, not officially—a bomb explodes in Nairobi killing ten Americans—some processes kick in," he said. "But I'm here to help. I didn't like what I saw up there." He sounded genuinely pained.

O holstered his .45.

I explained to Jason and Paul all that had transpired, from the visit to Limuru Country Club to Sahara to the maps. We agreed that Jason's task was to find out who Sahara worked for. He had three dead guys to start with. Our job was to keep digging and follow up on the maps we had found. Absolutely nothing was to be said to anyone. It was going to be the four of us against a powerful phantom. I didn't mention the laptop.

"But first, I have to bury my wife. I am going to take her home," O said as he started to walk away.

We parted ways just in time—the news teams had finally made their way. As they scrambled to the scene, the snipers melted out of sight—back into the world of ghost stories and the folklore about the American military presence in Kenya.

"Your mother, O, how is she?" I asked him nervously as we went back to his apartment.

"Diabetes—it's just diabetes ... best fucking news all day," he answered.

CHAPTER 5

MEETING HELEN

"The laptop, we have to get it to someone who knows about computers," I said to O, though I hated to be thinking about the case right now.

It was evening but he suggested calling Kamau and asking for a recommendation. We needed someone like him, able to improvise in situations that seemed impossible. I called Kamau and explained what had happened and what we needed. He said he would call me back in five minutes, but he called back in less than two and gave me an address.

"Who am I going to see?" I asked him.

"Helen, she is the best. Just remember that," he responded.

I knocked on the neighbor's door and asked him if the rope ladder was still up. I wanted to avoid the vultures circling down below in the courtyard. As I slid down the ladder it all hit me. At the bottom I sat staring into the rose bushes in the lessening daylight, crying.

I finally composed myself, made it quietly to O's Land Rover, and drove to the address in Kileleshwa, a formerly upscale neighborhood in Nairobi that had lost its standing only because more "posh"—as the Kenyans put it—estates had been built.

At the gate, the guard asked me who I had come to see, and

he guided me to the servant quarters. I knocked, waited, knocked again, and then she answered the door.

"MacBook. Here," she said, pointing to her palm. I gave her the laptop.

"Come in. Strip naked," she ordered.

I laughed and said no.

"Do you want my help or not?"

"I'm not a male prostitute—in any case, I would rather I was paid in cash, not in kind," I said. I was glad to be talking to someone who was not weighed down by the tragedy of Mary's murder.

"You are all bloody—I'm not going to let you in like this. What the fuck, man? Get your mind out of the gutter," she said, opening and lifting up her hands so that the MacBook looked like it would fall any second. "You need to shower—and you need a change of clothes."

She went into another room and came back with a towel.

"You would rather stand by the door than get naked? Are we in fucking kindergarten? Get on with it. Look, I'll get naked just to show you it's no big deal."

She took off her shorts and, when she got to her underwear, I quickly undressed, piling my clothes on the floor and leaving my Glock on top. She gave me the towel and directed me to the shower.

"Are you going to shower with that?" she asked when she saw me eyeing my Glock. I picked it up and put it on a little side table by the door.

"The water will be cold—this is the servant quarters," she warned.

The thing is, she was beautiful—beautiful in a strange way, I thought to myself as I took a cold shower. She was the opposite of Muddy, shorter, stockier, and with a short afro. Her teeth were oddly spaced out and her forehead seemed to recede into her hairline. But she was beautiful. I got out of the shower and wrapped myself in a towel. She pointed to the couch and I looked back at her in surprise.

"Humor me," she said. "It's all I have."

Shit! She had laid out a long yellow dress for me to wear. I had to laugh. Why not? It's not like she would just have men's clothing lying around for a tall American detective to put on. I wiggled into it. It felt cozy and, in spite of myself, I liked how it hugged my hips.

"I am clean and I am dressed," I announced.

"This laptop, tell me everything about the owner," she said as she put a cup of hot tea in front of me.

"Why?" I said to her. "All I know about him is that I'd like to kill him."

"This computer has some heavy shit around it. There are two things about security, any kind of security. Either it is built around the owner, or the owner adapts it to his or her personality. Do you see what I'm saying?" She didn't wait for me to answer, or rather ask her what she meant.

"The bottom line is there are no objective security systems. At the end of the day, Mr. Detective, no matter how sophisticated a system is, it's only as good as the user. So what I am saying to you is this—if I know the user, then I have the human aspect of the security system. If I do not get to know the user, there is no way I am breaking anything. This is something they don't teach you in hack school—you hack a personality, not code—assuming of course you are good to begin with," she explained patiently. "Had you ever heard of me before today, Mr. Detective?"

"No, I haven't," I answered.

"I'd like to keep it that way—no triggering some shit somewhere that comes down on me. So start talking!" she commanded.

She was weird but she made sense. Even the cold shower made sense—why should she be polite and let me in all bloody? And being naked—what was the big deal anyway? To get to Sahara, I had to tell her everything about the case. It felt good to sit there and talk through it as she took notes.

"This Sahara of yours, what kind of man is he?" she asked. "How would you describe him?"

"Patient, knowledgeable, confident, cruel, controlling, and efficient … the kind of man who prides himself on making the least amount of wasted moves," I answered, realizing that it sounded like I admired him.

"Age?" she asked.

"About sixty, fit but losing the battle."

"Hairline?"

"Balding and grey, a well-trimmed goatee. There was something professorial about him."

"Why do you say that?" she asked, looking up from her note-taking. I couldn't quite say why.

"Let's try another route, Mr. Detective—what kind of fucking language did he use?" she asked.

"Simple language—he wanted me to understand—and he was that way with his men. It wasn't perverse—he genuinely wanted me to understand him. At times, it was like he was speaking to a student about to flunk a final exam," I said, starting to see some sort of logic in her questions.

It was like a police sketch artist with an eyewitness, you corral in the details—a nose, a chin, eyes—until you have a whole face. Now that I was on this side of it, I understood what it meant to assume that a witness knows more than they think they know.

"What was he wearing when you met?" she asked. I described the clothing he and his men had been wearing.

"The outfit—it sounds like he should have been in a suit or corduroys, not a safari shirt," she said.

"Yeah, he apologized for that—said that he knew Africa wasn't just wild animals or something like that," I explained.

"What were his exact words?" she asked, suddenly looking up.

" 'Africa is not a country,' " I answered, thinking that these were the kind of questions we should ask witnesses, questions that tried to get to the essence of the suspect and not just the color of his clothes.

Helen clapped her hands together in excitement.

"I love that. I love the fucker! I think I have him!" she exclaimed.

She stood up and, placing her hand on my shoulder, she guided me out.

"Detective, don't forget your gun," she said as I got to the door. I piled it on top of my bloody clothes, hiked up my dress, and walked to the Land Rover.

At the gate the guard looked into the car and laughed, saying, "A man goes in, a woman comes out."

I didn't respond.

"Looking good, sister!" he yelled as I drove off.

O was just finishing patching up the broken patio windows when I walked in. He looked at me in my bright yellow dress, my Glock resting peacefully on top of my pile of clothes.

"How did it go?" he asked, as if this was something that happened every day.

As soon as I was done explaining, it was time to leave for Kisumu to make Mary's burial arrangements—I had no idea what to expect but I knew I just needed to be there for my friend.

"My mother, she can't see you like this. You need some makeup," he said with a serious look of concern on his face before he broke into laughter. I had some clothes in O's guest bedroom and I changed back into a man.

Muddy hadn't come back from picking up Janet. I called and she said she was sitting with Janet in her dorm room, talking, so we left for Kisumu without her.

CHAPTER 6

MOURNING MARY

I didn't speak the Luo language but I could tell that something was going terribly wrong. When O and I arrived in Kisumu the night following Mary's death and walked through the door, his mother, an old dark-skinned woman, eyes with bits of unseeing grey, had hobbled to him. They spoke for a little while and she let out the most gut-wrenching wail I had ever heard. She did it three times and soon the compound was alive with elders. Some of them were crying. Others were trying to comfort O, who stood stoically, like a man waiting for an answer. This went on for a while. Tea was prepared; bread sliced into triangles and spread with jam and butter—a snack I had come to associate with weddings—was passed around. Then O spoke for a long time.

I watched without understanding his impassioned plea. I had never seen him speak in front of people, and with his tall frame, piercing red eyes, and a voice that at different times sounded cajoling, pleading, and proud, he had a commanding presence. When he was done, the elders huddled in the corner. O came and sat by me and we watched them whisper animatedly among themselves. I couldn't bring myself to ask O what was happening—this wasn't one of our cases.

"I'm glad your mother is feeling better" was all I could say to him.

"She came back from the *hosi* this morning," O said, falling into Nairobi slang.

Finally his mother, her hands and voice shaking, tears in her eyes, said something to O. He stood up, said something angrily, gesturing at everyone, and took off. Everything had happened so fast. His mother tried to say something to me but I couldn't understand. An elderly man came over to me and translated it into English.

"She says she loves her son, that in death she forgives Mary. However, her hands are tied. The clan has spoken. She has to do what her people want. In time he will see it was the right thing to do," he said.

"What do you mean? Mary won't be buried here?" I asked him in disbelief.

"Should our people simply lie down and be trampled upon like weeds?" he asked as he started to guide me out.

"Is that you or the mother saying that stupid shit? That is her son, out there in pain because her daughter-in-law was shot in the head," I said to him. I was confused and angry.

"The people have spoken, we now have one voice," he said and smiled gently at me, as if I were a child and would understand someday.

He placed his hand on my shoulder. I wanted to hit him.

"Fuck off," I said to him, and he let go. I turned to look at O's mother; she cast her eyes down and started sobbing as the elders enveloped her.

"Tell Odhiambo we are sorry," the old man said to me when I got to the door.

I found O lying back on a reclined passenger seat. We had an eight-hour drive ahead of us and I was not looking forward to it.

"All this time wasted ... we could have been working," he

said, more to himself than to me. I started the car without saying a word.

"They won't let me bury my wife," O said, looking straight ahead after we'd been driving for an hour or so in silence. "I bought that piece of land, and built that house for my mother, and they will not let me bury my dead wife." He sounded like he was a bit amused by the ridiculousness of it all, as if he couldn't believe it.

"Why? Isn't that the custom?" I asked.

He helped me piece together the reason why. Mary was a Kikuyu and O, a Luo. Living in Nairobi, isolated from their fellow ethnic groups, it had never been an issue—as far as I could tell. In fact, until it was time to bury her, I, as an outsider, couldn't tell they were from different ethnic groups. They spoke to each other in English but I had always assumed that it was for my benefit. I suppose it's the difference between interracial marriages in New York and in some backwater Midwestern town.

The elections were tomorrow and the resulting tensions had only heightened ethnocentrism. The president, a Kikuyu, was being opposed by a Luo—it seemed as if Mary's death had fallen along the same ethnic demarcations. O's family didn't want to bury a Kikuyu woman. Would Mary's family want to bury a woman married to a Luo? I couldn't ask O. I passed on his mother's message to him. Now it made sense. Weeds, I knew that term in the context of Rwanda—Muddy, a Tutsi, had been called a "weed." In the Kenyan context, the Luos and Kikuyus saw each other as weeds.

"You and me, Ishmael, we come from a different world—we have us on one side and criminals on the other—and what matters is getting the criminal even when ethnicity and race run interference. You know what I mean? That's where we draw the line. In my mother's world, one's ethnicity matters more than life and death itself. She is my wife. I am her son. She is her daughter. But not today—today, ethnicity is god," O lamented.

O's marriage had added another dimension to his duality—to his ability to be violent and cruel when in the cruel and violent world of our investigations, and to be loving without residual feelings of guilt when in the loving world of Mary. That balance had collapsed. Now the duality that allowed him to be a Luo married to a Kikuyu had also collapsed under the pressure of the day's ethnic politics—and it was costing him his home and a burial place for his wife.

I could see a bit of it. When I took Muddy—an African refugee who did spoken word—to the U.S. to meet my parents, how would their black middle-class sensibilities take it? I was supposed to marry up—that's what they had liked about my ex-wife and her corporate-ladder climbing. When I said I wanted to become a cop, it was not so much that they hated the profession, though it made them uneasy; it was because it was beneath us. So their son who was a cop working in Kenya was marrying a Rwandan refugee who did spoken word? They would have something to say about that.

"What did you tell your mother ... the clan?" I asked him.

"I told her that I loved my wife and that they might as well have killed me too. I asked her how I could bury my wife elsewhere and still call this place home? How can I come back here? How do I forgive that? And how do I live with myself after costing Mary her life? I asked her all those questions and you know what she told me? She said she understands my pain but this was no longer just about a man and his wife, but about what our people want," he explained, anger carrying each word.

"O, she seemed genuinely in pain," I said to him.

"Pain without action is useless to me," he replied tensely.

"Hey, I don't know a lot, but this much I know. You cannot blame yourself for Mary's death," I said, not even sure if I believed that myself.

O laughed a laugh that was somewhere between incredulity and anger. The kind of laugh that told me that if we hadn't been friends, his response would've been more forceful.

"Jesus, Ishmael, what the fuck? If she hadn't been married to me, she wouldn't be dead. It's that simple. I am responsible for her death. And so are you. And so is Sahara. We will all have to pay somehow. It's just the way it is now," he said, pushing himself against the passenger seat as if trying to still himself.

I felt like shit for having said what I said. I had to agree that he was right. The fact was that without him, without us rattling the bushes, Mary would still be alive. We hadn't killed her—yet we had. Even after we found out why she had died and brought those responsible to some form of justice, we would still be responsible for her death.

The bottom line was that I could not imagine what he was going through. I had never lost anyone close to me—I had lost cop friends, but I'm talking about someone I truly loved, who I saw every day, who I lived and fought with. I couldn't imagine what it was like to have that gone—what the first morning after, and then the next and the next … what that emptiness was like.

We were now close to Nakuru, and I was about to joke about going to Lake Nakuru to see flamingoes, when we turned a corner and found ourselves in front of a group of young men armed with rocks, bows and arrows, and machetes that I guessed to be part of the Chinese machete shipment seized earlier in Mombasa.

They were chanting "Down with Kibaki! Up with Raila!" Some of them were still in their school uniforms, while others, nicely dressed, appeared to have joined the crowd after work. It looked more like a celebration than a war party. We slowed down and drove through them, until they suddenly stopped moving and we had to stop as well or run them over.

I rolled down my window. I could smell alcohol on their breath. They said something to us. I looked over at O.

"They want to know what we are—which ethnicity," O translated.

"American," I said, finding the whole thing a bit amusing—fucking bows and arrows?

"*Kipande*?" Now, that I knew meant "ID." O showed them his badge and they sobered up for a minute. O asked them something.

"We are Kalenjin, warriors ... like Rambo," one of them replied and laughed, pointing at me.

"Or Terminator," another one said. O shook his head. They waved us through. Luos were okay and Americans were most welcome.

"What if we had been Kikuyu?" I asked him, feeling unsettled by the whole thing.

"A few insults, your mother this, your mother that, a few slaps ... that's it—they are just kids," O replied.

"You keep saying that," I said to him.

"And you keep being American—it comes in handy, you know ... goodwill ..." he retorted.

There was something I had to tell him—my fuck-up with Sahara—how if I had shot the driver, Sahara would have been dead or ours. He listened and was silent for a while.

"It's okay, Ishmael, but let me tell you something—understand that this world, our world is not what it was two weeks ago—you cannot order it to some moral code," he said.

"They opened the door, Ishmael—they opened the fucking door—and you know what? We never really had a choice but to enter their hell. And I am not talking about some simple revenge shit and what it requires, I am talking about justice. You have seen what they are capable of. To get Sahara, to get justice, we have to use their fucked-up moral code. Either that or we walk away … Right now!" He banged his hand on the dashboard.

"You let Jamal walk … why?" I asked him.

"Jamal—where is the justice in killing him? When it came down to it, he tried, even if it was to save himself. We owed him our lives from way back when. That debt has been paid," he said.

"Did you know your gun was empty?" I asked.

"Did I know my gun was empty?" he repeated my question without answering.

My friend was hurting—his wife was dead, his family had abandoned him when he needed them the most, denied him the kind of closure that comes with being held close by family as he grieved. I vowed to myself to be there with him when he walked through the door that Sahara had opened.

Wanting to lose myself in the case, I was dreading going back into O's apartment, but as we neared his door, we could hear laughter. We went in to find Janet and Muddy going through Mary's clothes. Janet was holding up a mini-skirt and boots, an outfit that was so unlike Mary that I too couldn't help laughing.

Janet rushed to O and started crying. Muddy stood up and I walked to her. We held each other and my world felt real again.

Then she patted me on the shoulder, went to Janet, and guided her back to the pile of belongings.

O rolled a joint and sat with them among piles of Mary's books and clothes. I opened a bottle of whiskey and sat down too. With a joint passing between O and Muddy, and a bottle between Janet and me, we mourned.

O took us back to their early days when they had just started dating—a cop and a schoolteacher, who happened to be Luo and Kikuyu—"as if we didn't have enough differences."

When they first met, he hadn't even made detective yet. He was a constable called to her school because someone had broken in and made off with grounds maintenance equipment, wheelbarrows, shears, and the like. He saw her as she was walking to lunch. He tried to get himself invited along. She said no. He kept coming back to her school and questioning potential witnesses until she said yes.

"That case of the missing *wheelbarrow* has never been solved to this day," he declared to our laughter. "But the case of lonely hearts was."

Muddy suggested finishing the exams Mary had been grading, but the math was too difficult for us. We didn't stop to think about whether we were doing the right thing when we passed all her students—Janet was going to take Mary's last gift to her students in the morning.

We couldn't get ourselves to cook. There was a twenty-four-hour Kenchic around the corner and I rushed there to get some chicken and chips. When I came back, it was to find Kenny Rogers blaring throughout the apartment, his raspy country voice belting out the almost soulful "She Believes in Me."

Neighbors knocked on the door and I opened it, thinking they had come to complain, but it was to join us. Seeing there wouldn't be enough food, they went back to their kitchens and came with whatever leftovers they had. On the sitting room floor where just hours before Mary had lain dead, all sorts of dishes were laid out—*ugali*, fish, chapattis, boiled maize and beans, cabbage and eggs and a curry of one thing or another, fermented milk and porridge—you name it. It was as if all of Kenya's ethnicities were represented in the dishes.

"Hey, Muddy, I missed your performance," Janet yelled, to drown out the calls for "The Gambler" to be rewound.

Muddy stood up a bit unsteadily and let her dreads hang out. That got the attention of the mourners-turned-party revelers.

"A song, a painting, a poem, a word is a story. So let me tell you a story, a story about …" She seemed lost, and smiled, as if inviting us to tell her what the story should be. She continued after the pause.

"Let me tell you a story about a word—one word that is as old as the very earth we walk on, a word that crosses boundaries, that swims underneath the currents of culture, a word that is a language, a word that is the language. Let me tell you a story about the word 'love.' When love was born, love was living. This love that was newborn and old, an old woman, this love decided to walk the earth. And young love said to older love, or was it the other way round? Love said to love, Love is birth, Love is living and Love is death, Love is gentle, Love is fierce, Love is violent, Love is living and Love is death, Love is God and Love is the Devil, and Love forgets more than it remembers, but tonight, this morning that is still a night …"

She took a few deep breaths that cut through our quietness.

"Love is the vehicle that drove us here, Love is Mary, Love is O, and Love is us. I love you, O."

No one said anything and for that one moment, I felt

love like it was a human being walking among us, a physical thing, something that I could touch. That was not the poem she had performed at the Carnivore, not even close. It was something new.

Then there was the sound of a rewinding cassette, a few miscues to the beginning of "The Gambler," and we went back to singing along. As the party continued, some of the neighbors went to the kitchen, found food containers, and packed away the now twice leftover food into O's fridge. Dishes were cleaned, and the floor cleared of bottles and mopped. It didn't matter that most of the neighbors hardly spoke to each other, that they were from different ethnicities, or that they had to go to work the following day—they kept O company till six in the morning, talking and laughing about things peculiarly Kenyan, peppering me with questions about America and Muddy about Rwanda, and occasionally all of us sang along to a Kenny Rogers song.

Finally, everyone was gone and we were left sprawled on the sitting room floor. It was time to start staring at our reality.

"Next move?" I asked O in the haze of the smoke.

"Kikuyu land, tomorrow we go to Kikuyu country." Then he looked at Janet. "And you back to uni."

Janet reached for his hand. He handed the joint back to Muddy and cupped Janet's hand with both of his.

"Who's going to take care of you without me here?" Janet asked him.

"Not you, Janet … Mary would kill me if I let you interrupt your studies—especially with your math skills," O teased before choking up.

"You are the star still shining in my world, Janet. Your life is ahead of you, we are your past," he said, wiping tears away from his eyes.

I looked away so that I wouldn't cry. Muddy sighed and laid her head on my lap, her dreadlocks sprawling onto the floor.

We turned on the 7:00 a.m. news. The counting of the electoral votes was still going on, with a live update of the tally—it looked like Kenya would be swearing in a Luo president.

"Two for two soon," O said, referring to Obama. "See, I told you there was nothing to worry about—the most peaceful election of all time."

"Tell that to a powder keg," Muddy muttered.

We were still a unit of some sort. I wanted to believe that we still worked. We needed to sleep.

I had barely closed my eyes when my cell rang. It was Helen and she had something for me. I could tell she was excited.

"I'm here to return the dress," I said to the watchman, to preempt more jokes from him.

"Go on, Miss," he said without skipping a beat. I found the door open so I knocked as I walked in. I called out Helen's name but she didn't answer. Her office door was closed. I knocked again, still no answer, so I pushed the door open. She had her headphones on, swaying to whatever she was listening to, and I let out a sigh of relief.

Her office didn't look like a hacker's—there were only two computers sitting on a desk in an otherwise empty room.

"The servers aren't here … and I'm not telling," she said, smiling at my surprise. "I know, I know, you want to get on with it."

She went on. "Your guy, I knew it—he is an anthropologist or historian of some sort. He studied at UC–Berkeley—most probably some African-related shit, and he loves watching American football and basketball games. He reads a lot of African stuff—archaeology—old stuff. And that's not all," she said, seeing the look of disappointment on my face. "See this?"

She showed me videos of some scouting missions Sahara had gone on with his men. Each one of them began with footage of the entrance to a location and the security—in each place, their Range Rover was all but waved through—then the front desk, and soon enough, the lower rooms. They had done their homework before settling for the Norfolk.

"This is plenty already—how did you get in?" I asked.

"My profile of Sahara. An old white man who probably taught at a university, efficient, a person who values simplicity. In spite of the security protecting his laptop, he found a way of circumventing it. He didn't grow up using computers, he's a pen-and-paper person. You know how back in the day people hid safes behind paintings? Pretty much the same here—he hid things behind other things. He hid them where you would never think of looking unless you knew him," she explained. "Let me put it this way, if I hadn't gotten a sense of the old fuck, it would have taken me months to try and break into folders that had nothing in them," she said, looking at me to see if I understood.

"It was that simple?" I asked her.

"You know the difference between simple and simplicity? Think of a child's poem—simple, but try to write one yourself and you realize it's simplicity masked as simple. But hey, I'm not offended," she answered, half smiling, half scowling. "One other thing, though. There is an encrypted file—that will take some time, but I think I can break it open. That's the file you want, because it was important enough for Mr. Arthritis to follow protocol with it."

"Can you make a copy of the file? I'm thinking I can also have the guys at the embassy look at it," I said. "More hands on it the better, we need to move fast—these guys are already a year ahead."

"No, too risky ... You would have to take the whole thing to them," she said, pointing at the computer. "Or the hard drive ..."

"Then I will leave it in your capable hands," I said, trusting she would find a way.

"I don't have the most sophisticated equipment in the world, I have to improvise ... unless you offer to buy me the expensive shit I need ... but probably not on your salary—Kamau told me this was a personal favor," she said.

"Not on my salary. But Sahara can afford it," I said, as I gave the several thousand dollars I'd taken from Sahara's driver to a surprised Helen.

"I'll call, don't call me," she yelled. I rushed back to O's with a DVD of the footage of Sahara and his men scouting locations.

O and I went through the scouting tapes carefully. They corresponded with the locations marked on the maps that I had retrieved from the Range Rover. It was time to call Hassan and Jason—we needed more manpower and equipment to check out all the locations. We had a lot on our plate as it was with Mary's funeral.

We started out our meeting with Jason and Hassan chitchatting about the elections. The elections had thus far gone well enough; no violence and no major irregularities were being reported. Raila was still pulling ahead of Kibaki. Hassan had deployed uniformed police to likely trouble spots, but he was confident that by the end of the following day we would have a new president without violence. The predicted blood-letting had not happened.

We moved on to the case. They weren't happy that we had kept the laptop from them.

"I don't like this—we agreed—full disclosure," Jason said.

"What did you think? That some Americans with high security clearances would storm into O's house and kill his wife and all would be well?" I asked Jason.

"Only a person working with Sahara would know we had it. We wanted to see if someone would come asking," O lied. It worked to quiet any protests.

"So?" Hassan asked.

"No, but it's only been a few days," O answered.

I explained about the map locations and showed them the DVD footage.

"Your computer guy broke his security?" a surprised Jason asked. I didn't correct him on gender; the less he knew about Helen, the better.

"Yeah, only he could have done that. Weird little guy— terrorists and hackers have the same look—haughty, haunted, and hunted. But hey, we need a game plan—we need to check out all these places as fast as we can. We need help, good help. We can't do it by ourselves—we have to bury O's wife," I reminded them.

The Al Qaeda charade was using up a lot of resources, but Jason and Hassan promised to free up some people to check out the locations in the DVD. They were going to divvy up the work, but we would start things off by checking Kenyatta International Conference Center (KICC) on our way to Limuru. Since the

Electoral Commission's command center was at the KICC, it was all the more urgent. Jason made a call and arranged for some bomb experts from the embassy to meet us there.

"Jason, the terrorist list—anything yet?" O asked him as we left. "Anything we should worry about?"

"Nothing. I have your backs," Jason answered. "If anyone makes a move on you, I will run serious interference and let you know."

The KICC brings to mind one word—"hubris." Not because the place didn't have a function: it was where national and international conferences were held, where the wedding parties of the rich and famous were catered, and where, often enough, foreign diplomats met. It's just that the place was built to immortalize Kenya's first president. Inside, there was a tall statue of the late Kenyatta, and whereas in real life he was an old man, stooped and decrepit, the statue was pure magnificence—eleven or so feet of gleaming gold.

"Chop off a toe and you can build a home," O joked.

With Jason's man, O and I followed the path Sahara and his men had taken through the building, down to the basement. We found nothing—there were no traces of any explosives, no hollow sounds, and no newer shades of cement or painting. We even went over repair records from the last two years—nothing. They could very well have planted a bomb in one of the rooms but it seemed unlikely. Sahara would have been going for maximum effect. But we decided to split up anyway, and check the lobby and also the first floor. Nothing.

We were off to Limuru to ask Mary's parents to take their daughter back. O's people had said their piece. If Mary's people agreed with O's and denied her a burial place, she would effectively be an orphan.

I called Muddy to let her know we were on our way to Limuru. She lived close to Mary's parents, so she suggested we pick her up, and afterwards we could sleep over at her place. It was a good plan, except that Muddy was so tired that she passed out in the backseat of the Land Rover. I should have been sleeping, too, but so should have O, who was driving.

"Is this usual?" I asked him.

"Is what usual?" he asked in return.

"You didn't let me finish," I countered, but it was more that I was wondering how to ask the question. "Is it usual that ethnic hatred doesn't dissolve after death? I mean, shouldn't death bring people together, if only to bury their loved one?" I asked, fumbling into coherence. I just couldn't shake the feeling that all the bad things happening were in preparation for a major catastrophic event.

"Look, wasn't it illegal in the U.S.—on pain of death, on pain of lynching—to fuck a white woman?" he asked angrily. "You're going to have your black president, I know, but it's too early to start lecturing."

"What the fuck, man, look around you—bomb explosions, elections, machetes, and Mary, we have to beg for fucking six feet of dirt to bury her?" I said.

"Welcome to Kenya—*Karibu Kenya*," he said. In all the time I had known him, he had never talked to me like I was a tourist.

"This *hakuna matata* shit you Kenyans have going—it's going to blow up in your faces," I replied in kind.

O was silent.

"A few days ago, at Muddy's performance, I knew what to expect, I knew Mary would be there the next day, and the next—the only thing I had to fear was the pain of leaving her in grief. Today, I don't know tomorrow anymore. Let us bury Mary. This shit will figure itself out," he finally said.

"Did you ever think of having children?" I asked, deciding to let it go. It wasn't like there was anything we could do about Kenyan politics. And now that I had ten rings for Muddy, kids suddenly didn't seem like such a bad idea.

"Yes, but there was always tomorrow. You cannot love, truly love, unless you believe you will always have tomorrow—otherwise your life together is a wish, a regret. Yes—we wanted children," he answered.

"Hey, when are you going to do it?" O asked, meaning the proposal.

"The ..." I was looking for a code word for the beaded rings in case Muddy was just closing her eyes. "I couldn't throw ten rings into a hat ... our lives, everything is upside down," I said.

O lit a joint and rolled down his window, the cold Limuru air jolting me into full alertness.

"That is the worst code I have ever heard," he said, his chest heaving in and out in silent laughter. "You love the woman, propose. Even if bullets are flying around you, get on your knees and ask. You cannot live thinking that tomorrow you are going to die, or that you'll lose the one you love ... Life ... life ... would be just too much work."

We turned on the radio just as Kibaki was being announced the winner. Raila had been leading. Kibaki's last-minute surge was suspicious, to say the least.

"You better wake Muddy up. Shit, Ishmael, this is really bad,"

O said as he stopped the car and tried calling the headquarters. No answer. He tried Hassan, still nothing.

I woke Muddy up and explained what had happened.

"In Rwanda it took the suspicious presidential plane crash, in Kenya this is it, last-minute rigging," she said, her voice betraying an anxiety I had never heard before.

O handed her the joint—she took a few puffs and threw it out the window.

We were about thirty minutes away from Mary's parents' house. We decided to continue. We figured it would take a day or two before the violence spiraled into sleepy Limuru—and we just might have enough time to bury Mary.

CHAPTER 7

AND THEN IT RAINED

The makeshift roadblock and the ten or so young men armed with machetes, knives, stones, flashlights, and kerosene lamps running toward us took us by surprise. We tried to reverse, but behind us another roadblock had been hastily erected. The Land Rover could take most terrains—but we were surrounded by trees.

We had been overrun by events. Now it was a question of basic survival.

O jumped out of the car, went to the trunk, came back with two AKs, and handed one to Muddy. Muddy and I stepped out, leaving the engine running and the lights on.

I had faced death many times before, I had even walked into a KKK camp alone, but this was different. If they got to us, O, a Luo, would be killed on the spot. For Muddy, unable to pass because she spoke Kikuyu with a Kinyarwanda accent, and me, who could barely ask for water to save my life, it could go either way.

We were armed with new guns, and they had machetes and old guns that looked like hunting muskets, but there were three of us and they were at least twenty, counting the ones manning the roadblock they had erected behind us. If some of them were ready to die, they would get us.

But we had an advantage. I reached into the Land Rover and

turned the lights to high beam, blinding the young men coming toward us—an old trick that made them approach cautiously.

There was still the matter of those edging closer and closer from behind, the glowing red taillights acting as a beacon.

O sent out a growl from his AK into the air—and everybody stood where they were. Muddy hopped back into the Land Rover, crawled all the way to the rear, and opened the door so that with her AK she had us covered.

O motioned for me to speak to the young men. I understood. His Luo-accented Kiswahili would only heighten the situation.

I lowered my Glock and walked toward them.

"I am an American." Never before had those words sounded so hollow and devoid of meaning. I stupidly thought I might as well have also announced that we came in peace.

"And we are here to make burial arrangements for a friend," I added.

There was some murmuring and then two young men stepped forward—one of them held a gleaming machete and the other an old hunting rifle. The one holding the machete spoke in Kikuyu, but it was not until the other one holding the musket started translating that I understood what was going on—the leader didn't speak English and needed an interpreter.

"We have no quarrel with you, Mr. American. You can leave and greet Mr. Obama for us when you get back home. Eh, Mr. Obama, that Luo, he is very lucky to be American," the leader said through the interpreter, pointing the machete at me.

"Can the others please identify themselves?" he asked.

"My name is Muddy and this is my home," Muddy yelled from the back.

"This is not your home. You are our guest and we treat guests with respect. You too may pass," the man replied.

"And the third person? Who are you?" the man asked, pointing at O.

"I am a Kenyan, just like you," O shouted back. I saw them start but another growl from O held them back. We could not afford to draw first blood. However, we could remind them they had lives to lose.

"Identify yourselves!" O challenged them.

"We are the protectors of our land and wealth," the leader said proudly. "Your people are killing our people and for that you have to pay," he added, as a *matatu* came from the other side of the roadblock. The passengers were ordered out. I could make out flashlights going over identification cards. All the passengers climbed back in except for one man who was herded into the surrounding bushes as he pleaded for his life.

"Let the man go, just let him go—what has he done to you? Do you even know his name?" I asked the leader.

"Do you know what they are doing to our people in Kisumu? Did you hear about the church in the Rift Valley? Little children, women—screaming—burning to death?" the man asked me. The passion in his voice—this was not going to be easy.

"That man, he had nothing to do with it. Nothing at all—this is not justice, this is murder," I said to him, thinking I could nudge the little flame of humanity I heard in his voice into empathy.

"Murder? Justice? You think I care? It is one less of them," he screamed at me.

He yelled something in Kikuyu to his men. We heard loud screams and then silence except for the rustling as the murderers emerged from the bushes. The man was dead. There was nothing we could have done for him.

"Let me say something," I said to the leader when his attention returned to us.

"Speak, Mr. Obama," he gave me permission, sarcastically.

"The Norfolk bombing, most of the dead are Kenyans, there were some Kikuyus, Asians, Luos, and many others who died. We are the detectives working that case and I haven't heard my friend say this justice is only for his people and not the others. You understand? He is working for Kenyan justice. And if you kill him, the murderers who planted the bomb will not be brought to justice. Your people will have died in vain," I appealed to him.

"The dead are already dead. But we can make sure their children live without fear," he said. "You, we have no quarrel with. You can go. But you will never save your friend."

"Listen to me. My name is Odhiambo and I am here to bury my wife," O shouted defiantly. With that, they knew who he was—their inter-ethnic marriage would have been fueling anger for years.

"Make your move," he goaded them, letting out another roar.

This is it, I thought to myself. Instinctively I raised my weapon to the man's head. The translator shakily raised his musket to mine.

"The gun I'm holding is a Glock. You will be dead long before your man here has a chance to fire that thing—if it doesn't jam," I said to the leader, waiting tensely for the translation to register. "But look, even warriors have to eat." I reached into my back pocket and came out with the rest of the money from the Range Rover.

The leader took it and slapped it against the machete. The translator lowered his musket and I lowered my weapon as well. I thought how ironic it was that Sahara's money was buying our lives and those of the young men we would have taken with us.

"We need more—for that weed," he said, pointing at O. "We

need more, or you leave him behind." That was the last of the money—and the longer we stood bargaining, the more we were losing our advantage, the more the stalemate was receding, as they plotted and found weaknesses in our three-person defense. I had to make a move.

"Fuck off … I'm done here," I said to him as I grabbed the musket and shot the translator in the head. I elbowed the leader in the face and he fell backwards, his machete clattering away from him. The young men started moving forward, but I was pointing my gun at the head of the now-kneeling leader. He looked behind him and waved at them to stop.

I stood him up and took the wad of cash from his pocket. He motioned to me that we could go. I yelled out to O to start the car and he slowly drove to where I was standing.

I hopped in, grabbing the leader by his shirt, and pulled him along so that he was running by the Land Rover. The young men moved away. We drove through the makeshift roadblock in complete silence, except for the yells of the leader, who was begging for us to stop. I released him as soon as we were in the clear.

"There was no saving him," Muddy said, in reference to the man who had just been murdered. "I've seen this before. We should have killed the whole lot of them."

"I could have made my move earlier—I could have made my move as soon as I walked up to him," I said, before I leaned out the window and threw up. Did I execute the translator or was it an act of self-defense?

"No, you couldn't have … you needed the time to make a plan. Your instincts … you were right not to shoot the leader, they would have overrun us," O said.

I didn't ask him why he had been goading them. It seemed like there was a part of him that wanted violence to break out, no matter the consequences ... to lose his grief in it. I knew that because I too wanted to square off with something, with someone, and here was the difference between us ... someone deserving.

We turned on the radio to the BBC and that was when we realized the extent of it all. Our experience was just a taste of what everyone else was going through. We could hear alarm in the reporter's voice—in the slums of Kibera and Mathare, violence had already broken out—ethnicity pitted against ethnicity.

In Kisumu, Kikuyus were being pulled out of their homes and cars and killed. The police had killed unarmed protestors from the opposition. Some of the opposition leaders had gone back to their constituents to organize them into militia. Abroad, different ethnicities were collecting money for their brethren. Some white tourists had been beaten up. The police deployed in the rural areas had broken along ethnic lines, and had gone on a killing rampage.

In less than an hour, the country had become unrecognizable. The violence that had been circling around us for so long, touching down every now and then, had descended on the whole country.

Mary's father, Ngatia, opened the door. The kerosene lamp flickered back and forth and he beckoned us in before it gave out. We followed him into the sitting room, where we found Mary's mother, Mumbi, sitting by a charcoal burner. They lived alone and, judging from the photographs with frames blackened by burning charcoal, Mary was their only child.

One photograph showed the father addressing young school kids—he used to be a headmaster. The mother was a teacher too—which explained why Mary had become a teacher. On a long wooden table, there were trays full of bread with jam and butter and kettles of tea—for the mourners who had not yet arrived.

No one was going to come, not with the looming violence outside. They pointed us to the bread and tea and then shuffled along and brought three chairs to the fire. We did not sit down. I stretched my hands to warm them and noticed they were still shaking.

They were listening to the news and Ngatia was having a beer. Muddy quickly filled both of them in about the young men with machetes and explained that we had to move.

"I can only hope we have time to bury my daughter properly. When is the burial, Odhiambo?" Mumbi asked O in English.

"That is why I am here," O said, and he explained what had happened with his relatives. By the time he was done Mumbi was crying. Muddy leaned closer to her and took her hands. The father hadn't said a word, but now he looked at O.

"You have killed my daughter ... and now you cannot even bury her," Ngatia said in such a tired voice that I felt waves of pity going through me.

"Yes," O said. "Because of me she is dead—but she was dead to you a long time ago. See what your hatred has brought home?" He pointed at the radio. "It is people like you and my mother who taught these young men to hate. What kind of a father disowns his daughter?"

"You want to know what kind of a father? I'll show you," Ngatia said, standing up to get his walking stick.

"Enough!" Mumbi yelled at both of them. "We were wrong—I always thought there would be a time when we would welcome her back. One cannot stop being a mother or a daughter. We were angry, we did not expect her to die," she added more quietly.

It made sense—we get angry at the ones we love and, as long as they are alive, there is some hope of reconciliation. One never factors in death.

"Now he wants us to bury her? When a woman marries, she marries into the man's family. We cannot bury her!" Ngatia said to Mumbi.

"Hey, I know we need to talk. But we have to go," Muddy reminded us. The five or so minutes we had spent talking—that was already too long.

Just as we were getting ready to leave, there was urgent knocking at the door. Someone shouted something before running off.

"They are coming for you," Ngatia translated.

We rushed to the door and cautiously opened it. No one was there but we could make out flashlights tearing into the darkness. Muddy and O rushed to the Land Rover and came back with their AK-47s, with O holding three vests and Muddy two flashlights.

"By now, they will have some regional cops with them," O said as he gave one of the vests to Muddy, and the other two to Mary's parents.

There wasn't much time to debate over our three choices— drive through the mob, stay and fight, or escape through the fields. There was no way we were driving without risking an ambush. To stay and fight wasn't an option either, sending us into the open would be easy—all they had to do was set the wooden house on fire.

Making our way through the surrounding tea plantation made the most sense. There was one disadvantage—with Mary's parents in tow and in the Limuru darkness, we would be slow.

Ngatia swigged the last of the Tusker with an impish grin.

"I might as well die happy," he said.

Mumbi wanted to pack a few things, but with only minutes to spare, we could allow her to take only a family portrait, with a toothless baby Mary smiling out of the black-and-white photograph.

"It is just a house," she said to herself as we made for the door. She reached over to turn off the kerosene lamp. Muddy stopped her—we needed them to think that, with the light on and the car outside, we were still in the house.

Muddy made sure the curtains were drawn shut. She turned up the radio. More reports about ethnic violence erupting—we did not need telling, we were in the thick of it.

"Listen, O, you take the rear, Ishmael, I want you to take the right flank—I will take point. Mother, stay behind me. Ngatia, take the right," Muddy instructed, and looked at O. He reached into his holster and reluctantly gave Ngatia his old .45.

"I hope you learned to use this when you were killing your own people," O said with derision. Ngatia took the gun and removed the safety.

"I did what I thought was right then—and tonight I will do what I think is right again. Yes, I fought with the British against the freedom fighters. Today, I will fight whoever stands between me and my family," Ngatia said as he weighed the .45 in his right hand. "My regrets are mine, not yours."

I understood—he was an Uncle Tom, one of those who had picked up a gun against his own people in their struggle against the British. I had been called an Uncle Tom for joining the police force but I wasn't like Ngatia. I hadn't been out there hunting black freedom fighters. I could feel tension building in our soon-to-be-besieged group.

"Let's go! I know we need to talk—but let's do it on the move!" Muddy ordered.

She had taken charge. Muddy's military training, from her time in the Rwandan Patriotic Front, had kicked in, and it was a good thing, because neither O nor I had any training, much less in guerrilla warfare. We stepped out into the darkness and made our way to the back of the house. Out in the distance we could hear single gun reports: more victims by the roadblock.

"That is the *gotora*. That is what we used. I can recognize it anywhere," Ngatia said. "One shot at a time, if you are lucky."

But just when we were thinking it might not be so bad, we heard the pronounced sound of an AK-47.

"They definitely have the local cops with them," O said.

We were no longer just facing machetes—the gang now had the aid of well-armed police. We were no longer the outnumbered but better-armed group—we had nothing going for us except the darkness, our training, and just a little bit of time.

"Our priority is the AKs—take them out," Muddy said, to the sound of more gunfire.

"Element of surprise? Have they given up on that?" I asked.

"It's a mob. Shoot anything that moves that is not us, but our priority is the big guns," Muddy replied.

"What if there are others, like us, trying to escape? Are they to be shot too?" Mumbi asked.

"I am not the Red Cross, Mother," Muddy answered curtly. Then, catching herself, she added more gently, "Hey, it's just that I want you alive to bury your daughter."

"We cannot do the work of those coming to kill us," Mumbi said, stopping as if to turn back. The mob was getting closer and closer and we could see flashlights searching into the darkness. Muddy grabbed her hand and pulled her along.

"Keep your eyes open for others trying to run," Muddy said as we waded through the tea plantation.

Looking back, we could see fire and smoke spiraling out of what had been their house. As the mob steadily gained on us, the house seemed to burn even more furiously. We could see from their flashlights that they were spreading out—and it started to seem like hundreds of flashlights were running on either side of us.

"They are trying to outflank us," Muddy said as we huddled together in the dark. We had switched off our flashlights, and we could barely see each other.

"There is no way we are going to make it out," O said.

"What do we do now?" I asked.

"We go back the way we came," Muddy said calmly.

"You must be crazy. We go back there and we are all dead," Ngatia whispered, expressing what I was thinking.

"Surprise—they will not be expecting that," Muddy said.

"She is right … it makes the most sense. Football … switch to the least defended part of the field," O agreed, using his own brand of logic.

"Look!" Muddy pointed to the growing flashlights on both sides of us. "Their rear guard is now weak. We can smash right through that."

"What makes you think they will not come after us?" Ngatia asked.

"You do the unexpected. We break their rear and we break their will to fight—at least for today. We got to do it now," Muddy said.

"I have to bury my daughter—I am not dying today. We shall do as you say," Mumbi said to Muddy.

"Make a single file, harder to see us or bump into us. We get close—we fan out—semi-circle—protect the flanks," she instructed. "Mumbi, you stay with me. O, on the right, Ishmael, the left. Ngatia, you take our rear."

"One last thing, it's going to be close, it's going to be nasty and bloody. You will be afraid. If you run, you die. You have to be cold, methodical, and decisive. Take your time—they won't— they will rush and try to overwhelm—that is their power—the numbers—capitalize on their mistakes. Make them fear you," she said in a whisper. "Listen for my signal." She tapped her AK-47. "And then let them know we are here to work."

"My daughter, yes, let us bury her here with her people— instead of in a strange land where she is not wanted," Ngatia said urgently. One would have thought he was talking about burying a Kikuyu woman at the North Pole. Ethnic pride, or the realization that he could die any second now, had changed his mind.

"I cannot fight, but I can pray," Mumbi said. My mind flashed back to my own mother, safely tucked away in Madison. That was exactly the kind of thing she would say, and it would sound right.

"Pray for them too—they need your prayers more than we do," Muddy said. I could detect a smile in her voice, the kind O wore when contemplating violence.

With that, we turned around, with all my training screaming against Muddy's call.

Flashlights and paraffin torches getting closer and closer—the yells, insults, threats of what they are going to do us—I don't need an interpreter now—*I will gut you alive and fuck your women as you bleed to death* sounds the same in all languages. We are moving fast toward what has now become their rear. I now know the taste of fear, and it's the smell of a burning house and the musky smell of the tea plants, as anonymous flashlights and, behind them, men intent on killing you, close in.

I have my Glock—and I'm wondering whether there is solace in not dying easy. The fear, I have come to know it well over the years, my whole body, my whole being, all the thoughts and fibers are now primed to fight or flee. Fleeing is not an option here. So it's fear and fight. Fear is primal; fear is what I and the people besieging us have in common. They are afraid, more afraid than they have ever been, because they know we can kill—some of them saw their friend's head exploding in the full glare of the Land Rover lights. Death and blood are no longer abstract— something that you do only to other people. They know that, they are afraid—that is why they are yelling and talking about gutting and raping.

My advantage is that I know my fear. When it comes down to it, I know how to bathe in it, to luxuriate painfully in it, until the moment when I need to let go and let my instincts, honed by years of training and adversity, take over. I wouldn't survive in a world where there is no fear. Only once have I really known despair and that was just a few days ago, when I thought we would all die and there was little I could do about it. But here I am out in the open; with my hands armed and feet free, I control my destiny.

And then when Muddy calls to me in short bursts from her AK, all I am left with is a violent clarity about what must be done—to kill and kill until I remain alive. I fire my Glock into the flashlights, picking one at a time, hearing a scream of pain as a flashlight falls to the ground.

I fire at a spit of light, then I hear the recoil of a *gotora*. I fire and advance into their rear. Muddy is doing the same with Mumbi behind her. O falls behind us and I can hear short busy bursts.

A few rows down, I hear an AK-47. It's not us, and I calm the fear that comes with knowing the efficiency of the weapon. I crawl on my belly and hide between some bushes as two machetes swish past me. I kill them both, shoot them in the back and advance, and keep crawling on my stomach, waiting so I can pick out the AK. An AK fires in my direction and I stay down as a minty wet tea-leaf smell wafts my way. Guided by the silhouette and his long police overcoat hitting against the leaves, I shoot at the mass. He falls. I crawl to him. I can feel his warm blood against the coolness of the dead leaves on the ground. I slither, groping for his extra magazines—I find them, tuck my Glock into the small of my back, and pick up his AK.

"I have an AK," I shout to my comrades.

More AK fire coming from the rear and once again I wait, and then continue crawling until the policeman is almost standing over me. He sees or senses me, but it's too late to recoil his arms and clear the length he needs for the AK. I edge just a little bit closer, spin onto my back, and fire the AK into his chin—he topples backwards. I can feel a sudden burst of rainwater but I know it's blood splattering on my face. Before he hits the ground, I am on one knee, firing into whoever is behind.

We slowly, mercilessly, and methodically dig a hole through their rearguard. We sound more organized. The young men and what is left of the police force lose the will to fight. They slow down, and keep slowing down until ahead and around us there are no more flashlights. We make it to the clearing and back on the path to the house. It's only then that we realize that Ngatia is not with us. As we start to wonder, we hear O's .45 reporting back to us, followed by a yell, then silence.

"Mother, we have to go. You have a daughter to bury," Muddy says as she gently pushes Mary's mother, now catatonic and staring at her burning house and life, into the Land Rover. They didn't torch the Land Rover—they needed it more than they needed Mumbi's house.

"I am too old to be alone," she says to me as she gets in. Everything she had ever worked for, all she had loved, she has lost everything except her own life—and at her age, how can one start all over again? All she had to look forward to was burying her daughter in a country that had gone to hell.

"Your husband, he gave his life so we could escape. He held them back until we were in the clear. Then they overran him. We are here because of him," I say to her, though I'm not sure. He could just as easily have tried to make a run for it.

"There was a lot of good in him," she says.

I suddenly double up and heave and heave but nothing comes out.

Muddy places her hand on my shoulder. I shudder at her touch and she spins me around, so that I am looking at her, her face glowing from the flames of the burning house.

"How many of them were armed?" she asks.

"I don't know, Muddy—all of them—some of them," I say.

"Not all of them had guns, not all of them could even have had sharpened machetes. You understand? Some of them were just young, jobless, hopeless men. Peer pressure forced some of them to belong to the gang. If Amnesty comes here tomorrow and they count the bodies, this will be a massacre, no matter what we say. But you know what you know—okay? Should we have left Mary's parents to burn with the house so that we could escape? Should we have let them kill us? Fuck you! Fuck you and your fucked-up conscience, you chose to live so you killed," she says, hitting me in the chest.

"Muddy! Enough," O yells from the driver's seat. "Enough— we need to get the fuck out of here!"

I don't say anything, even though I understand her.

"Sometimes your guilt is disguised self-righteousness," she says as she goes to the front to sit with O. She's taking it person- ally, as if I were passing judgment on her. But I wasn't, it was just me reacting to staying alive in so much death.

"This shit, Muddy, it makes me wonder about you in Rwanda—whose side you were really on," I say to her. The words just come out of me. I know I am being mean, but I can't help it.

She turns and looks at me for a while without saying anything.

"They had a choice not to massacre innocent people. We were the ones without a choice," she says finally.

I don't ask her which "they"—in Rwanda or tonight in Lim- uru. We make it to her place and we sit up all night waiting for them to regroup and attack. They don't, and sunrise finds us with O lost in thought, trying to make his omelette.

"We have to send her home today," he says, as he absent- mindedly slops the worst omelette he has ever made onto my plate. "No matter what, we bury her today."

Before burying Mary, we had to find her father where he had fallen the night before. The tea plantation looked like the war zone it had been, bodies all over the place. Just a few hours ago, these bodies, now bloody and carelessly strewn, had been alive. As Muddy had guessed, the young men had not come for their dead; they were probably too busy plotting how to avenge their deaths to bury them, or, more likely, scared of seeing the carnage that they had caused. We each picked two or three rows to weave in and out of in our search.

It was O who stumbled onto Ngatia. He called us to his row urgently. We rushed there as if we expected to find Ngatia miraculously alive. For the first time since I had known him, O was doubled over, throwing up violently. Ngatia had been hacked into little pieces. Only his head, with deep gashes, was left intact. They had taken it all out on him, and his body reminded me of the dead young man we had found in the forest. It could just as easily have been us lying there in bits. Around him, there were three of his attackers, shot to death, and in contrast, their death seemed kinder and gentler.

Mumbi let out a wail and knelt by what was left of him. She removed her wrap and gently started filling it with Ngatia's remains until she could fit no more.

Muddy tripped on something and, looking down, we saw it was O's .45. We couldn't tell whether Ngatia had hidden it or whether it had been buried in the struggle that had ensued, but it was empty. O reloaded and tucked it into his empty holster. It was as if he had been expecting to be reunited with his gun.

Mumbi tried hoisting the wrap that had now become a sack onto her shoulders, but it was as heavy as it was bloody. O and I grabbed one end each and we hauled it to the Land Rover.

"Why would they do this? To die is to die," I asked once we were in the car.

"You don't know, do you?" Mumbi said. "That is how the Kikuyu treated their traitors. Traitors were cut into little pieces." She paused.

"Yes, he was a traitor—he helped the British. He was a home guard. He was a coward, but no one deserves to die like a dog," she added bitterly.

"Why did you stay with him?" I asked her.

"Why does anybody stay with anybody? I loved him … and people, even the worst of them, change," she said simply. "But that is not why they killed him. They killed him because his daughter married a Luo. But that makes his murderers worse— they are traitors to the human race."

"Mother, did he change?" Muddy asked.

"No," she answered as she leaned her head against the window. We didn't have far to go to get to what had been her home but I reached out and pulled her toward me so that she lay her head on my chest. She sighed and closed her eyes.

"At my age, what am I going to do all alone?" she asked.

We had no answers, except first to bury Ngatia and Mary. We could bury Ngatia at the back of what had been their house— now a smoldering skeleton—and then leave to get Mary's body.

The four of us dug Ngatia's grave, taking turns digging and shoveling out the soil until we were six feet into the ground. Mumbi said a quick prayer and then we started on Mary's grave. A few hours later, hungry, dirty, and thirsty, we were off to pick up Janet, buy Mary a coffin, and bring her back home.

By the time we were driving back with Mary's body, the young men had regrouped, but we were at that point where we didn't care. The transition from casual lawlessness into the hell of anarchy wasn't difficult to adjust to. As detectives we lived on this side of the world anyway. Within the logic of anarchy, everything just made sense. We had to bury Mary. Some people would try to stop us. To bury Mary we had to go through them or die trying.

I was finding myself living more and more in one moment, trying to get to the next, moments held together only by the need to stay alive, to protect my own, and to see to it that those I cared about were buried. Pulled into this vortex of violence and more violence, my principles of justice were becoming rudimentary— us against them. I knew it even without knowing: I had become dangerous and I had to keep finding a way of getting back to a place of sanity.

Yet I could not but think that we were at war with people who just a few days ago had been civilians. Here, in Kisumu, in Nairobi, and in the Rift Valley, Luos, Kalenjins, and Kikuyus were killing each other in the name of the fat motherfuckers who were now discussing the future of the country in the comfort of the KICC.

We got to the roadblock and O slowed down like he was going to stop. The young men started approaching and O stepped on the gas. They recognized the Land Rover roaring toward them and they scattered in all directions. A little farther down the road, we jumped out and waited for them to come at us. They stayed hidden—they had understood our message, that we were ready to die if they were.

Funerals in a time of war are lonely affairs. For Mary's burial, the only people in attendance were O, Mumbi, Janet, Muddy, and Joe Sherry. Joe Sherry, so called because of his love for sherry, had dated Mary before O, and I gathered that it was Mumbi who had called him. He owned a bar close to Limuru called the Red Nova that we went to once in a while. The bond between them must have remained strong if he had risked his life to come here, but then again, as a Kikuyu, he would have had an easier time at the Limuru roadblocks.

With all things being equal, her students and fellow teachers would have been there. Mary's relatives and O's would have been there as well—and she would have been buried in Kisumu. As it was, six people buried a life that had touched so many.

O was dressed in black corduroy pants, a dress shirt, a tie, and his ubiquitous safari boots and black leather jacket. The rest of us were dressed as cleanly as we could manage. Muddy and Janet had picked out Mary's burial outfit: black shoes, a slab of a green dress that we used to joke was her school uniform, and a cowry necklace that brought out the beauty she was always trying to hide from her students—but she looked every bit the schoolteacher that she had been.

O was stoic, except for his shaking hands as he threw the first fistful of soil onto her coffin and a painful wince at the drumming sound it made. He came back to where I was standing and put his hand on my shoulder as if to console me.

As she edged closer to the grave, Mumbi said she had something to say about her daughter.

"I know we have to be fast because our times will not allow for a long farewell, but I have already buried a husband in silence. I will tell you a story. When Mary was very small, our culture did not allow her to sit with men as they slaughtered a goat and drank *muratina*—the traditional brew. When she asked why, her father told her it was because she was not a man.

" 'What is the difference between a man and a woman?' my daughter asked.

" 'Men wear trousers and women don't,' Ngatia answered, thinking that was the end of it as Mary walked back to the house. A few minutes later, she walked out wearing, or rather being worn by, her father's best pair of pants.

" 'I am a man now,' Mary said when she made it back to us. Defeated, the men had to let her stay. My daughter never let difference stop her from becoming what she wanted and marrying the man she wanted. In her own gentle constant way, she was better than all of us. As her mother I failed her," Mumbi concluded, and broke into tears.

Janet was crying. I was worried about her. I looked at her, her youth shining through the greyness of the funeral, the ethnic war, and the Norfolk bombing. What was going to happen to her without Mary?

She had survived worse, but as I was slowly learning, it wasn't just a question of surviving the worst—it's easy to survive when you have nothing to lose since life itself is the victory. The hard part is when you discover that there is a lot to live for, and it keeps being taken away from you, trying and losing, hoping and losing, loving and losing. O followed my gaze and he gripped my shoulder tighter.

As I picked up a handful of soil to throw over Mary's coffin, I had two thoughts—one was that I was sublimating my own pain by worrying about others, and the second was that I had to keep O alive for the sake of Janet. How I would keep him alive and from what, I didn't know.

Joe Sherry left by himself—he was safer that way—and the rest of us, including Mumbi, drove back to O's. When we could, we would take Mumbi back and help her rebuild, but in the meantime she could stay at Muddy's for as long as she needed. For now, we wanted everyone together—this little family of people who otherwise might have been strangers, brought together by love and violence. What was that saying? A family that eats together stays together? I smiled at the strangeness of my thoughts.

"A family that suffers together stays together," I said aloud, and we laughed.

An hour or so after we got back to O's, Jason showed up unannounced. It was a relief to see him. It meant movement on the case. We introduced him to Muddy, Janet, and Mumbi.

"I've heard so much about you," he said to Muddy.

"From whom? Or should I say, from what file?" I asked him.

We talked about the crisis in the country and I briefed him on all that had transpired with Helen. That brought us back to the case.

"Two things …" He paused. "Can I talk freely?" he asked suddenly. Before we could answer, he continued.

"Kenya is no longer safe for you—not for a while, anyway. There are some people asking about you. The only reason they haven't found you is the chaos—and they're afraid of getting caught in one of those roadblocks …" he said, smiling as if to suggest that at least the violence was good for something.

"You, how did you get here?" O asked him.

"I know what they don't—a white man in a car with diplomatic plates is safe. Fucking mercenaries are fucking cowards. You know why? Because they want to live to spend the money," he said.

"How do you know they are mercenaries?" Muddy asked.

"Because they are not mine—and no one knows who they are … independent contractors—call them by whatever name," Jason answered.

"We can bait them, let's grab them—they can tell us who they're working for," O said, excited by the prospect.

"They won't know much, Sahara won't risk it," Jason said.

"Then what exactly have you done for us? We have given you a lot more than you bring to the table. Hey, do you have leads on the fuckers who killed my wife? You have everything, DNA, prints. What is it that you do, exactly? Could you be more useless?" O said angrily.

"I can give you the official line and send you after some lowkey Al Qaeda operatives somewhere. Or I can tell you the truth as I know it—I don't know shit, no one knows who these guys are, and no one wants to find out. They are American, I agree with you. But Paul wants to believe they are Americans who have been turned by the terrorists—like that fucking kid, the American Taliban, John Walker. So he'll keep going after Al Qaeda, Al Shabaab, anything with Muslim blood in it," he explained.

"We have to find Sahara. It's the only way out—he is the key," I said.

"That's why I'm here," Jason said. "I don't think he's in the country. I think he's back in the U.S. He's safest there. Even if he isn't, our best chance of finding out who that fucker is lies in the United States."

"Well, then, get some of your men on it," Muddy said.

"I can't, like I said, all hands are on Al Qaeda," Jason said, sounding a bit like his old self. "But hey, what if there was a way we could find him quietly?"

We looked intrigued.

"The United States—you have to go to the U.S.... Only way we are going to see this thing through. You have to go back to the beginning—he got those four young men from somewhere in the U.S., they were trained somewhere, there is a trail somewhere in the U.S., and you have to find it," he said, trying not to appear too excited.

He waited as we processed, or rather laughed through, what he had just said.

"We are on all sorts of lists. How the fuck do we get in?" I asked him.

"I have one word for you—Mexico," he said, lifting his hands up to highlight the name as if it were on a billboard. "You want this solved, you want justice or revenge, you go in through Mexico. Besides, the safest place for you right now is with Uncle Sam—no one will think of looking for you there."

"So we get to Mexico and then what? We can't fly into the U.S.," I said. "You gotta do better than that, Jason."

Before Jason could answer, Muddy jumped in.

"Jason, you're good. We sneak in like refugees, illegally," Muddy said with a laugh. I could tell she liked the idea.

"Muddy's right. You have to sneak in. Mexico is another Kenya; the dollar goes a long way there," he said. I looked at him, expecting him to laugh, but he was serious.

"Mexico? What about Canada? We can fly into Canada. Nobody watches the Canadian border," I argued, finding it incredible that we were even taking his suggestion seriously.

"No. Canada is too risky," Jason said emphatically. "If you get flagged, you can't bribe your way through the airport. Shit, think about it—black people driving into the U.S. through the Canadian border? You will be profiled. In Mexico, the dollar is the law …"

"I'll be damned if I'm going to sneak back into my own motherfucking country," I interrupted, angry because I knew it was the only way. We had one lead—if we could call it that—and that was the University of California. We just had to start there. We had to find Sahara.

"Mexico … it has to be Mexico—been thinking about it, tried other options, only Mexico works," Jason went on, as if trying to convince himself as well. "There are other logistical calculations. I have a person I trust in Mexico," he added as he opened his briefcase.

"Why? I mean, what do you get out of this?" O asked Jason.

"I told you before, I can't protect my country without the whole truth; like a doctor, you can't treat a disease you don't understand. I get the truth and you get justice—and we can do both quietly. It has to be done quietly. Quiet is the only way we get out of this one," he answered.

From the briefcase, Jason produced three Kenyan passports, one for O and the other two for Muddy and me. I opened mine to find an old passport photo, blurry yet recognizably me. My name was no longer Ishmael Fofona—it was James Mwangi. I leaned over and looked at O's. His name was Patrick Onyango.

"Look, Muddy, they will need you … a beautiful woman

creates an aura of goodwill," Jason explained as he handed Muddy a passport.

Muddy laughed when she saw her name.

"Jane Mwangi, your trophy illegal immigrant wife," she said to me. I liked that—the wife part—but I was also thinking that it made it all the more difficult to propose with my ten beaded rings. It would look like I was doing it because the idea had been introduced into my head by Jason.

Jason gave us three Social Security cards clearly stamped "eligible for work," three large envelopes containing airline tickets to Mexico City, fake driver's licenses, and ten thousand dollars each. Operating on a cash basis meant no credit cards and no paper trail.

For what was going to be a long journey, the travel plan itself was simple enough. We would fly into Mexico City, where Jason's contact would meet us. His contact would take us to Tijuana and get us across the border and eventually into San Francisco and Oakland. From there we would be on our own.

O's cousin Michael, who lived in Oakland, could shelter us for a few days. O would tell him we were coming to the U.S. to look for work. He might suspect something when he saw that an American was with O, but he wouldn't ask questions. They had known each other since they were little kids and they had the kind of trust that had been tested over the years.

Jason was right, we were going to be safer in the U.S. No government agency would think of searching for us in the great underground immigrant networks, and if they did, where would they start? Who would they send inside without them sticking out like a white man in an African village?

"Just don't get pulled over or arrested for anything," Jason warned us, as if following my thoughts.

How we were going to work a case where Sahara's fascination with the University of California was the main lead, and work it as illegal immigrants, I had no idea. In reality we had more than that—we had photos, fingerprints, and DNA from the three dead white men. We knew our guy from Ngong Forest had a sickle cell trait for which he was taking medication. We knew what Sahara looked like, and that he was not done, and we had a laptop that Helen was hacking.

Janet was going to be safe at the university and Mumbi would stay with relatives in Nairobi.

Mary was gone. We had buried her. Her father was dead. Unpredictable violence was erupting all over the country.

It was going to be a relief to board that plane to Mexico.

CHAPTER 9

BETWEEN TIJUANA AND A HARD PLACE

Mexico. We were on our way to Mexico. For fuck's sake, how was it that in just the span of a few years I was returning to my own country as an illegal immigrant? Yet after everything I had seen in the last few days, a black American detective sneaking into the U.S. through Mexico shouldn't have raised any eyebrows.

Leaving the U.S. the first time around to settle in Kenya hadn't been easy, but Muddy was there and I simply had to go back to her. I recalled the first time I had seen her on stage, doing spoken word with a serious sensuality that commanded respect as much as it did admiration. There was always more to Muddy. I knew it from the moment we met. Yet, even for love, leaving all you have known and all you could ever become, all you had in fact hoped to become, is not easy. I had to leave friends behind, I had just been promoted, and I did often wonder whether as an only child I had betrayed my parents.

In other ways, it was easy to leave. In Kenya, my skin was like everyone else's, I was part of the majority. Not that I was an insider: the accent, my "Americaness," was apparent to those I interacted with and I had come to accept it as part of me. What I had refused to accept was being called *mzungu*—it was a fighting word, like a white man calling me a nigger.

To be away from home—to live as an immigrant among people who were black like me—would there ever come a time when home could be anywhere we wanted it to be? I had chosen

Kenya—would there ever come a time when Kenya or any other place would choose me? Truly embrace me as one of its own?

I had to learn Kiswahili. Yes, most Kenyans wanted to practice their English, a sort of rap English, with an American, but still, O, Muddy, Janet, or even anyone at Broadway's Tavern—they could all have been my teachers. But there was a part of me that resisted, that made me want to never fully belong, and I had begun to suspect that, deep down, I wanted it that way—there was a part of me that wanted to remain American. The dreams I enjoyed most were those in which I was eating heart attack food—meat lover's pizza from Domino's or the properly named Kill Me Quick Double Cheese and Bacon Hamburger at the Paradise Bar in good old Madison, Wisconsin.

I was sure about one thing though—I was excited that I would be home, back in the U.S. California and Wisconsin were worlds apart, but it was still home. If we solved the case, maybe I would take Muddy to Madison to meet my parents! Shit, maybe I would get to propose in Madison, by Lake Mendota.

"You planning on coming back with us?" Muddy, sitting between us, asked O, who was looking out pensively into the clouds.

"Of course, where else would I go?" O answered.

"No, I mean … are you planning on surviving the case?"

"Do I look suicidal to you?" O asked defensively.

Muddy cast a glance my way, but I pretended I wasn't listening.

"You might fool Ishmael, but not me, O. I know that look!"

"What look?" he asked.

"The look of a man or a woman who is not planning on coming back. I know that look from men and women … even children who had lost everything. In Rwanda, they held their AK-47s and marched forward, never looked back and never stopped. They kept walking, fighting, until a bullet stopped them. And for the unlucky ones, the war ended," Muddy said, flipping through the in-flight magazine, trying to be nonchalant.

"Just because that's what you did doesn't mean that's what I will do," O said.

Muddy didn't take the bait.

"At some point you . . . you have to think things through—see yourself in the light of day and the truth that surrounds you. I did not close my eyes when I was being raped and tortured. I certainly did not close them when I was killing . . ." she responded.

"Sounds like the beginning of one of your poems," I said to her.

"Fuck off, fake husband," she said as she put her head on my shoulder and promptly dozed off.

O and Muddy, sometimes they spoke in a different register— a language that, even though it was in English, I could never fully grasp. At an intellectual level I knew what she was telling him—plan to stay alive, and don't be too gung-ho about seeking revenge or turning this into a suicide mission. I knew this because I was worrying about the same thing, but when it came from Muddy it felt like she was speaking to O on another level, and, gruff as he was, her words would have communicated something to him that I myself could not say.

O finished his drink, leaned against the window, and went to sleep. I was exhausted as well—too exhausted to sleep. Flipping through the in-flight magazine's guide to Mexico, I was envious of the people who ate at the glossy, luxurious restaurants, shopped in the malls, visited the museums, and took romantic walks on the beaches. I took consolation in the thought that just like I had seen a side of Kenya the tourists would never see, so would I experience Mexico, through its underbelly.

O was clearly having a nightmare. I didn't wake him up; this was the most sleep he had gotten since Mary's death. I lifted two blankets from the floor, careful not to wake Muddy either, tore into the plastic with my teeth, and covered us both. She nestled deeper into my shoulder. Not long after, I too was off to sleep.

James and Jane Mwangi and Patrick Onyango had no trouble getting through airport security with their tourist visas. There were no double glances and checks—compared to what we would have undergone at a U.S. airport, we were practically waved into Mexico. To be fair, not that many Africans are trying to enter Mexico illegally.

The first thing we saw on reaching the gate was our false names hoisted high up in the air above a sea of placards. We cut through the crowd and found a tall, skinny, fit man dressed in blue jeans, beat-up old sneakers, and a black dress shirt. He appeared to be in his fifties, and had I seen him on a Mombasa beach, I would have thought him Swahili—he was black, lighter than me, but with coppery skin. His short afro was neatly combed. His eyes conveyed the kind of humor I had come to associate with Kenyans, as well as relief that we had made it.

"You must be the black gringo," he said to me, and then turned to Muddy. "And you, you have the look of a flower, truly a rose among thorns," and he pointed at O and me.

"Naturally, a man gravitates toward beauty," he said as he took her hand and squeezed it, letting out a delighted laugh.

The Muddy I knew would have delivered some kind of retort or, in some instances, with drunken fools, a backhand slap, but now she smiled almost shyly.

"And you, my friend—we are not neighbors, like with this

black gringo—but we come from the same place—mother Africa. All of us," he said to O, placing his hand over his heart and making the sign of the cross.

The mythical Africa that everyone, even Africans, craves ... I had yet to see it, I thought to myself.

"Me, my name is Julio—and I am at your service," he announced. "I will provide you with a ride from Mexico to the United States of America." And he made a gesture indicating a bumpy ride.

"Of all the places I have ever wanted to go ... Mexico was not one of them. Not even in my wildest dreams," O said, breaking into laughter. "But here we are."

"*Órale!* It's good, then. Let's hit the potholes. My friend," Julio said, turning to O, "you will find many, many, many similarities between our fine country and yours."

We got to Julio's car—a Mercedes-Benz that looked like it was being held together by rusty coat hangers. He opened the trunk and we threw in our carry-on luggage. A surprise was waiting for us—on the outside, the car was a beat-up old Mercedes. Inside, it was brand-new—still had that brand-new smell—and it had gadgets I hadn't seen before, like an iPod Touch that plugged into the car's music system.

Julio laughed as he looked at our surprised faces.

"In my line of work, appearances deceive, two faces—always," he said.

"And what line of work might that be?" Muddy asked him.

"In Mexico, a man must have many hands in many pockets. I have as many lines of work as there are pockets. Many hands like an Indian god," Julio answered. I noticed that he kept looking at the rearview mirror. We all looked back too, but didn't see anything.

"We cross the border tonight?" O asked him.

"No, my friends—you get to see more of Mexico. Two days' time. Jason called me too late, I have to plan. If we rush … mistakes in Mexico are very expensive," he said.

Two days of waiting was going to feel like a long time, but I for one did not see a need to protest. We needed to rest, regroup, and do some hard thinking.

"How do you know Jason?" I asked.

"My friends, it looks like my deception did not work very well," he told us. We looked behind us again and saw a black SUV gaining on us. My question was lost to the moment.

"Enemy or friend—best not to find out." Julio stepped on the gas and the Mercedes lurched forward, picking up speed, and the SUV became smaller and smaller as the distance between us grew.

Suddenly, he veered into a dirt road, stopped, and ran to the trunk. He called us over and we found him removing our luggage. Just when we were about to protest, he lifted the mat. His trunk had a false bottom and all around his spare tire were guns—Glocks, two M-16s, the universal AK-47s, and something I had never seen in the trunk of a car before, grenades. He motioned to us to choose our weapons—O and Muddy armed themselves with AKs while I reached for a Glock. We could see dust rising as the SUV picked up our trail. We piled back in and roared off.

"Ambush," I shouted over the noise. No one heard me, so I yelled again, "Ambush them."

"In Mexico, everyone you want to kill has bulletproof windows," Julio said.

"Do you?" Muddy asked him. He smiled.

"Of course. But they're no good when they're open," he said

as he rolled up his window. We followed his cue and double-checked that all the windows were rolled up tight.

The SUV was now a few hundred feet behind us. They opened fire. The bullets rained on the rear window, leaving small pockmarks. They let out another burst that skirted all around us.

"The tires, they are trying to get the tires," Julio shouted.

Then out of nowhere a gate appeared—and someone opened it before we hit it. The SUV came to a screeching halt, furiously backed away, and drove off.

With the gate behind us, I now saw rows and rows of barely standing slum houses, made of corrugated iron and stitched together with rusty nails and rope to make odd-shaped boxes. Looking up the hill, I could see heat rising from the tops. If it weren't for the skin color of the inhabitants and the bright graffiti decorating the shacks, I could have sworn I was in Kenya. I didn't understand what we were doing in a Mexican slum, much less why the SUV had stopped.

But what was going on soon became apparent, as four jeeps with heavily armed young men joined the Mercedes to make a convoy. Old women were smiling and waving at Julio while little children in ragged clothes ran alongside us. On the tin rooftops, I could see armed men perched, barely managing to hold on. No one was going to bring war to this slum unless they were ready to pay a high price. It was Julio's slum. Relief set in.

Julio didn't think we were the SUV's targets.

"Only Jason and I know you are here. And in Mexico, everyone is a target," he explained with a laugh. "And sometimes you do not know who wants you dead until you are dead already—and what good does that do you?"

We drove up a muddy road full of potholes. Just when I was wondering how the Mercedes would make it all the way up the hill, we came to a tarmac road with lights running alongside it. Where it ended, there was a huge fortified gate that opened on to an extravagant lawn. The next thing I was expecting to see was a McMansion. Instead, I saw a number of identical-looking houses, lower-middle-class-type homes made out of brick—about ten of them.

"You are living well," Muddy said, pointing downhill to the slums, where the candles flickering through the windows resembled a night vigil.

"*Mamacita*, you judge as fast as you are beautiful. We haven't even broken bread," Julio replied.

"Our lives are in your hands ... you can understand why we are a little bit concerned—the SUV," I said to him, trying to sound casual.

"What do you do?" O asked him. "We need to know."

"Let her ask. Questions about what a man does should come from the rose, not the thorns," Julio said with a laugh.

"I have asked," Muddy said. I could tell from the tone in her voice that she was getting irritated. We came to a stop in front of one of the houses.

"You know. You know what I do ... This is Mexico. A secret is a dollar or two away. That is how the SUV found us. There are no secrets here but you, you are big detectives so you know that. You want to know, who is Jason? How I do know him? What is a CIA man doing working with an Afro-Mexican from the slums? That is what you are asking. So I want to ask—what is a black gringo doing in Mexico trying to tunnel his way into his own country? The Africans I can understand, but you, my friend, why? How do I know I will still be breathing and walking on my two legs after you are gone? We all have questions, my friends," he said, and for a moment I thought he would show us the true colors of a drug dealer living literally on top of his people.

But then his face softened. "Come inside. We put something

in our bellies, and then we talk as much we want," he said as he opened the car door. "Besides, and I am not trying to scare you, if you face the truth, what choice do you have? Like you say, your lives are in my hands. No?"

"Ain't that the truth. Amen to that, brother. You got a joint? Such a long journey to get to your part of the world calls for a celebration," O said.

"Do I have a joint? Is this African *loco*?" Julio asked, genuinely amused. "Do I have a joint?"

And just like that, the tension that had been building since we spotted the SUV was gone.

We walked into one of the brick houses. It was dark but as soon as Julio reached for a switch, the place was flooded with noise, lights, the sound of beers and whiskey bottles being opened—it was a surprise party. There was no time to ask questions; bottles of tequila were shoved into our hands and a few moments later Muddy and O each had a joint.

Every person Julio greeted had flowers or a cheap gift—a beaded necklace or a belt—for him. One old man even had a chicken for Julio, and another a cigar—*Cubano, señor,* he said to much laughter—someone even gave him a Fanta. It reminded me of those stories you hear about doctors in rural areas being paid in kind.

I walked over to Muddy and O—I didn't want to, I didn't like their high talk—but there was no one else to talk to.

"A drug-dealing Robin Hood?" Muddy was saying while laughing.

"No, Muddy, Julio is a drug-dealing revolutionary ... like the Cuban, Che ..." O said.

"Che? What the fuck, O? What the fuck are you smoking, O?" Muddy asked as they broke into conspiratorial giggles.

"Muddy, that is your problem—the example doesn't matter. You fixate on the example and not the principle of the statement," said O.

"But your example is proof, you know, like in a science experiment, if your experiment is wrong, you cannot say the ..." She paused, looking for a word. "You cannot say the ..."

"Hypothesis," I interjected and let out a groan.

"You cannot say your hypothesis is correct," she finished.

"Don't you guys care about what's going on? Here we are in Mexico, we just almost got shot, we're with a drug-dealing slumlord following a case that for all we know should have been solved back in Kenya," I said. Muddy leaned into me and brought a bottle of tequila to my lips.

"Fake husband ... That SUV could have been our death carriage. It could also have belonged to Julio. There is nothing to know yet. Drink up," she instructed.

It's not like I needed much persuasion. Julio was right—for the moment he was all we had. In this compound, we were his guests. If we didn't want to be here, then we might as well have taken our chances in Kenya.

Our host was being celebrated. The music kicked in hard—guitars and drums and wailing but happy singers tried to outdo each other. We joined the party. Muddy and O smoked up and I held on to the bottle, drinking the madness of the last few days away.

The night continued until it faded into morning. Breakfast, or brewskyfast as Jason would have called it, was served and the music, drinking, and smoking went on.

At about 7:30 a.m., Julio stumbled over to us.

"My friends, it's time to go open it," he said.

"Open what?" I asked.

"You wanted to know what I do. Allow me to start with why," he replied mysteriously.

We followed him as he led a long procession of drunken men and women, with guitarists dispersed among us playing different tunes and people singing different songs—chaos. We went through the slum picking up more and more people, until at the bottom of the hill we came to an oasis—a massive new school. I hadn't seen grass or trees as we walked down, yet here pavements cut across green lawns leading to four new stone buildings with red-tiled roofs.

The whole procession walked around the school, meandering in and out of the new classrooms, the teachers' lounge, the lab, the students' dining room, and the newly built pit latrines.

The students, all dressed in green shirts, shorts, and dresses, were assembled in the square that the buildings ringed. The teachers were sitting up on a platform. And the principal, a short, rotund black Mexican—I still couldn't get over the black Mexican part—looked regal in an armchair. A bell rang and the principal stood up to speak to all of us, as people in the procession drunkenly shushed each other. Julio walked over and said something to one of the teachers, who then went and joined the principal.

"Distinguished guests, parents, and fellow teachers, this is a great day," the principal began, as the teacher translated his words into English for us.

"Our children will no longer be illiterate—we shall no longer dream of sending them to schools that we cannot afford. In this school, which we have decided to call the School of Free Dreams, any child who wants to learn will be educated ..." and he went on for quite a bit about the virtues of education before finishing to drunken happy cheers.

Julio walked up and shook hands with the principal and with each of the teachers as the students clapped.

"Sweat and blood. Let us never forget that. Now I declare the school open—let the learning begin," he said. Some parents were crying while others laughed, and the students walked quietly to their classrooms. The procession made its way back up the hill.

"This is great, Julio, but what happens to the school if something happens to you?" I asked him.

"I have done what you gringos call investment ... no, endowment. The money is there to run the school ... in a U.S. bank, of course ... they are too big to fail, they say, so my money is always safe ..." he began, but then he was engulfed by a crowd of people coming to thank or congratulate him.

When we got back to the compound, he called to the three of us and told us to follow him. "Now I will show you what I do," he declared.

He took us to one of the small buildings. Inside, we found his employees: naked men and women packing cocaine into bricks. He took us to another house, and it was weed. Each of the houses was a processing zone for weed or cocaine brought in by armored trucks that were just rolling in as we left with the last house. The houses weren't divided into rooms—they were just empty halls with chairs and long tables and weird-smelling chemicals.

"This is how I built the school," he said when we were done.

"With American noses ... the gringo nose is very good for business. They sell us the guns, we sell them the dope. No blanket of lies between us." He laughed, but we were too stunned to join him.

One of his men came and called him. We followed him to the gate—there were about twenty men in ragged clothes waiting for him.

"They are looking for work. This ..." he pointed at the houses, "is the only work that pays."

He said something to the men and they pointed at one man. Julio reached into his pocket and gave him a wad of pesos to share, I gathered. He then pointed them to the trucks that had just arrived and they rushed to unload them.

"My friends ... life here is very hard. Go get some rest and then tell me what you are doing in my beautiful country. I know what Jason told me, but Julio likes to hear for himself," he said. He called over one of his men, who guided us to rooms in the only two houses that weren't part of the factory.

Both Muddy and I stank, from travel, from weed, from tequila, and from not having washed or brushed our teeth or changed our clothes since we'd left Kenya—but we were happy to be alone together, just the two of us, and finally naked. Despite our lack of sleep and our stinky breath and armpits, we kissed, caressed, and made love before collapsing in the mid-morning heat.

O, Muddy, Julio, and I were sitting in a bar called, simply, Cantina. It could have been a bar in the slums of Kenya; it was so devoid of comforts that even the walls seemed out of place. Yet it was lively, with men and women talking loudly over cigarettes and tequila. There were some musicians on a makeshift stage picking at their guitars, riffing off each other, and they seemed to be enjoying playing with each other even more than entertaining the bar. Every now and then, a drunken patron would join them and sing along for few minutes before getting thirsty and going back to the bottle.

Soon Muddy was on stage—performing a poem with a man wearing a cheap guitar loosely across his shoulders, like it was an AK-47, his fingers moving rapidly to produce a slow deliberate sound, like a train chugging up and down hills, straining when going up, and braking when going down to maintain speed.

Muddy was speaking just above the guitar, sometimes missing a step, at other times catching up—a Tower of Babel speaking to each person in their own special language, to individual needs, fears, and hopes. The English teacher who had translated for the principal at the school was standing next to Muddy, rendering her words into Spanish, gesturing animatedly, performing alongside her.

"Water ... is like blood—it flows—water dies. But water lives if it's in an ocean, if in its bed there are many, many like us, many like bones—odd-shaped, a jigsaw puzzle of the dead African bones that hold the Indian Ocean, and the Atlantic, and the Mediterranean, and the Pacific. In the Sahara, the Sahel, in the Mojave, in the Chihuahua Desert—these barren lands strewn with odd-shaped bones, each oasis draws life from blood like us. Blood is like water, it flows and it dries, but not if it's a memory."

"Look, who is that?" she asked, pointing at a faded painting with thin cigarette soot and cobwebs running down it. The teacher repeated the question to the bar.

"Yanga," a few disjointed voices yelled back.

"Gaspar Yanga, or to call him by another name, Dedan

Kimathi Waciuri," she said. "But today, let's just call him Love."
She got down from the makeshift stage and joined us at our table as a complimentary cheap bottle of tequila was brought over.

"Muddy, you are *hermosa*. It would take at least ten English
words to describe what *hermosa* means in Spanish … Beautiful,
complete, unparalleled, handsome … do you want me to go on?"
Julio said, laughing. The whole bar was quiet, listening to the
teacher's translation.

"Of course, go on, Julio—some girls love diamonds, I love
words. I would love to hear the rest of them … that was only four,"
Muddy replied. I felt a twinge of jealousy.

"Start the count, then: without end, deep … *órale*, perhaps I
lied a little lie. It is six English words for one word of Spanish.
All I am saying is you are beautiful in a deep Mexican way," Julio
said, raising up his hands in surrender.

"Obviously Julio does not share your gift," O said to Muddy.
When the teacher was done translating, the little cantina trem-
bled and threatened to crumble as laughter and conversation
broke out and drinks were ordered.

I had come to treasure such moments, when the case, the
poverty and violence, the drugs, the politics, foreignness, what
we had left back in Kenya and what I was going to find at home
didn't matter. Only this moment, untainted by any of those
things except for a feeling of being here, mattered—the cantina
could have been down in hell, or in heaven, and only all of us
laughing would have mattered. What makes such a moment
happen? Five minutes earlier or later, that moment wouldn't
have been possible.

At last, Julio, sounding serious, said, "Okay, let's get down
to business. Let's go back to the house. We can come back here
after we're done talking."

CHAPTER 10

THE PROPOSAL

"We leave tomorrow morning," Julio said, after we had settled down for the promised serious business talk. "In normal times, it would take us two hours—if we are crossing the border legally—but there are no more normal times in Mexico. And you, my friends, want to go in quietly—so it could take a day or two."

He was trying to spread out a small pocket map on a table sticky with beer, and when he succeeded, he indicated two crossing points.

"I have made arrangements for your travel from San Diego to San Francisco. Once I deliver you to your man, you are on your own ... when you are ready to come back, you call me and I pick you up in my limousine," he instructed, as if it were the simplest thing in the world.

"Jason, how do you know him?" O asked.

"Jason, me and him have been friends for a long time. Jason—one day he comes to me and he says, I will give you guns and intelligence. In return, you keep your ear to the ground—listen for Arabic. He says, after 9/11 his foreign policy is, yes to drugs and no to terrorists. He laughs, high as hell. We shake hands and we have been good friends since," Julio explained and waited for the information to sink in. "Simple as that."

"I know we are capable of many things, Julio—but you are asking me to believe that the CIA is working with drug cartels to fight terrorism?" I said.

"Ishmael, simple economics—what I am telling you is this—we do not want terrorists coming in through Mexico. The gringo noses turn against us. Business, you know? If one of us gets greedy and wants some oil money, the United States government cannot stop him from smuggling in terrorists through a tunnel. But we can, because we know each other's business—it is my business to know what is happening in other compounds because my life and livelihood depends on knowing," he explained.

"Julio, we are on the terrorist list—anyone who knows who we are will think you are breaking your fucked-up agreement ..." Muddy said.

Someone called Julio. He looked at his phone.

"Then know that Jason and I risk a lot here. But you also know that Jason is who he is, just like I am who I am," he said and wandered off.

I felt I could trust Julio more than I could Jason. It was the same way I had always felt I could trust Jamal, even after he betrayed us to Sahara—they both were criminals, but they were always in their element. Perhaps I thought I could trust Julio because I knew that, fundamentally, I couldn't trust him. His mandate in life was to sell drugs and protect the school he had built, and everyone was useful to the extent that they served or detracted from his mission.

Jason, on the other hand, was a political instrument, even though he thought he was acting independently. In the end he was around for as long as politicians in Washington found him useful. He had taken us this far but it didn't mean that he would not sell us out if it would serve a higher purpose—as defined by him.

The difference was that Jason wanted us to trust him and Julio didn't care. I guess we were all predictable in our own ways.

O was going to do whatever it took to kill the men behind his wife's murder. Muddy was here because in spite of her attempts to leave a life of violence behind, a part of her was addicted to the smell of gunpowder. I had never known her to turn down a fight. She could have decided to stay home and look after Janet and Mary's mother, but she was here. And I followed a case to the bitter end because that was how I defined myself—it was all I knew, it was all I could stand on.

O hadn't said anything. I looked at him, trying to catch his eye, and he nodded back.

"I will work with the Devil if I have to," he said.

"But will you play by his rules?" I asked him.

"There are no rules," Muddy said. "We want the motherfuckers who are setting off bombs and killing women in their homes in Nairobi. The only rule is to get them. Just like the only rule in this fucking slum is to get your child into that school with some food in their belly," she added.

"This is a long way from Broadway's—the stakes are higher and unforgiving," I said, knowing it wouldn't matter.

With or without us, Julio would be here, building a school or a clinic while selling drugs and killing people, destroying some homes and lives in order to save others. Jason would always have a job, maintaining some sort of balance between drugs and terrorism. The question was, could we have made it this far without them? The more I thought about it the more I thought, yes—we could have gotten here without them. But it would have taken us much longer to get those passports, to put together the money and find ourselves a coyote for the trip through Mexico. That kind of time we did not have.

"So, my friends, what do you really want?" Julio asked as he came back and sat down. Muddy and I looked at O.

"My wife ..." he started to say, but he choked up.

"We also want justice for a young man, killed and left out in the wild, and for the bomb victims," I added.

"And the beautiful rose in love with the AK, what does she want?" Julio asked.

"My ghosts, they leave me alone when I am busy," Muddy said, puffing at her joint.

"Look, my friends, we are all grown-ups here—you are here—you can walk away, hop on the next plane back to Kenya. If you want exile, I can get you to Cuba, or you can stay here. You will not do that, because you have work to do—and it is important work for you. So we get it done and call it a day," Julio said. His phone rang again; he looked at it and excused himself for a second time, in a hurry.

I asked Muddy if she wanted to go for a walk. I had never thought I would feel safe enough in a slum to take a romantic night walk with the woman I loved. We walked until we came to the cantina. Opposite, a woman had set up a small table from which she was selling all sorts of things, cigarettes and matches, potato chips, pens and beaded chains and rings like the ones I had brought with me from Kenya. We went over to her. I gave her five dollars and pointed at Muddy, and she piled bracelets and necklaces on Muddy's wrists and around her neck. The woman tried to give me change, but I refused it.

Right there, I went down on my knees in the wet nasty mud, and in front of this woman and her makeshift shop, and with Muddy asking me if I was okay, I proposed with the ten rings from Hammer ... sliding each one of them onto her ten fingers—and she laughing at their flimsiness.

"Yes," she said. "Yes, I will marry you. Ishmael, I would marry you ten times over—you didn't even have to ask."

She pulled me up.

"Of all the places, Ishmael—a fucking slum in Mexico?" she said, more to herself than to me. It just made sense—I didn't know why, but it did. I marveled at how beautiful she looked—it was as if I was seeing her again after a long time, I told her.

"With this background, any woman would look beautiful," she said.

The trinket seller took both our hands, led us to the cantina, and loudly called for drinks. She was saying something and the schoolteacher translated for us,

"She is saying—*A drink for that woman—she needs to be drunk where she is going.*"

When the waiter came over, the woman pointed at me, indicating that I would pay for the drinks she had just bought Muddy and me. I did, and we made our escape back to Julio's.

At about 5:00 a.m. there was urgent knocking on the door. I opened it cautiously. It was one of Julio's men and, after getting dressed and wondering if anyone ever slept in this slum, we followed him to one of the drug-processing houses. The employees, still naked, were running out. We rushed in to find, amid the still-to-be-processed cocaine, the English teacher, our translator, tied face up on one of the worktables—naked and roughed up. He was shouting something in Spanish but on seeing us, he quieted down, his chest heaving in and out, hand and leg muscles quivering from the adrenaline coursing through him. And then, in a gesture that I thought was cruel, asked the teacher to tell us what was going on.

"They came for me at the cantina—they say I am an

informant and that I told the police that Julio would be picking you up from the airport. They say I am the only one who had the information. They say they have more evidence but they will not show it to me. They say my life depends on my telling them who I really am. If I lie they kill me, if I tell the truth, they let me live," he explained.

Julio pulled us aside. "I need to know what he knows, and I need to know who else he has talked to," he told us.

"But how do you know it's him? Shit, torture, fear, duress—you get unreliable information," I said to Julio, thinking back to Sahara's logic.

"I found him like this—my men roughed him up and naturally I do not want to undermine their authority. But know that here in Mexico, everyone talks," he explained.

"What are you trying to achieve exactly?" Muddy asked him.

"Your lives in Mexico and across the border depend on no one knowing who you are—you get that, my friends? This is for your own good, your own safety—my own as well. You can stay here in this room or you can go back to the cantina and hope that we are still driving to the border tomorrow morning," Julio said, trying to hold in his anger.

We decided to stay.

"How long have we worked together?" he asked the teacher.

"Five years, almost five years," the teacher answered, translating both question and answer.

"In those five years, you have come to know me very well?" Julio asked.

"Yes, and you have really looked out for me," he answered regretfully.

"*Órale, hermano*, I want you to take those five years of

knowing me and hold them close to your heart. Answer me one question, do you think you are lying on this table because of mere suspicion?" he asked.

"No, but I am telling ..." the teacher started to say.

"Listen to me, because it is very important ... mostly to you ... Also to all of us, but most of all to you. Think about your answer—take your time and think—my brother, your life is in your hands," Julio advised him.

I was trying to figure out what Julio was doing to the English teacher. If he had sold out Julio, his gamble would be that Julio didn't have enough information—therefore needed a confession. So if he kept quiet, Julio couldn't know for sure. And if he hadn't sold out Julio, he would have to trust that Julio would believe him, because Julio had nothing on him.

Julio had raised the stakes, though, with the simple question—How well did he know Julio? How safe was he in either telling the truth or lying? Would Julio come at him with mere suspicion? If the answer was yes, then he could try to bluff his way out of it. If it was no, then he would have to fess up. Julio was starting to look like Sahara to me.

At last, trying to speak bravely, the teacher said, "I am Detective Roberto Gonzalez. I work with the Mexican anti-terror unit. You are harboring known terrorists, it had to be reported."

Julio held his men back.

"Who did you tell about our friends here?" Julio asked.

"Only my *jefe*."

"I would forgive anything else. But not from one who has become like a brother to me," Julio said as he took an army knife from one of his men.

I could see the teacher's stomach muscles tense instinctively. I was not going to let this happen.

"If this is on us, you have to let us handle it," I said, stepping in so that I was standing between the two of them.

"No, gringo, this is between me and him ... unless you want to start a little trouble," he said calmly.

"I am a cop, too, Julio. I'm not going to stand aside and let you kill another cop," I said, feeling the familiar fear creeping through the small of my back, adrenaline starting to rush in. O casually positioned himself closer to one of the men, while Muddy, who was close to Julio, remained where she was.

I knew O wanted to get to the U.S. for Sahara and that nothing would stand in his way. But witnessing another cop getting killed in front of us, and because of us, though in the larger scheme of things it was Sahara who was responsible—even O couldn't justify that. It would cheapen his revenge—and revenge has to be self-righteous, or at least have the pretense of being self-righteous.

"Let us not do anything stupid. We have time, enough time to kill and to die—so let us talk, my friends. Explain to me why this *pendejo* should live. Tell me why I should let him live," Julio said, looking at his men.

"It's a question of principle, Julio," I said.

"So now you are a man of principle, eh, gringo?" Julio said, twisting "gringo" so that it no longer had a friendly ring to it.

O walked over to Julio and pulled out two chairs so that both of them could sit down.

"I have shot men in the back. I have tortured. I have let an innocent man be hacked to death with machetes so that I could bury a dead woman—my wife. I will do a lot worse to destroy the men who killed her. When I am done, they will know what my wife's name was worth. I am not telling you all these things so that you think I am a tough man, but so that you know how serious I am when I say I will not let you kill that man, because his life is the only thing separating you from me. We have to draw the line here, Julio, and I am asking you to understand that, because I would rather go after the men who killed my wife than die here. But I will die here to keep that line standing ..." O said, speaking barely above a whisper.

I couldn't have said it any better. All I knew was that if we stood aside and let Julio kill a fellow cop, I would no longer be who I thought I was, or wanted to become, or could become. Letting the man die would be a kind of suicide followed by an afterlife of pure hell in which love and the things I thought I deserved and could earn would have no meaning. I hadn't understood it until now—that was why O let Jamal walk.

Julio looked over at Muddy. She shrugged back at him.

"His wife, she was a schoolteacher, too," Muddy said. Something about that jolted Julio so that he raised his eyebrows in surprise—as if now he understood.

Just one of those details that makes people human to us, I thought to myself.

"Here in Mexico, we respect the dead very much," Julio said very seriously. "And so that you can honor your wife's memory I will respect your wish and not kill this man. Our debt to the dead is more important than the principles of our professions."

Julio started talking to his men in Spanish. I could see he was explaining what had just transpired because he kept pointing at O, and the teacher seemed more relieved with each word. His men looked skeptical—their rules told them that the teacher had to die, but the more he talked, the more they started to look sympathetically at O, until finally one of them walked over to where O was sitting, shook his hand, and then untied the teacher.

"How did you know it was him?" Muddy asked Julio. He

beckoned to one of his men, who came forward with a laptop. Julio typed in an address and turned the laptop so we could see. There, in full color, was a rookie cop photo of the teacher.

He turned the laptop around for the teacher, who looked at the photo in pain and confusion. It went against police protocol—that file was supposed to stop existing the moment he went undercover.

"Do you want to know how much your life was worth?" Julio asked him.

He opened another file. It contained a photo of one of his men handing a suitcase over to the police chief, and another one of the chief beaming down into the suitcase as he looked at the money.

"Five thousand U.S. dollars," Julio said. "That is all it took. Five thousand dollars for your life. Judas sold Jesus to one person, but your *jefe* has sold you and my guests many times over—because of you."

"Shit, even in Kenya the chief wouldn't sell an undercover cop. Some things are just not done," O said. I wasn't too sure about that.

"Bring the other one in," Julio instructed his men, just as I was thinking it was over. A vaguely familiar man was brought in, all bloodied up. He was in shock and he kept feeling for something around his neck until one of Julio's men took a rosary from his own neck and gave it to him.

"This was the man who introduced me to my *hermano*," Julio said, pointing at the teacher. Julio handed the teacher his knife.

"Mercy, Julio. A gun, I beg," the teacher pleaded with him.

"No, my brother, now you have a real choice. Your life for his," Julio said. The man looked straight into Julio's eyes, and without hesitation, he took the teacher's hand, the one holding the knife, held it steady, and lunged into it. The knife sliced into his stomach and he cried out in pain. The teacher removed it and plunged the knife into the man's heart and he died. No one moved as the dead man slowly slid down to the floor.

"That is how to die," Julio said, wiping away tears. His men, too, were silently sobbing. I had heard of fucked-up Mexican machismo—but now I'd just seen it.

"This brave man—we have to make sure his children and wife lack for nothing," Julio said as we left to prepare for the border crossing.

Having spoken out for the teacher, there was nothing we could have done for the second man. It was like the man back in Limuru, the one who was hacked to death as we listened. After letting the teacher go, Julio had to show that he was still ruthless; otherwise his hold on power would slip. He had shown that he could forgive, but it was a forgiveness that showed no mercy.

CHAPTER 11

THE BORDER CROSSED US

Just a few months ago, we had been so sure of the world we lived in. For Jason, and I must admit for myself as well, there was no way a black man was going to be president in our lifetime. We couldn't have been surer, and now it looked like we were going to be proved wrong.

For O and his fellow Kenyans, that a civil war would break out was unimaginable. And for O, that Mary would be dead seemed impossible. Just a few months ago, the world, even in its most uncertain times, was still a known quantity—but here we were now, with everything in flux. Here I was, making my way as an illegal immigrant back into a country that in a matter of months might be inaugurating a black man like me.

The teacher was driving and Julio was sitting next to him; O, Muddy, and I sat in the back. Julio had decided to bring the teacher along—a cop might come in handy, but it was also to try to turn him. The teacher had already been initiated and tied into Julio's gang when he killed that man—I was sure there was a knife with his fingerprints on it tucked away somewhere—and now he owed his life to Julio and to us. Besides, at the end of it all, Julio had a genuine brotherly bond with the teacher.

Obama, the soon-to-be president-elect, I hoped, was already commanding such a stage that Bush preferred to stay in the White House and out of sight. The radio was replaying his statement on the Kenya crisis—he was hoping for a transition to democracy. What was the likelihood, I wanted to scream to all of Mexico? What was the likelihood of a black U.S. presidential candidate talking policy about the African country that his father was from?

"Gringo, let me break it down for you. Everyone is pushing something. The motherfuckers in Iraq, democracy is a drug … forced into their veins. They nod in and out, the oil is piped out— you see what I mean?" Julio was saying.

"You keep telling yourself that. Democracy, no matter how fucked up, is not a drug. Drugs are you, Julio. Look at your country, thirty thousand dead," I said defensively.

"But with your guns. Drugs kill; bombs kill. Boom, you are free but dead! Better be high and alive. No?" Julio responded and laughed the kind of laugh that told me he didn't believe in what he was saying.

"You don't have to deal," I said to him angrily. The more I missed home, the more I defended it, the more I longed for it.

I had only seen Tijuana from afar. Driving out of the slum, we had caught the tail end of the city, vibrant with bold colors. There were buildings from centuries ago standing next to skyscrapers, and it gave the place an odd feeling, as if the past were here in the present.

People were going about their business and, if it weren't for them taking cover when a car backfired, one would never have thought that the fear of people like Julio ruled the city. It was hard to reconcile what I was seeing with the terror the city's inhabitants felt every day, the terror of knowing that being innocent wouldn't stop a stray bullet from a policeman or a gang from hitting you. Nairobi was also beautiful, Limuru even more so, but that had not stopped the violence.

The city suddenly opened up to the desert, where in contrast everything around us was the same—sand, desert, the occasional thriving cacti, and long-suffering stunted trees. Peaceful in its constancy—like an ocean, or the plains.

An hour or so from the border, as if conjured up from the desert nothingness, two clouds of dust suddenly spiraled toward us from both sides. When they got closer, we could make out four desert ATVs roaring away, bouncing from dune to dune—I could see why they were named dune buggies. If this had been a race I would have been admiring the display of skill; they were like surfers out in an ocean, riding wave after wave. Soon, we could make out four heavily armed men in protective gear and desert camouflage.

"Aren't we still in our lovely Mexico?" Julio asked the teacher.

"Yes," he said.

"Then what are these *pendejos* doing out here? Be ready for anything," Julio told us.

"We can't get arrested," O said, as he and Muddy checked their AKs and placed more magazines by them. I readied my Glock. The teacher wasn't armed, and Julio gave him a 9 mm.

"Who are they? Border patrol?" O asked.

"Welcome to your new life as an illegal immigrant—the Minutemen, white militia, they protect the borders," I said.

"You mean they protect their own?" Julio said sarcastically.

"If they know who we are, they didn't cross the border to take prisoners," I said.

They revved their dune buggies, spinning their wheels and raising so much sand and dust into the air that soon we couldn't see more than two feet around us.

O tapped the teacher's shoulder and asked him if he knew what was going on.

"*Órale*, take it easy. I took precautions—I am the only one who knew we were coming this way. We cannot outrun them. We see what they want, no?" Julio answered.

"Bulletproof windows—we are safe in here," the teacher said.

We checked our weapons as we waited for the dust to settle. The militiamen beckoned Julio over. Instead, I rolled down the window a few inches.

"Is there a problem?" I asked, trying to sound as friendly as I could.

"You American?" one of them asked.

"Yes—trying to head back home," I answered, putting on my best innocent-tourist expression.

"Taking the long route, ain't you? What you doing around here, anyhow?" the same guy asked.

"I could ask you the same, ain't you a bit out of your way?" I said in turn.

"We ain't got no jurisdiction out here … Now, why don't you step out of the vehicle so that we can see who we talking to? We can talk face to face … *mano a mano*," the man said.

It was a gamble but I asked Muddy to cover me. I slid my Glock into the small of my back, took off my shoulder holster, and gingerly opened the door as Muddy slid into place.

"Come on down, we ain't gonna bite you," their leader said.

I walked over to him—the four men were spaced out so that they were surrounding our car. I could see they had headsets on so they could hear each other, but they couldn't all see each other. I knew O, Muddy, Julio, and the teacher had each picked their target. If it came to it and I couldn't get to my gun before the man in front of me did, all I had to do was fall to the ground.

"Like I was saying, we ain't got no jurisdiction—just like when them Mexicans cross over and shit all over the jurisdiction on the other side. So the better question is, what you doing way out here? We don't see many Afro-Americans around here," he said, drawling out "Afro-Americans."

"Well, here we are, two Americans talking on this side of the border about jurisdiction. You came to us—what do you want?" I asked, trying to sound firm and polite at the same time.

"What we want to know is whether you're carrying some Mexicans—you could be one of them black coyotes. So, why don't you ask your friends to step out the car, we get our Mexicans and the drugs, and you can be on your way?" the leader said, making it sound both reasonable and threatening.

"Out here, you have no authority," I said, motioning towards the U.S., a vague shape a few miles away. "What you are doing is interfering with my investigation," I added, thinking how true that was.

"Well, that may very well be true, but we sure could use some proof … you got a badge? Or perhaps a number I can call?" he asked, so sure that I was lying.

I walked closer to him so he would either have to step back or push me backward to use his weapon.

"You rent-a-cops are quite something. I'm undercover—why would I have my fucking badge with me? And the longer you keep me, the more questions they will ask," I said angrily, having decided to play the part that I was playing in real life anyway. He hadn't expected that tone and it gave him pause.

His friends were getting impatient, as I presumed mine were as well, and now that they had heard me over their leader's headset, they would be a little less sure of the course of action to take. They had been expecting, at the very least, a simple Stepin Fetchit routine.

"Just walk away—hop away on your toys and pretend we never met. I can carry on and you can continue playing your games," I said to him, knowing that there was no way this was going to end well.

"You got one of yours in the White House, almost, but not out here in wetback country. You dig, my brother? So this is what you are gonna do. You are gonna call your little friends and ask them to step out the car one by one. Then we are going to search your vehicle. And then I will want to see some undercover identification," he instructed, sounding like he was talking to a junior partner.

"Dumb fuck—you think I have some Mormons in the car? I ask them to step out and they step out shooting," I said.

He pulled back, trying to raise his M-16. I edged closer in so that I was holding his gun down at an angle, pointing away from me. I still hadn't gone for my Glock, hoping that, somehow, we would all come to our senses and have a good laugh, and then we would be on our way.

"Hey, that's not all I have to say," I said before he could respond. "I'm going to reach into my pocket slowly—I want to give you something—for you and your men."

"Very slowly," came the inevitable warning.

"Here is five thousand dollars—they see me giving it to you, I go back and tell them you took a bribe and we are all safe, and you can have a drink on the Bureau. Just take it and move on and I can put down in my report that the Minutemen have good judgment," I said, trying to sound as convincing as Julio had been when he gave the teacher the choice of truth, lies, or death. He hesitated.

"What I am telling you is that you were dead the moment you stopped us. And now I am giving you money to stay alive," I said to them all, via the leader's headset.

He was starting to waver. Whatever he had against Mexicans

was not principle. Way inside Mexico, confronting a black man with a car full of people whose intentions and capabilities he didn't know, reason was telling him to take the money and run. As he put out his hand for the money, I reached for my Glock, closed in, and raised it to his chin.

"I'm going to walk away now," I said. "You make a move and you will be the first to die."

I could see the fear growing in his eyes—the tables had turned.

"Hey, fellas, five thousand dollars for nothing? Let's get outta here!" he yelled out to his men. I backtracked to the car and climbed in.

"They were trying to get us out of the car—I think they know who we are," I whispered urgently as the leader made a big show of putting the money in his pocket. They rode off and we continued on.

"Think they are coming back?" the teacher asked.

"Regardless of whether they know who we are, that was their reconnaissance—try and gauge our strength. Not bad at all," Muddy said.

"And now we also know who we're dealing with," I said.

"They will be back. Stop the car—I'll climb up on the roof," O said to the teacher.

"We are safer in the car," Julio said, tapping the windows.

"Inside we have only four guns—on the roof, I have an advantage and we have an extra gun—five on four," O explained.

It made sense: sitting in the middle, Muddy couldn't very well shoot over O or me, and if they took out the tires, we couldn't stay in an immobilized car indefinitely. We had to fight our way out.

"When you see them, stop the car," O said.

Stopping the car was counter-intuitive—a moving target is harder to hit, so they would expect us to try to outrun them. Stopping would throw them off and we would be able to pick our shots.

"It's going to be bumpy," the teacher said as he spun the wheels and churned up a sand storm to camouflage O's move.

We hadn't gone very far before we saw the four-wheelers coming furiously toward us from both sides. The teacher stopped the car—as we had expected, they had been anticipating a chase, and so they stopped a few hundred feet away to think about their next move. Then they started up again—they sped toward us as they fired and we could feel their rounds tearing into the jeep like a hailstorm. I heard the disciplined roar from O's AK, and the four-wheeler coming at the teacher spun in the air and came crashing down into the sand. The driver tried to find cover but it was too late. O cut him down.

I waited, feeling the tapping of the M-16 fire getting more and more intense—and just when I thought I couldn't stand it, the driver of the ATV nearest to us hit a small dune and reached for the wheel with both hands. I waited one second more for the four-wheeler to steady, and just as he was reaching for his weapon again, I let out one shot—the man's head jerked backwards and the four-wheeler crawled to a stop a few feet from our car. Julio and Muddy were still firing at the remaining vehicles. From the roof, O joined them—it was now three guns to two. One of them tried to turn back but it was too late, as both machines and the men inside came to a dead stop. In a matter of seconds, it was quiet again.

We stepped outside to ID the men. I went to the leader first. In an inside pocket of his jacket, next to my wad of cash, was the man's wallet. I opened it. There was a photograph of the man, his wife, and two young children in a park. I stared at it for a moment. The man stirred—he was barely alive.

"Why didn't you walk away? You should have walked away," I said to him as he groped for the wallet. I gave it to him and he shakily looked at the photograph.

"Why?" he asked.

I looked at him, trying to understand what he was asking. Why had we fought back? Why didn't he walk away? Why was he dying? Why were we in Mexico? Why had I betrayed our country? He was gone before I could ask him what he meant.

I was about to put his wallet back in his jacket but remembered it had my prints—as did the M-16. I tore off one of his sleeves, dipped it into the tank of his four-wheeler, and put his wallet and weapon on top of it. Then I asked O for a lighter and set it on fire.

There was nothing useful on any of them. Did they really know who we were? It seemed more than likely. If so, it meant that Sahara knew we were coming, and that was bad news. The good news was that the U.S. government didn't know—otherwise it would not have been four militiamen.

We drove off. A few hundred feet behind us, the four-wheeler exploded into flames. The man's question kept playing in my mind. That question, asked into the vacuum of death, when there was nothing else left to lose or gain, that question as a dying man's confession or curse—that question—I knew that question would fuck me over, someday soon.

An hour later, we came to a stop. Julio took out three shovels from the back of the car and led us to the bottom of a sand dune. He gave the teacher, O, and me a shovel each and pointed to where we were to start digging. We dug for about ten minutes until we hit what looked like a trapdoor. Julio pulled it open and we all went down a ladder to the beginning of a tunnel. He fumbled around and found some flashlights.

"Whoever is last, close the door—the wind will cover it with sand," he said nonchalantly. "Sorry about the accommodations, this is not the kind of tunnel that has electricity and air-conditioning. This is a poor man's drug tunnel."

We crawled for about an hour before the tunnel suddenly opened up into a basement. Julio knocked on a door in the wall once, paused, then twice more.

"You know what that says?" he asked me.

"No," I answered, curious.

"My knock say 'Ju-li-o.' Get it? I spell my name," he said, laughing. We were too exhausted to laugh with him.

The trapdoor opened and on other side was a well-dressed old woman who reminded me of O's mother, aged and wrinkled but not bent.

"What are you doing here, Julio? Aren't you the big *jefe* over there now?" she asked him in English.

"I had to deliver them across myself," he replied as he pointed at us.

"They must be very special packages," she said, beckoning us in.

"Welcome to the United States of America. You are now officially illegal immigrants," he said to us.

"Come … let us get you something to eat and then you can bathe," the old woman said to us, as if we were children, not fiercely armed and dirty strangers. She led us to her sitting room, which was immaculately clean, and I noticed that we were tracking dirt all over the place.

"Don't worry, labor is cheap over here—someone will clean up after you," she said, laughing. She handed us towels and blue overalls to wear, leaving us to decide who was going to shower first.

After we cleaned up, Julio called us together for what appeared to be a drug meeting. He went to another room and came back with three phones and a bunch of SIM cards.

"Change them every other day! Don't use only cash—that will make some people suspicious. Here are some prepaid credit cards. Buy new ones in poor neighborhoods—use fake names. Your weapons are like Samson's hair, your strength and weakness—if you are arrested with them, you are fucked. You could go in Gandhi-like. But to find clean unmarked guns is hard work, so take what you have," he said.

"Operate like this is the 1960s—that is the only way to defeat your more sophisticated enemy. They have the satellites, you will have only what you can see; they will have their sophisticated weapons, you will have only what you can point and shoot; they will have their computer networks, their international connections, the Internet will be at their beck and call, you will have word of mouth. In other words, my friends, stay as you are, operate as if you are still in Africa," Julio drilled us, and then laughed. I laughed along, too: it was the best damn speech anyone could give three fish out of water.

It was time to leave for Oakland. We stepped outside the house into a hot, glaring sun and climbed into a blue van with NINJA CAR CLEANERS on it—the logo was a picture of Mr. Clean dressed like a ninja. We were off.

I was in the U.S.—that much I knew objectively. I was a U.S. citizen and this was my country, but I didn't feel like I was home. At the same time, with the election coming up, I couldn't have picked a more exciting time to come home, in spite of the ugliness we had left behind in Kenya and in a Mexican desert.

CHAPTER 12

BACK IN THE U.S. OF A.

I was home, but home was largely unrecognizable—San Francisco wasn't Madison, by far. For one, late November in Madison was bitter cold and snow-covered. In San Francisco, the night was cool, all right, but it felt more like a nice Wisconsin spring.

Yet, at the same time, it was home. American English! I had never thought of language as anything other than words, but to be surrounded by it after so long, to wallow in it, to understand everything around me—it was as if a long-dulled sense had awoken. Even when I couldn't make out a whole conversation or even a single sentence in the noise of people and machinery, there was a sense of familiarity, of being home.

And this din was American. The hum of noise was mine—the Caterpillars and jackhammers working through a darkness lit by large floodlights, loud people walking down the street, all the smells of different cuisines from cheap and expensive restaurants, the smell of perfume coming from well-dressed men and women going to the bars and clubs. Yes, this wasn't Madison, but it smelled and sounded like home.

When I worked undercover as a cop, there were times I felt desolate and lonely—it was like living parallel lives, trapped in one body. But even then I always knew that a single phone call could change all that—I had a whole police force behind me, which meant that, at the bottom of it all, I had a government behind me. This felt different—I didn't have a single lifeline. Yes, I could ask for favors from people I trusted like Mo, my journalist friend in Madison, but even they could only do so much for me.

Now I felt like my cover was too complete—a single arrest and I would be tried as an enemy combatant. I was a man without a country at home. On the other hand, it wasn't so bad: I had O and Muddy here with me and we were all working this case together.

From the door of his house in Oakland, Michael sleepily beckoned us in. Where O was tall and lean, Michael, though just as tall, seemed to fill the doorway. Shaved bald and wearing a big smile and a thick blue bathrobe that barely covered his belly, he looked every bit the consummate Kenyan middle manager. He let us in, mumbling something about having to be at work in the morning—he worked at a nursing home. He pointed to the fridge, two couches, and a bunch of sleeping bags in the sitting room, and went back to sleep.

"How did he know that we would be five and not three?" I asked O. O hadn't told him we were coming with Julio and the teacher.

"He didn't, he just assumed we would be many," O answered.

"I find that to be very curious. Why?" Julio asked, joining me in my suspicions.

"It's an African thing," Muddy said.

"You motherfuckers better chill out and enjoy your African hospitality," O explained lightly. I didn't need convincing and I went to the fridge. It was full of barely cold food—fish, *nyama choma*, collard greens, and *ugali*. The long road had made us ravenously hungry and I didn't bother looking for plates or spoons, I just laid out the food on the low coffee table in its big aluminum trays. There were some Tuskers in the fridge too. I passed them around and as we ate, we discussed our next move.

"Are you in any hurry to get back?" Muddy asked Julio and the teacher. "I mean, surely your thriving business can survive a few days without you? Then we can enjoy the sights."

"What are you asking?" Julio said.

"We could use your help—your Ninja Cleaners gives us a good cover. Two of us have never been to the U.S. before, two of us are cops used to doing things with the law on their side, the simple way. Look, Julio, we need you, we need you to help us stay underground," Muddy said.

"If you stay, I stay. Then we go back together," the teacher said to Julio.

"Let me make a call," Julio said and stepped outside. We waited, sipping tiredly on our beers until he returned.

"Jason, he like that I stay and watch over you," he said with a smile on his face.

"What did you really say to him?" I asked him.

"Let us say that you, my friends, are good for business. You were right, my dear rose," he said, turning to Muddy. "From here I can run my business."

Sometimes I doubted whether without Muddy we would ever get anything done. She was right—we needed Julio around.

There was one other piece of business to take care of: the teacher. We needed to know what he would do. We had saved his life, and he had proven himself. Now it was a question of whether he trusted us enough to let us continue with our work without him raising the alarm.

"I have nowhere to go except back to Mexico. To live here in

America … is death to me. My former life is dead, what life will I be born to? I am police—that is all I know to do. Julio, help me get the bastard who sold me out … It is the only way I can go back in," he said. "Once I'm back in, you and I, we know each other well now."

He did have options: he could stay in the United States illegally, he could go to the DEA and offer his services and knowledge, he could go into the drug business himself—many police and military personnel had—but he was right. Each option was like death. He had only one choice, and that was to go reclaim his life. It all depended on just how badly Julio still wanted to ruin or kill him.

Julio was silent for a minute.

"I will help you, but remember your life is mine," he said. The teacher, looking depressed, nodded in agreement.

This was our life, shifting alliances and allegiances, and we hoped with each shift that somehow the world, even as it remained the same crooked, crime-filled place it had always been, had changed for the better. With the teacher back in the force, a corrupt chief would be out. And the teacher had already been compromised by Julio. For him, the teacher, alive and back inside the police force, was worth more than dead and buried somewhere in a Mexican desert on their return trip.

Julio would get to turn him after all. With at least two things resolved, we inflated five of the seven air mattresses—it was true that Michael had just assumed there would be many of us and had prepared all the beds that he had.

While O was in the kitchen looking for omelette ingredients, I turned on Michael's computer—he had the Kenyan *Daily*

Nation as his homepage. Muddy leaned over my shoulder and we skimmed through the front page. The violence had intensified, but there were two positive developments. The idea that Obama should make a unity visit to Kenya was being floated—it'd be good for his campaign if he brought peace to a country while still just a candidate, and if anyone could, it was him. The United Nations was also sending in a former UN chief to broker peace and the Elders were planning to visit.

This was the first time I'd heard of the Elders. I looked it up on the Internet—it was an organization composed of the world's most influential retirees—Mandela, Clinton, Bishop Tutu, Jimmy Carter, and others who still believed in doing some good, though I couldn't help wondering cynically what they could do now that they couldn't do when they'd held their powerful offices. Nevertheless, the idea that the world was a village and yet needed global leaders was interesting.

I guessed Obama's visit wouldn't happen at the height of the violence—too dangerous, physically and politically. And after the Norfolk bombing, with Sahara still on the loose, it would be foolhardy for the U.S. Embassy in Kenya to allow such a visit. We had to find Sahara—without him, everyone was holding on to only a small piece of the puzzle.

The United States had launched a drone missile attack into Somalia, killing some operatives from Al Qaeda, Al Shabaab, or another organization. Of course, the real culprits were still at large, because they were going after the wrong guys. It was time to really question whether Paul was just a hapless diplomat who went along with the powers that be, or whether he was actively part of the disinformation detracting from the Sahara mission.

I had the feeling that the case was getting away from us, that we didn't have the skills or the power to solve it, that we were being sucked into the eye of a hurricane.

Julio and the teacher were still sleeping, but they woke up as soon as O walked back into the sitting room with a big pan half-covered by a massive omelette. He had put in anything he could find in Michael's fridge—beans, *ugali*, fish, beef, and even fries—but it was damn good.

Over breakfast, we discussed the best thing to do. We had to make it to the university and see what we could find out there. Muddy, O, and I would go to Berkeley while Julio and the teacher remained behind to buy car-washing supplies and Ninja Car Washers uniforms—to turn our shell of a cover into actual immigrant jobs.

Helen, our "African Hacker," as I had taken to calling her, had decided from her profile that Sahara not only had a connection to the University of California, Berkeley, but that he had probably taught there—something to do with Africa. Muddy and I took a cab to the university and marched straight to the African Studies Department. We were going to present ourselves as a black couple, African and African-American, interested in the program.

"Can we learn more about what it is you do here?" we asked a beautiful white woman with thick blond dreadlocks and dressed in African clothing.

"My Kiswahili name is Amina," she said as she shook our hands. "It means 'feel safe.' But you can also call me by my American name, Leslie," she added with a self-conscious laugh when we said nothing.

"Pardon me, I was just admiring your dress," Muddy said. She introduced us using our cover names.

"You must be Kikuyu ... your name suggests so," Amina said to me pleasantly.

"No, I'm actually from here ... the United States, I mean. My parents gave me that name," I said.

"Oh, I understand ... black power," she concluded, and then paused. "Oh my God, where is my hospitality? May I offer you some tea?"

"Thank you, Amina, tea would be lovely," Muddy said. I was dying with laughter at this proper-sounding Muddy.

Amina made a call to the office and dashed off with a coffee pot. The assistant director, a tall, stocky white man with flaming red hair, came out and led us to his office. It reminded me of many of the offices of expatriates that I had visited in Kenya—there were the drums and clothes, and long shelves of books that displayed his knowledge.

There were also the usual Maasai photographs: one of him surrounded by Africans, a scholarly face among a sea of smiling black faces, another in which he was wearing a beaded crown, next to him a slaughtered bull with its bright thick red blood streaking through sandy earth. He smiled when he saw me looking at the photograph.

"They made me an honorary chief ... called me the red chief on account of my hair," he said. "I used to be a vegetarian until that," he added, pointing at the bull. "How could I live on grass like the animal, they asked? I had no answer."

I gave him our Kikuyu names.

"Chief ... my husband and I, we feel we need to know more about Africa. I am an African and he is from here, but we need to know more so we can ..." Muddy started to say.

"Let me guess," the white African Chief interrupted her. "You are from … wait, wait, don't tell me, you're from Rwanda," he said, almost jumping up and down in his chair.

"Yes, my, how could you tell?" Muddy asked, sounding genuinely surprised except that from her tone I could tell she was putting on an act.

"I have an excellent ear for African accents. Were you there? Did you really see it? Sad times … Did you lose someone? Why do you have a Kikuyu name?" he asked her.

Muddy didn't answer.

"Excuse me, I get carried away when I meet people like you—survivors—it takes courage and strength. You are the reason I am what I am. I should not have asked. What can I do for you?" he said apologetically.

We explained that we had met a professor from the department, probably retired, but we had lost his contact information. He had had a profound effect on us, he had told us about the program, and we had promised to look him up when we came to campus. He went by the name of Sahara—his African name. At which point the Chief said that it happened all the time, friends of Africa took African names.

We described Sahara, but the Chief said that we could be describing most old white college professors. He entered a few keys into his computer, waved us over to his side, and scrolled down a list of current and retired professors associated with the program.

"Any of these names seem familiar?" he asked. None of them did.

He gave us his card and some brochures and suggested we spend some time online learning about the program—we could come back next week if we had questions before applying.

As we left the office, we saw that Amina was pouring water from the coffee pot onto some Ketepa tea bags. So, to be polite, the four of us sat around her receptionist desk, sipping lukewarm Kenyan tea.

"Hey, what are you guys doing later in the afternoon? It's African Festival Week. I promise it's going to be a blast—come, I'll show you around," she offered, and gave us a flyer. We were just about to turn her down, when she said, "Hey, you can't say no—everyone who has ever done anything in Africa, they will all be there. You can leave Africa, but Africa will never leave you."

"Your professor might even be there," the Chief said.

The conversation spiraled down to cuisine and culture. When we left, the Chief and Amina were laughing about their last encounter at an Ethiopian restaurant: the hot pepper had been watered down—the food wasn't *really* African.

"I have an idea. I once asked Jason why he joined the Foreign Service, and he said it was because he went on a study abroad program. We need to look at their study abroad programs—love for the Foreign Service begins with Peace Corps–type programs, a visit to a foreign country ..." I said excitedly.

"Where are you going with this?" Muddy asked me.

"Sahara's men, there was something about them ... Someone somewhere must have recruited and trained them, and a campus is as good a place as any. Shit, the army, the CIA, corporations, everyone recruits from the colleges. Why not Sahara? Think of Amina ... she would be attracted to a company promising to do some good," I talked it through to Muddy.

"Well, let's find out," she said.

A colorfully dressed maternal woman who had a busy mouth

ran the study abroad office. Muddy told her we were journalists working on a piece for Kenya's *Daily Nation* about Berkeley's programs. What we wanted to do was go through a list of
their students spanning two or three generations. Specifically, we
wanted to write about students who had been to Africa.

"You're in luck, honey, everything is computerized," she said
to us as she turned on a computer monitor. "What years?"

"When was the Peace Corps founded?" I asked her. "Sixty-
two, wasn't it, by Kennedy?"

"I see you've done your research, dear. It was 1961. Let's see,
1961 to the present ... if we narrow the search to Africa," she said
as she typed, " ... not many hits in the early 1960s. You know,
Africa was not that popular back then ..."

"Why is that?" Muddy asked.

"Your guess is as good as mine, honey. All I can tell you is
that you'll find very few alumni for the early days," she replied.

That was good for us, since our search dates would range
from the 1970s to the early '90s, assuming that Sahara's men were,
give or take a few years, in their late thirties.

"Do you have a flash drive?" she asked. "It's okay, I know
those damn things can be expensive." She rummaged through
her drawer, found several, and picked one. "The students, they
forget them here and never come back for them," she said, looking with pity at the poor African journalists.

She gave us the downloaded data and we thanked her,
promising that we would send her the piece as soon as it was
published.

Next, we went to the university library and used a computer
there to go through the flash drive. A few minutes into it, Muddy

pointed to the screen and I tensed. We had something. In 1985, five students, four of them white and one of them black, had traveled to South Africa. These were the days before the U.S. declared sanctions against the racist government there.

There were a few photos of them marching with black students against apartheid. But it was the last photo, in which they were looking into the camera somberly, their eyes without the luster, smiles, and laughter of the earlier photographs, that suggested something profound had happened to them. My guess was that they had seen more violence than the university newspaper would dare publish—dying and dead schoolchildren still in their uniforms, shot by the security forces. These were our guys.

The write-up concluded with the information that their meeting with the university president led to the University of California becoming the first university to fully divest from apartheid South Africa—to the tune of three billion dollars.

That kindness they had about them that felt so out of place—it made sense. It was hard to believe that these kids would, a few years later, plant a bomb in Kenya, kill one of their own and die in a small apartment in Nairobi after shooting an unarmed woman in the head.

The write-up didn't mention where they were from—but we had their names. Neil Jackson, Harrison Bush, Ronald William, and John Rhodes. And our dead man—Amos Apara. There was no Sahara, but now I knew if we looked hard enough, we would find him. We could work with this.

I stepped outside the library and called Helen. She was still working on getting past the security on Sahara's laptop. In the meantime, she would hack into the school database and get us the listed addresses for where the men had lived.

I went back inside and we continued going through the flash

drive, sure we wouldn't find Sahara. But if we followed the dead
black man—Amos Apara—I had to get used to the fact that we
now had a name—he would eventually lead us to Sahara. We left
the library feeling much lighter.

The African Festival Week was unlike anything I had ever seen.
It was half celebration and half mourning; Kenya, up in flames,
was still fresh in my mind. But slowly I relaxed and forgot that
we were here to look for Sahara or anything that might help us
with the case.

At the festival, Muddy and I could eat, drink, and hold
hands and just be an engaged couple in love. We could dance
to the Malian musician on stage, playing his *ngoni*, which made
beautiful muted thin and stringy sounds that were well comple-
mented by a blues guitarist's lazy electrified notes, the congas,
and the drums. I had seen Muddy happy, but I had never seen
her carefree—without a worry in the world, so in the moment
that every now and then she'd even skip about when pointing
something out.

I was dressed in a flowing blue African shirt and blue jeans,
while O was wearing a white shirt over black corduroys. Muddy
had set her dreadlocks free and she was wearing a long hippie-
looking African dress. You could say we were disguised as ourselves. The outfits had another advantage: they concealed our
weapons and bulletproof vests.

Julio and the teacher were wearing modern Mexican outfits; at least that's what they told us, as Julio made us repeat the
names of everything—guayabera shirts, which looked African
to me, and sombreros, jeans, and sandals. It was Muddy's idea to
play up the ethnic dress.

We divided up, O taking the teacher and Muddy taking Julio, and went in search of Sahara. After two hours of walking around, peering into every face, we converged at a makeshift bar that was selling Tusker beer. In true Kenyan form, we ordered two each and some beef kebabs and found a place under the tent to sit down, watching people walk by. This had been a long shot, but there was no harm in hanging around in case Sahara came to the festival later.

"Mr. Mwangi, you are not asking," O said to me, reverting to our cover names.

"What question?" I asked him.

"I thought by now you would have asked what I thought of America, your country," O said.

"Well?" I said.

"I knew we were many but I did not know there was a place where we could be … all together, black people from all over. And walking together with Asians and Europeans—you know what I mean? I like that. Makes me think of what's happening back home," he answered pensively.

Amina walked by, dressed every bit the part, looking more African even than Muddy, who had forsaken a head-wrap so that, as she had explained, her dreads could soak in the American sun. I caught up with her and we walked back to the tent together. She had a quick beer with us—she was meeting friends—but she was having a party later and she invited us along.

At Amina's, Muddy and O were smoking up a storm while I was getting deeper and deeper into the blues. The teacher and Julio had left with the rest of Amina's guests, a motley crew of graduate students interested in one or another aspect of Africa.

"Hey, Mwangi!" O called out, high and very drunk. "Do you know what it's like to wake up one morning, kiss the woman you love goodbye, go to a hospital to see your sick mother, and come back to find your wife dead? Do you know anything about that kind of ... of ... suddeneity?" he asked me as he got up to dance, or rather sway back and forth.

"Suddeneity is not a fucking word," Muddy corrected him, and she took a deeper hit from her joint.

"No, I can't say I do," I answered, already hating where the conversation was going.

"Heeeeey, Bwana," Amina said, raising her hands up in the air. "My father ... my father died in a car accident in fucking Kampala, one day we were talking over the phone, the next day he was dead and we were trying to get him back home. Some people hit giraffes, and some die in war. We're here, aren't we?" she said as she blew smoke into the air and coughed.

"Don't stand in my way," O said to me, ignoring Amina's comment but reaching for her hand.

"Hey, fuck off," Amina said, and slapped his hand away.

"I'm sorry—that came out the wrong way. Okay?" he said to Amina before continuing. "What I mean is that the closest you can get to knowing yourself is when you're looking for the motherfucker that tried to kill you—that's it. And you wanna know why?" he asked drunkenly.

"Why?" we chorused back, some of us lagging behind like we were preschoolers.

"Because you have to ask yourself—why does that motherfucker want to kill me? And why did he miss me and kill my wife?" he said, pointing at an imaginary enemy.

"And then you have to ask—how the fuck do I kill him?" O said. "Do you know that you have to get to know his soul? I mean you have to know his soul. That is how we get Sahara." He slapped his hand on his knee emphatically.

"What do you guys do? I thought you were looking to enroll ... PhD program and all," Amina said, trying not to sound nervous.

"Do you really care?" Muddy asked her. Amina thought for a minute or so.

"Shit, I don't care ... I don't know why I thought I cared," she said, which led to another high philosophical debate about why we need to know things or people and what it means to truly know.

Perhaps the idea that you could really get to know someone's soul was an overstatement, but, thinking of Muddy, I thought, I hoped, that you could get at least part of the way there. I guess this what Helen the Hacker meant—you hack the person, not the computer. We still didn't know Sahara that well. In fact, we hardly knew him at all.

It was time for Muddy and me to leave. O and Amina both looked at us as if to ask what had taken us so long. By the time we made it to the door they were kissing. Two wounded people had found each other. I wanted to say something about it to Muddy but it occurred to me that whether O woke up missing his wife less, or even more, it would not change the bottom line—she was gone. That was his life now—a constant longing for what he had lost.

Muddy and I took a cab back to Michael's. Julio and the teacher had started on a bottle of tequila. Still high from the festival, they decided we should walk to the Mexican neighborhood that was just few blocks from Michael's house, in search of bar to call *mi casa*, as Julio put it.

This was something I had forgotten about the United

States—in Kenya each ethnic group had a territory that they claimed as theirs; in the United States, the territories were neighborhoods. We didn't have far to go before we made it to the Bajo Tierra. The bar was more like a dugout; from the street you went down a few stairs that led you through a short, brightly colored tunnel.

The bar itself was old-fashioned, none of those flashy digital jukeboxes and fancy lights. The only concession to modernity was a small ATM in the corner.

We had a beer, took the keys to the Ninja Cleaners van, and left Julio and the teacher having a good time. I guess they were becoming friends. Back in the van, we turned on the AC and made love like we were teenagers, our flowing African clothes getting in the way, with Mexican pop music playing in the background.

There was still one more day of the festival left and I was hoping it would count for something.

CHAPTER 13

OLD FRIENDS

He wouldn't have recognized me. He wouldn't have been expecting me to be in the U.S., let alone at an African Festival in Oakland; and in my outfit, to him I was anyone other than myself.

Nor would I have seen him, except that on this second and last day of the festival I'd stopped giving in to the seductive music and food and I had gone back to work. Even then it took me several passes to realize that the surfer dude sitting at a table drinking Tusker beer and chatting away with friends at the makeshift bar we'd been at just a day before was the man I had let go in Nairobi, who, naked, had still somehow managed to get a motorcycle and rescue Sahara.

Convinced it was him, I called Muddy and O. Julio and the teacher hadn't joined us, they had some business to take care of. I didn't ask what kind of business. I went over to the bar and ordered a Tusker, watching him, ready to move. Muddy and O soon joined me and I discreetly pointed out the man.

We needed him to come with us quietly, so we could talk without urgency and fear of interruption. In Kenya we would have just grabbed him, right there where he was. Now we were completely at a loss about what to do—being on the right side of Kenya's blurry law had spoiled us. Were it not for the seriousness of it all, it would have been comical. Like pickpockets, we had to wait until an opportunity presented itself.

At last, he and his friends were done with their beer and we followed them out of the festival as our man chatted and laughed without a care in the world. We followed them down a beautiful street with trees and flowers along the sidewalks. Finally, he waved goodbye to his friends and hopped up a flight of stairs to an apartment complex. It wasn't hard to tell which apartment was his. A light came on, a window opened, and Lingala music piped through it.

The question again—what do we do? We finally had something major, a direct connection to Sahara, and we had no idea what to do.

"We are ghosts, no one knows we are here, or even thinks that we could be here—there is no motive to trace. We could just go in, grab him, and be gone in a few seconds," O said, with a voice that made me pity the man.

"We have to talk to him first," Muddy said.

"And take him where?" I asked them both.

"We have the van, we can find a quiet place," Muddy replied.

"We would have to get rid of it—and it's good for our cover," I countered. There really was only one thing to do: for Muddy to knock on his door as we hid. When he opened it, we would burst right through and interrogate him inside. It didn't matter that now he'd know we were here in the States. Either O or I would kill him.

There was a problem with that idea, though. It was one thing when we were all in the same busy bar tent at the festival, and we were part of the scene. It was another for Muddy to knock on his door. He would be cautious, and if he was in fact a central part of Sahara's team he would immediately recognize her.

Muddy agreed to do it anyway.

"It's the best we can do … what are we gonna do? Tail him

until one night he decides to pee in a dark alley at three in the morning?" O said.

We waited until someone entered the complex, and just when the door was about to shut, we rushed in. I could feel the familiar tension that now bordered on excitement. Leaning against the wall on either side of the door, we prepared our weapons as Muddy knocked. The man asked who was there.

"Where's the party?" Muddy asked him through the door.

He opened it, leaving the security latch in place.

"John Adams said this was the place to head to after the festival?" Muddy lied.

"No one by that name lives in this building, I think," he said. Muddy apologized and started to walk away.

"Do you have his number?" he asked helpfully.

"Yes, he gave it to me but my cell doesn't work in the United States ..." she answered.

"Oh, where are you coming from? By all means, come in and use mine ..." he said, opening the door.

Muddy followed him in. We heard a thump and walked in to find the man lying on the floor, unconscious, and Muddy holding her gun by the barrel. We tied and gagged him, and then O slapped him back into consciousness.

"If you scream, we will have no choice," O said to him as he removed the gag.

"I wasn't going to do anything to her ... phone, she wanted a phone. I will pay—how much?" he said, after a few seconds of trying to comprehend what was going on.

Muddy slapped him.

"How much do you think I'm worth?" she asked him.

"I don't understand. I was just trying to help—ask her," he said, looking around for a way out.

"Like you helped that man escape me in Nairobi?" I said. I could see the recognition on his face—it slowly turned into fear.

"Shit, shit, shit! I had no idea what was going on—I was just a driver ... you know, just their driver," he pleaded.

"What is your name?" I asked him.

"Pete," he answered. "Peter Arnold."

I found his wallet on the desk. The driver's license gave the same name and address.

"Pete—everything you know," Muddy said.

"I had no idea they were going to kill your wife," Peter said to O.

"How did you know?" I asked him.

"Know what?"

"That it was his wife and no one else who died?" I asked.

"I didn't say that, wait, what I meant was—that's what Jim, Jim Delaware told me in the Range Rover," he said hurriedly. I didn't react to his mentioning Sahara's real name; neither did O or Muddy. We were here in his apartment, he assumed we knew everything; all we had to do was keep him talking.

"Things were happening fast—how could he take the time to explain who had died and who had lived?" I asked him. He looked at me but he didn't answer. He must have been thinking that, having let him walk away once, I was going to do it again.

O, who had been quiet all along, pulled up a chair and sat so that he was facing Peter.

"Listen to me very carefully. You are already dead. You should have died in Nairobi. You didn't, and that's okay. We are here now to make it happen. Go back to the moment we walked in through that door and tell yourself, I am dead. Then, I want you to try and earn your life back," O said calmly, even helpfully. O's eerily calm demeanor scared Peter into talking.

"Look, guys, I have changed ... I'm only thirty years old, you know—I'm just starting to figure out life, trying to live my life—Kenya, all that is behind me ..." Peter pleaded. His face, having gone white at first, was now beet red.

"I don't care about your future, tell me about the past ..." O interrupted. "So let's talk." O untied Peter's hands and sat back down.

"My name is Peter Arnold," the man said again. "Until that morning, I drove for Jim Delaware and his men—you know, shit, I was just a backpacker, just wanted to see the world but I was always broke. I knew my way around Nairobi—the flea-bag motels, where to get a cheap meal, you know, people always thinking I was loaded coz I was white, but I was just trying to see the world, broke as hell. I was a *mzungu*, right? I was Bwana Peter. One night at Florida 2000—I was just trying to get laid and I take this fine-ass woman to the back—she doesn't look like a prostitute or anything, but after we're done and get back to the bar, she asks me for two hundred dollars, two hundred for a *fucking* BJ. I have no money—and she goes crazy, and every-one at the bar is looking at me like they want to kill me. Here comes Mr. Moneybags, and he slaps two hundred dollars on the table—gives her another twenty and asks her to get us and her-self a drink. Later he offers me a job as his driver. I accept," he explained.

It was time to change tactics, time to up the game. If Peter knew we would be going Cop 101 on him, then he would have anticipated all this.

"Peter, let me ask you something," I said.

"Yes?" he responded.

"Did you expect us at your door tonight, or tomorrow, or the day after, or ever?"

"No, I don't understand, I can't, how did you get here? How did you find me?" he asked.

"How did we get into the country? How did we find you? I'm not saying we know everything, there is a lot we don't know, but you can be sure we will find it all out. What you should be worried about is whether you'll be around to see us fail or succeed," I explained.

"Also, Peter, understand that we cannot arrest you, threaten you with years behind bars—it's life or death. Your life is in your hands," O said.

"Amos Apara, tell us what happened," I said to him. I could see he was surprised that we knew the man's name.

"I don't know—they didn't take me everywhere—like, I drove them to scout out places. When the Norfolk happened, I thought it might be them—but I had driven them there over a year ago, so I let it go," he answered.

The grainy security tape we had recovered had shown five men getting out of the van, but it sounded like they did their reconnaissance in the Range Rover. It was possible that he had been kept out of the loop.

"What happened to Amos?" I asked him again.

"He just stopped showing up," he said.

"And you didn't say anything?" Muddy asked.

"I asked where he was. And the boss man ... you know, Jim ... he said Amos had gone home—but the way he said it, with a smile, it was as if he wanted me to know that something had happened to him—like he was giving me a warning," Peter said. "I could feel the tension between them sometimes—you know, it was as if he didn't always agree with whatever they were doing. I mean, like sometimes they wouldn't talk to him—they were ... businesslike."

"Were they always like that?" O asked.

"No, before they were chummy—like friends… made jokes about women, sometimes about Africans—you know, American humor," he answered, looking at me. "What are you going to do with me? I'm doing well, right? Giving you what you want? Yeah?"

"Stay with Jim," O said to him, ignoring his plea.

"Jim? He knows everything about Africa—some kind of history buff, like, one time we were driving down Kimathi Street and he goes into the whole Mau Mau thing. Out in the bush, he would be pointing out different plants and trees and calling them by their Latin names, even told us about the formation of the Rift Valley. He was like a father-figure kinda guy—but he never talked about himself," Peter said, beginning to look a bit relaxed.

"Is that why you came back for him? You had a clean break. You could have just walked away, but you didn't," I said, trying not to raise my voice in anger.

"Money, I needed cash—it was payday—I needed the money. I had to come back for him. Five thousand dollars is a lot of money in Kenya, or anywhere. It was all for the money," he explained.

"When was the last time you spoke to him?" I asked.

"Last night. He was supposed to come to the festival, but he's having a party tomorrow night. He wanted to see if I could shuttle some of his guests from the airport," he said, to our surprise.

I could feel my heart pounding—we were this close to the man we had come to know as Sahara. O leaned back into the chair and Muddy decided to get some ice for the back of Peter's head.

O tied up and gagged him so we could go to the kitchen to

decide on what to do next. As valuable as he had become to us, we could not take any chances with him yet.

Peter was what he was—an American taking advantage of his whiteness in Kenya—that was no crime. He had been used, but that wasn't a crime either. There was no depth to him, neither more or less—he was what you saw: a surfer dude. We could kill Peter and try to storm our way into Sahara's party. But there would be such a massive manhunt for his killer that, even though there would be no evidence linking us to him, it was unnecessarily risky.

Or we could use him. The plan we eventually agreed on was simple, because we had to keep it simple. We needed to know who the guests at Sahara's party would be and, if possible, what they had come to celebrate and talk about. Peter had some of the names and their arrival times; we would run those by Jason and Helen to start with. And we needed to spend some quality time with Sahara.

It was also time to bring Mo and the *Madison Times* into the picture. I trusted her and we needed whatever we found to be out in the open as soon as we left the U.S. We would be safe to the extent that there were no more secrets for Sahara and his handlers to protect.

That left the question of how to get to Sahara.

Our best cover so far had been as illegal immigrants from an anonymous Africa. I suggested we use the same cover to get to Sahara.

"How, exactly?" O asked.

"Think back to the assistant director at the African Studies Program, the white people at the festival, why Peter opened the door for Muddy, think of some of the whites you've met in Kenya—what do they have in common?" I said.

"It's easy to see why Peter opened the door," he said humorously.

"They all want to help Africans without knowing their names," I answered, smiling along. "We become those Africans to Sahara. We ask Peter to make a call saying that he just met some Africans who are running an illegal car-washing business—they come to people's houses. His guests could drive home in clean cars as a gift from Sahara, and they'll be helping Africans help themselves," I explained.

"It will make him look good," Muddy agreed.

"It's risky—there's a good chance Sahara knows we're here—but it's a risk we have to take," O agreed.

We went back to Peter and explained the plan. If he wanted Sahara out of his life, and if he wanted to live, we were his best chance.

We didn't recognize the four names Sahara had given Peter for the airport pick-up. Jason came back with nothing either. If they had no records, even discreet ones, what were they doing with Sahara?

I called Helen—no headway with the encrypted file—but she said she'd be happy to look over the names, and she was still working on finding out the addresses of Amos Apara and the rest of the crew.

Peter was now nervous about the possibility of something going wrong. I didn't envy him: no matter what happened, his life was going to change—for better or for worse. And the only way he could make it happen was by going through Sahara. He had some beer—Tuskers, of course—and I poured a glass for him. He gulped it down and picked up the phone. We didn't want to risk using the speakerphone, so he made the call with the volume turned all the way up so we could hear what Sahara was saying.

"Mr. Delaware, it's Peter."

"Isn't it a bit late to be calling?" Sahara asked him.

"My apologies, but I just got back from the African festival and I have something that will interest you ..." Peter said. Sahara didn't say anything.

"I met three Africans, they are here under very tough circumstances, but they are quite industrious ..."

"What are they selling, not curios, I hope?" Sahara asked with a laugh.

"They are really trying to make a go of it—they run a carwash business. Ninja Car Washers ..." Peter began, before he was interrupted by loud laughter from Sahara.

"What? Ninja cleaners? You can't make this stuff up! Oh, boy—I'm glad you called. Tell me more ..." Sahara said, trying to stifle his laughter and get his professorial voice back.

"Like I said, they are very industrious. You don't go to them—they come to you. I was thinking that for your guests driving in tomorrow, these Africans could wash their cars and make some extra cash. It's nothing, I know that, but it would be an interesting party favor—unique—charity. You know, like Kiva—real help for those helping themselves," Peter said with surprising conviction.

"Not a bad idea, Peter. Not a bad idea at all. There is this African proverb—God helps those who help themselves. Yes, give them my address. The dinner begins at six. Can they come around seven? That will give them enough time to clean the cars and dry them before the guests depart at eight thirty. Make sure they are on white-people time and not African time. And what are their rates?" Sahara asked.

"I don't know—something reasonable, I'm sure," Peter said.

"I like to help but I don't like to get ripped off," Sahara said, sounding like a concerned businessman.

"Where are they from? If it's Nigeria or Kenya, forget it," he added, now laughing again.

"You're in luck—they are from Ghana—they appear to be trustworthy," Peter said, laughing along nervously.

We had a whole day tomorrow before we were going to head over to Sahara's. We couldn't leave Peter alone. We would have to trust him to go to the airport alone, because it was too risky to go with him. But it was one thing to leave him alone for two hours and another to let him have a whole day to cook up other schemes. But we also couldn't take him to Michael's and expose our base. So we decided to stay put. We sat around drinking the remaining Tuskers. And then we tied up and gagged a protesting Peter when it was time to sleep.

Helen's call woke me up at 7:00. As I stepped into the kitchen, everyone stirred awake.

"The names of the guests, yeah, I found something and it doesn't make sense. These names are so fucking random. Ansfrid Godfrey, a former grants advisor for the Norwegian government, Bruce Jackson teaches African history and Kiswahili at Ohio University—he used to be Jimmy Carter's press secretary—and Dan Gordon is Bob Geldof's manager, you know Geldof?" Helen asked me.

"Yeah, the Live Aid guy," I answered.

"The fourth guy, Martin Kimani, he is an assistant manager at Kenya's Pineapple Growing and Canning Company—he worked for a year as Moi's special advisor before resigning," she said.

His resignation from the government of Daniel Arap Moi—the dictator who'd ruled Kenya from 1978 to 2002—alone made him seem like a nice guy. If it weren't for his association with Sahara, he was the kind of man you wouldn't give a second look to—the kind that made money quietly, dignity intact because he didn't grovel for contracts.

Now, I knew a bit about the Pineapple Canning Company because poor kids sometimes sneaked through the barbed wire to steal the fruit, and once in a while a Alsatian guard dog would maul one of them to death. It would make the news, but of course no prosecutions ever followed.

"How did you find out who they are?" I asked her, wondering what connected them.

"A girl has to have her secrets …" she said, laughing. "But I'll give you a hint. I peeked into a few international criminal databases—Interpol, you know—found nothing. Then I tracked their names by nationality and peeked into the intelligence databases and bingo. These guys are listed only because of who and what they work for. They are nobodies, the paper-pushers, you know what I mean?"

"Yeah, but they do have something in common—an interest in Africa, if we add Sahara," I said.

"But Africa is huge, think about it—it's like saying we have a common interest in Europe, China, and the United States combined. Remember what Sahara told you about Africa not being a country?" she said. "We need more names. We can establish a pattern that way."

"Tonight—I will get you more," I said. We would have access to car registrations.

"And I have the addresses you asked for," she said. She hung up and texted me the addresses. Now that we knew where Sahara was, I was interested only in where Amos had lived. We would get Sahara tonight, and then I would be able to tell Amos's parents not only what had happened to their son, but that justice had been served.

Peter left to start his airport pick-ups at 3:00 and we headed back to Michael's to brief Julio and the teacher. We had to trust Peter, or at least hope that between us instilling fear in him and his wanting to break free from Sahara, he wouldn't betray us. And we needed to start making travel arrangements to get back home, once again going through Mexico before flying out to Nairobi. Things would be happening fast now. This was good for O, for all of us—no downtime meant no time to remember.

Around 5:00 p.m., there was a knock on the door. It was Mo, and seeing her brought back memories of Madison and the realization of just how desperate I was to see my parents, my friends, even my ex-wife. We hugged and, leaning against me, she said hello to everyone else. Mo hadn't changed—beautiful, talkative— a mixed-race bohemian, as Muddy had once described her.

The first and last time they had met was in Rwanda, when we went to bury the white girl, at the end of the first case O and I worked on together. Without Mo, O and I wouldn't have survived the case—we would have been killed and the truth buried with us. Mo's exposé and the media coverage that followed saved our lives. We needed her once again. We briefed her about Amos, the bomb, Mary—and how and why we were in the

United States illegally. We would know more after tonight, we promised. The thing about Mo was that she had energy, and soon she had us feeling like we were bouncing off the walls.

"I see another Pulitzer on the horizon," Mo said when we were done. "Well, my friends, this is what we can do. Bring the story out in installments. We start with the bomb explosion, Sahara and his men, the death of O's wife, Al Qaeda and the Somalis as a cover. That is the first part—I can have that ready to go in a day but I assume you want to be back in Kenya before I run it. The second part—let's see what you come up with first, but most of it should be about the things you've uncovered. And the last installment will be about closing the case," she said, gesturing busily with her hands to show us how the coverage would play out.

Once her story ran, our being on the terror list would become a non-issue, but we needed to be out of the U.S. If it came down to it, the Kenyan government, or whatever was left of it by the time we got back, would be careful about giving up its citizens to the U.S. And if some bounty hunters decided we were worth capturing or killing for some people somewhere, we would be on even ground.

It was time to go. Julio was too valuable to come with us. If something happened to him … he was our ticket through Mexico. In any case, we couldn't explain a Mexican in an African crew, so we had to leave the teacher behind as well. We put on the blue Ninja Cleaners hats and overalls—they compensated for how they looked by being good for concealing weapons and vests.

"Better hot and safe than cool and dead, huh?" Mo said, after I complained about how hot I felt.

CHAPTER 14

THE MEETING

In the dry near-desert climate of California, Sahara lived in an oasis, or more precisely, an orchard. Off the main road and onto a rocky path, a mile or so from the highway, we suddenly came to a plantation of windmills. There were rows and rows of avocados, oranges, bananas, and pineapples growing in the imported black soil. We drove through the tangy smell of citrus until we came to a gate with two armed guards. In Kenya, they would have seemed ordinary enough, but in the U.S. armed guards at a residence called attention to either how dangerous or how important Sahara was.

They stopped us and looked into the van.

"Ninja Cleaners, huh! But you aren't Japanese," one of them observed dryly before making a call and waving us through.

As we went up the driveway, we saw Peter coming out of the house to meet us. The dinner meeting had been going on for an hour, and he had been hanging out in the kitchen waiting for us.

So far we had seen only the two armed guards at the gate. Peter had seen another two men in the house who looked like ex-military to him. Assuming he was correct, that made four. We had no ears in the house, no intelligence collected over months of tailing the suspect, no long-term informant attached to the man. We just knew that Sahara was in that house with ten guests and probably four armed men to protect him.

Understanding who he was and how much time he had

spent in Africa, we assumed that he would insist on meeting us before paying us. There would be no sense of completion for him if he just gave the money to Peter. It was one of those things that can't be explained unless you have lived in Africa for a long time. There is a personal touch in most interactions and a need for closure.

If you buy something from a store, it's normal to stay an extra minute and chitchat about this or that, or complain or laugh with the seller and the other customers. This was something that had rubbed off on me without my realizing it, until I came across fellow Americans who just seemed gruff and abrupt. Sahara would have lived long enough in Africa to be infected with this particular strain of African hospitality. That's when we would grab him.

There were five Porsches and Benzes to clean. Peter rolled a hose down the long driveway as we unloaded our new equipment: handheld vacuum cleaners, non-scratch pads, polish, buckets, and Armor All car wash. I moved from car to car, vacuuming, as O and Muddy wiped the insides. Then Muddy hosed the outsides, while O and I scrubbed, rinsed, and gave them a shine. I was also busy with something else: gathering the plates and registration papers. Under normal circumstances, cigarette butts and napkins for DNA and fingerprints off the GPS screens would have been gold, but without a lab, we had to work with a bare minimum.

The names—again, none of them were familiar to us. I texted them to Helen and she soon texted back a collection of the same kind of random details as she'd sent before. There were twelve men meeting with Sahara. Four of them we knew about already. The other five had also worked for powerful people: Thatcher's office manager, Reagan's personal assistant, Clinton's onetime legal advisor, Kofi Annan's special advisor, and an assistant managing director of the Mandela Foundation. Another three were associated with the IMF, the World Bank, and the U.S. Endowment for Democracy.

"So we have these guys, all connected to powerful people or formerly powerful people, meeting with Sahara. We know Sahara planted the bomb in the Norfolk. We know he scouted other locations in Kenya, but we didn't find anything. Yet he wanted to stop our investigation. So he wasn't done yet. There's gotta be more—Norfolk was just a beginning," O said as we quickly converged on one car.

We were talking and interacting normally, as people who made a living together would—trying to whisper and hand each other notes would simply look suspicious. If Sahara knew we were here, we would have to wait until he made his move. And if he didn't, there was no way in hell he would expect us to be out in his driveway washing cars.

"Yeah, but we also have Jason and Peter with two different agendas. Jason wants Sahara found, but Peter wants to continue the Al Qaeda campaign. Depending on who's in charge, we were brought in because we weren't expected to go far, or because we were expected to go all the way," I said, to add to the confusion.

"The key is the men meeting in Sahara's house. We find what connects them, we find out what is happening," Muddy said, sounding like a seasoned detective.

"Shit, guys, could fucking Mandela and Tutu and the rest of the do-gooders be planting bombs in Nairobi?" O voiced what we were all thinking. We had to laugh out loud.

"Or Jimmy Carter?" I said.

"It doesn't make any sense—Reagan, dead and a conservative, Thatcher, conservative, and Carter and Mandela are liberals—some might even say revolutionary. What could possibly bring them together?" Muddy asked.

"There are several possible scenarios here, right? It could be these guys are fronting for others—you know, using the offices of the do-gooders—a few using the rest. It could be a recruitment party. We don't know. But we can be sure no good is coming out of whatever this is," I said, even though it didn't quite make sense to me.

My phone buzzed. It was Helen on the other end and she was excited—she had something for us.

"Two things: am I a genius or a genius? Carter, Mandela, and Tutu all belong to the same organization—the Elders, you know it—moral influence to shape a world gone rogue. Oh yeah, and 'cigar in Monica Lewinsky's you know what' Smoking Bill Clinton is also associated with it. The four of your men who worked for Reagan, Thatcher, the IMF, and the World Bank—they are all board members of an organization called International Democracy and Economic Security Council, or IDESC," she said.

"What does IDESC do?" I asked her.

"They promote international democracy and economic security," she said with a laugh. "No dirt on them from anywhere." She hung up and texted me the address of the IDESC office. It was in Oakland.

I conveyed the info to O and Muddy.

"If our friends here weren't meeting with Sahara, they would just be another group of people trying to save the world," Muddy said.

O started laughing so hard that we joined him without knowing why.

"What was the South African's name? The guy working for the Mandela Foundation?" he asked, barely able to speak.

"Jack Mpande," I said as I looked at the text from Helen again. Even before he said it, I flashed back to the Norfolk and I was putting out my hand to greet Jack Mpande.

"Shit! They were trying to kill him—like they did with Amos. Jack Mpande—he was about to do something they didn't want. No one would have tied his death to anything. That's why the motherfucker isn't here. We get Sahara and then we go back and find Jack," I said, starting to feel the end of what I could not yet completely define.

"Think he might be back in S.A.?" O asked.

"You better make the call," Muddy said to him.

O called Hassan, explained the situation briefly, and asked him to hold Mpande. The chief didn't ask where we were, or if we had proof. He simply said he would find him if he was still in the country.

"For now, Sahara is our man," O said. We agreed.

The cars didn't need any more cleaning—this really was charity work—but we went over them again as if they did. Finally, when we'd killed enough time, Peter came and called us inside to eat. In the sprawling kitchen, the size of his apartment, we found elaborate dishes of *jollof* rice, peanut stew, some kind of fish, and Heinekens.

We didn't eat. Sahara was too dangerous and we had come in blind—we didn't want to risk getting caught off-guard. Then Peter left to drive some of the guests back to their hotel. Soon after the expensive engines roared off a tall white man with a crew cut called us to the sitting room to meet Sahara.

"He's very happy with the job you've done—he would love it if this became a regular thing," the man said to us in a booming voice.

"We try," Muddy said, as we wound up a long passageway. At last we came to a massive sitting room.

"Where is our employer?" Muddy asked, sounding as African as I had ever heard her.

"Oh, he's waiting to see you in the office," the man boomed back. "Mr. Delaware would like to know how much he owes you."

"Fifteen dollars per car," O answered.

I was trying not to speak—it would have been hard to hide my American accent behind a fake Kenyan accent.

"Mr. Delaware will like the price. You know, he will be happy to see some Kenyans making something of themselves. If I was you, I would double the price—this is America," the man advised as he reached for the double doors.

Without any warning, O kicked the man through the double doors so that they swung wide open and shot him in the back of the head. As I wondered what the fuck was going on, O rolled onto the floor into the office, got on one knee, and let out two shots in quick succession. Muddy took cover behind the wall, looked in once and then again, and let out a single shot. It had taken less than five seconds. I still hadn't gone for my weapon. By the time I made it in, four men were lying on the floor. Three of them were dead. The man Muddy shot was one of the guards who'd been at the gate, and he was bleeding from a bullet to the stomach.

"Where is Delaware? Tell me where he is and we will call you an ambulance," O said. Mary's death seemed to have made O more reasonable, more willing to let motherfuckers live. But I knew differently—he was so determined to get Sahara and avenge Mary's death that he was willing to make concessions that just a few weeks ago he wouldn't have made. And for me, who knew O, that made him all the more dangerous in the long term.

"He left, he is gone ... I don't know ... please, I don't want to die," the man said, staring at the blood pooling on the floor.

Using a letter opener from the desk, Muddy tore off a sleeve from one of the dead men and gave it to the guard.

"Press hard," she instructed him.

"Someone warned him—soon after the meeting—someone called him ... told him who you were," the guard said, now looking a little more convinced that we might let him live.

"Did he take anything with him?" I asked.

"A small suitcase and his laptop ... you gotta call now," he pleaded.

"How were you going to get in touch with him?"

He pointed to the man with the booming voice, dead on the floor.

"He was supposed to call," the guard said.

I went over to the dead man and retrieved his phone. I didn't have to go far through his contacts before getting to an entry with the name Big Chief. In the meantime, O and Muddy were rummaging through Sahara's desk, looking for anything that might be useful.

"Call him—tell him we are all dead—you were the only one who survived. The faster you get off the phone, the sooner we call 911," I told him.

"Mr. Delaware, they are all dead, all of them," he shouted desperately into the phone. "The car washers—my friends, all of them are dead ..."

"Calm down ... they are all dead?" we heard Sahara ask in disbelief.

"Yes, I don't want to die, help me," the man said. Sahara hung up without another word. The man dialed 911 and after he gave them the address, I took the phone back from him. We didn't need him giving the cops more information over the phone before we were in the clear.

O and Muddy didn't find anything. The wallets from the bodyguards contained no IDs. We didn't have a forensics team, or unlimited time to go through the crime scene. We were nineteenth-century detectives operating in the twenty-first. It was time to go the Oakland offices of IDESC.

We couldn't take the van. Now that things had heated up, Sahara most probably would have alerted his connections in Homeland Security, and they in turn would have alerted local cops. I took the car keys from one of Sahara's men. Soon enough we were driving off in a massive Hummer.

We needed to do three things, and fast: get to the IDESC offices, find out if Peter had betrayed us and get him to tell us where Sahara was, and then get the hell out of the U.S. To do that we needed to get back to Michael's, where, in the labyrinth of illegal immigrants, we would be safe. But first IDESC—there would be answers there. We were almost home, yet everything was still in the balance.

"How did you know?" I asked O.

"I didn't," O said from the backseat. "The thing was, Peter told Sahara we were from Ghana, and the food on the table was Ghanaian. But then the man said something about Kenyans. He was just making small talk, trying to make us comfortable. If he'd kept his mouth shut, they would have had us," he explained, as if talking us through a game of chess.

"You saved our lives back there. We were walking into a fucking firing squad," Muddy said, looking back at O.

"I'm sorry, guys, I was kinda slow—I didn't see it coming," I said, feeling the weight of having done nothing. It occurred to me that my edge was gone since I'd come back home. I had to pick it up a notch. If Muddy hadn't jumped in, O would have been shot by the third bodyguard.

At what point did Sahara know it was us? Did the men following us from the airport know who we were, or were they really after Julio? Or if we'd been betrayed, was it by Jason or Paul? The point was, we didn't know—we had no ears listening through any walls anywhere. We could only react—and hope we reacted fast enough to finally take the initiative from Sahara.

I had to think and act like the under-resourced criminal that I was in real terms. I knew this system better than O and Muddy. I had to be more resourceful.

As soon as we hit Broadway Avenue, we heard a loud explosion— and right away we saw smoke billowing above the city lights. We knew it had to be the IDESC office going up in smoke. Muddy looked at me. A black Jaguar was coming toward us. It looked familiar, even in the shimmery near-dark.

Nearing the Hummer, it slowed down and the driver started to roll down the window. It was him: he had recognized the Hummer—but a second later, he realized that it wasn't one of his bodyguards driving it.

"Sahara!" I shouted. There wasn't enough time for me to reach my Glock and roll down the window, so I spun the unwieldy Hummer into the Jaguar. The Jaguar nimbly veered away, so that I could only nip its back, and it roared off. I turned around and sped after it. O and Muddy rolled down their windows and fired at the retreating Jaguar, shattering the rear window. It was much faster than the Hummer—the distance between us increased as it tore through the streets, and the Hummer threatened to roll over with each sharp corner we took. Somewhere up ahead, the Jaguar turned into a side street and just like that, Sahara was gone.

And as soon as we slowed down, a black cop flagged us down. This much I knew—he was going to call the plates in before he approached us. Then he'd ask me for my driver's license: a good fake that could pass most of the time, but not when we were driving an expensive car registered to someone else. There was no easy way out.

I put the Hummer in reverse and stepped on it. Through my rearview mirror, I could see shock all over the cop's face as he fumbled and tried to get out of the way. The Hummer started to climb up the front of the cruiser and I stopped. O jumped out, Glock in hand, aimed at the cop. Muddy also jumped out, weapon drawn.

The cop raised his hands without us asking. I pulled his door open and secured his sidearm, then smashed in the surveillance camera and radio, and took his cell phone. I handcuffed him and led him to the Hummer. He was shaking with fear, but he was trying to be brave. I stuck him between O and Muddy, who keep their guns trained on him as we drove through the dark streets.

A few blocks away, I saw a closed car-wash station. We got him out of the car and half-dragged him into the car wash. I handcuffed him to one of the rails as he pleaded for his life.

"What are we going to do with him?" O asked. I didn't answer. I took out my Glock and signaled for he and Muddy to leave us alone.

"I have three children …" the cop started to say.

"Listen, brother, things are not what they seem," I said, pointing in the direction of Muddy and O. "I gotta make them believe."

"You don't have to do this, brother. Hey, man, I too get angry and want to bomb some shit—just walk, walk away, I won't tell anybody," he pleaded.

Now I knew. An APB was out on us. The cop had flagged us down because, at some point in the evening, Sahara had called in his last card.

"Brother, you have to trust me. I am undercover—I'm trying to bring down a terrorist cell," I said.

He yelled in fear as I raised my gun to his head. I fired two shots into the wall.

"They'll find you in the morning," I said to his confused silence. It was probably going to be sooner, but by then we'd be harder to find.

I ran back to the Hummer and found O and Muddy looking surprised.

"I didn't kill him—told him I was UC," I said, managing a laugh that was more of a grunt. "The confusion will buy us time."

The cop would believe me—and more important, he would appear convincing to those who were hunting us. He would believe that Muddy and O were the terrorists, and at worst, because he had encountered us and lived to write his report, that I had a conscience, or at best, that I was who I said I was: an undercover agent. Doubt that bought me that split second between "kill," "wound," or "handcuff" might come in handy.

Where was Sahara? He had taken a suitcase and laptop, and he was on his way somewhere—and I was sure that he was the one who'd firebombed the IDESC office. He didn't have an office anymore, and he couldn't go back home—not with one of his men in the hospital, probably telling the cops all he knew. It hit me then—he was going back to Kenya. He seemed like a man who had cut his losses. In the same way that, in the U.S., we could emerge from and disappear into the immigrant community, in Kenya he had camouflage in the tourist hotels and networks. In any case, we could no longer, without significant risk, stay in the U.S. It was time for us to go back too.

We came to a dance club that was open, drove past it, and parked the Hummer a few blocks away. We wiped it down. We couldn't fully cover our tracks, but we could put some time between the authorities and us. To get back into Mexico, we just needed to be an hour or so ahead of everyone else. We took a cab from the club to Peter's.

The main door to Peter's apartment complex was propped open. As we walked up the stairs, we heard loud Malian blues music. When we got to his door, we drew our weapons. It wasn't locked and we could hear voices talking above the music. I pushed the door open slowly, and smoke from weed billowed out into the passageway. Peter was having a fucking party. When he saw us, he ran over and pulled us into the kitchen in excitement.

"Am I free? Tell me I'm free ..." he said, looking from Muddy to O to me.

"He escaped. He knew—someone warned him," I told him.

Peter sank slowly to the floor.

"Shit, then he knows I set him up ... I am fucking dead," he said, life literally draining out of him.

Sahara hadn't killed Peter because Peter had sold us out—that was one possibility. The other was that once Sahara had figured out who we really were, then we became the principals. Only after killing us would he go after Peter, and then only if there was something he would gain from it. He was that pragmatic. His mission was more important than killing Peter.

Looking at Peter slunk to the floor, high and disappointed, I felt that there was no way he was the one who had betrayed us. If he was pretending, then, on the strength of such a convincing act alone, he deserved to live. That left Hassan, Jason, or someone working closely with Jason. Like Paul. It had to be Jason or Paul. That would have to wait until we got back to Kenya.

"Any idea where he might have gone?" I asked him.

"No, but one of the guests in the car talked about them going to Kenya," Peter answered.

"We need to talk to them, maybe to one of the guests staying at the Hilton," I told Peter.

"Two of them wanted to see some girls. Like I was a pimp," he said.

But in Sahara's eyes, Peter, whether deserving of death or not, was compromised. We couldn't use him to get to the guests. We had to find another way of getting into the Hilton and grabbing one of them. We could call in a bomb threat. Or we could set off the fire alarm. But both plans meant that the place would be swarming with cops and firemen. There was only one way— we had to get into the Hilton quietly and talk to one of them there. It was the riskiest but the least expected move.

CHAPTER 15

KILLING FOR O

Close to midnight, three Africans—two men and a woman, dressed in business attire—walked into the Hilton. They were laughing like they'd been out having a good time, and the woman had her high heels in her right hand and her left hand linked through the elbow of one of the men.

"Packages for Room 312?" O asked at the desk. The clerk typed something into his computer.

"Sorry, Mr. Kimani. No package has come in yet, but a Mr. Henderson left you a message a few minutes ago, saying it'll get here in the morning," he informed us.

That message was from Peter. It was to establish an identity for O, and at the same time tell us whether Martin Kimani was still in town. We had bet that, at this late hour, the clerk would just take the message rather than wake up the guest.

"And they say things are slow in Africa," Muddy said as we started to walk toward the elevators.

"Shit—excuse my language ... hey, guys, wait a minute. I can't seem to find my room key," O said, as he rummaged through his wallet. The clerk looked at O's wallet, and for a second, it looked like he was going to ask him for his ID.

"Nice try, but you're not sleeping in my room," Muddy said to O. "Maybe his?" She pointed at me and laughed along with the clerk.

"It happens, sir," the clerk said to O, as he gave him another key card.

It was that simple. Anyone watching us walking into Mr.

Kimani's room would have thought we were going in for a drink before splitting up. We were learning fast. A few weeks ago, we would have flashed a badge; now we had just pulled a con.

Kimani, dead asleep, didn't hear us enter. O gently shook him awake, as Muddy turned on the TV and I turned on the lights. Kimani looked around to make sure he was still in the Hilton—and before he could scream, O put a gun to his head.

There was a near-empty bottle of champagne on the night-stand; next to it, an empty glass and a bucket, in which an ice pick floated among thin pieces of ice. I poured some champagne into the glass and he gulped it down fast.

"You know who we are?" O asked.

"Yes, I know who you are," he replied, his eyes angrily darting from O to me and Muddy.

Kimani had one of those faces that you immediately identified with—dignified. He was what I thought an African looked like before I went to Kenya—the Africans in the movies—wise, tall, slightly balding, with a well-trimmed goatee and, of course, the eyeglasses that he had reached for and was now adjusting. We'd chosen him because he was black and African, and we could pass for him—we certainly didn't look Norwegian or English.

"But do you know who I really am?" he asked in return.

"Why don't you tell us," Muddy said to him carelessly.

He glared at her and I knew she was on to something. If there was one thing this guy wasn't used to, it was women talking to him as if they were equals.

"My name is Martin Kimani ..." he said and went on to list all his credentials.

O whistled.

"Walk out of here now and I promise you a safe return to Kenya," he said, now that we were sufficiently impressed.

"But how well do you know me?" O asked him, now smiling. If I were Kimani, I would have chosen my next words very carefully, but he didn't know that the tables had turned. Maybe in Kenya, before the bomb explosion and Mary's death, Kimani could "senior" and "superior" his way out of a meeting with O. Used to exerting power from the shadows, he thought that he could use raw power and money to buy us out. But not in a Hilton Hotel in California, where O didn't really exist, and not after Mary's death.

"I'm sorry about your wife. She need not die in vain. You can do some good. A scholarship in her name at Kangemi Primary School—all the way to university, a job guaranteed at the end," he said, sounding so genuine that I had no doubt he meant it. He was part of that old generation whose word meant everything. And so, when they were wrong, people like Mary died.

"Whatever you want I can offer ten times over. You walk out now—and in five years, you are the police commissioner. If you want to retire, how about a twenty-acre farm anywhere in the country? Perhaps you'd like a hotel in Mombasa?" he continued.

Muddy, as if understanding what was going to happen next, turned up the volume on the TV and Kimani lost a bit of his composure.

O stepped away from him.

"Take off your pajamas," he said, in a tone that sounded more like a suggestion than a command.

"I will most certainly not, I am old enough to be your father," Kimani said defiantly. "And not in front of a woman young enough to be my daughter," he added, pointing at Muddy, who merely shrugged.

This is what it boiled down to. Kimani had information we needed—and we had his life in our hands, and between the two was his dignity. And not just dignity but that inviolable bond that holds societies together—that even in great adversity is upheld. This wasn't just a Kenyan thing; in each society there are some things that are worse than death. For Kimani, it was for an elder of social standing to strip naked in front of a young woman.

O walked up to him and suddenly swung the butt end of his Glock so that it caught Kimani in the mouth and broke two of his front teeth, splitting his lips open. O picked up the ice pick.

"I'm going to ram this into your gums. You will scream in pain and then I will ram it into your throat to shut you up. Then we move on to the motherfucker in Room 318. Do you understand me?" O asked him, with that same smile still on his face. A smile that said he would rather Kimani gave us nothing, so he could do it.

Kimani took off his clothes and O marched him to the bathroom and pushed him onto the toilet seat. Shivering even though it was warm, he'd lost the dignity he had exuded a moment before. Now he was just a scared, naked old man.

"Now, tell us everything," O said, and Kimani, as if relieved to confess things he had kept bottled up, started talking through his two broken teeth, his split lips, and the blood that kept dripping onto the marble bathroom floor.

"Outcome! That is what we control," he began. If it weren't for the circumstances, it would have sounded like he was about to give a PowerPoint presentation.

"We look at a situation and we decide what the bottom line is. God wants people to reform, to be good. The Devil wants them to be evil. We don't care whether they are good or bad; we just draw the line at extreme good or extreme evil. Hitler and Gandhi, revolutionaries and terrorists, Mother Teresa and Pinochet—all of them are the same to us—where we find them, we execute them ... can I have some aspirin?" he asked as he winced in pain.

I went to his desk, found two Tylenol tablets, and gave them to him. He looked at me, defeated—I must have had the same type of look on my face a few seconds before Mary was shot.

"Who is *we*?" Muddy asked him. He looked at O, as if asking for permission to answer, and O nodded yes.

"I would like to get dressed ... I assure you of my full cooperation. Let's talk—like men," he said, trying to reclaim his dignity and eyeing Muddy.

Muddy went to the closet and came back with underwear, a suit, and a tie.

He took the clothes, dressed, and washed the blood off his face. He adjusted his tie and tugged at his shirt cuffs. The suit really did make the man: he was back to being the commanding elderly African.

"Please, gentlemen and lady—shall we talk in the sitting room over a drink or two?" he asked. I suppose that even we were taken by surprise by the transformation and wanted to see where he would take this, so we said yes and followed him out of the bathroom. He went the mini-bar and came out with three small Johnnie Walker bottles.

"You know how you can tell a man who has never poured a drink? He pours the whiskey before the ice," he said.

"What is IDESC?" I asked him, and he looked at me as if trying to judge how much I knew.

"Look at the most powerful men in the world. Think about them. The photos you know of them, the stories about them— there is always a shadow, the figure of an unnamed man in the background. What if the shadow was the actual man and the man the shadow? Did you ever think of that? That is the illusion of power. What we—the managers, the assistant directors, the press secretaries—discovered was that we wielded the real power. Directors come and go—who remains? The assistant director. The manager comes and goes; the assistant manager stays ..."

"What the fuck are you talking about? You're telling us that a bunch of middle managers are blowing up hotels?" I interrupted him.

"You are not listening to me. Do you know the term 'institutional memory'?" he asked.

We shifted about uncomfortably like we hadn't done our homework. I had heard the term—the Madison Police Department had a racist institutional memory even though it had a black chief—but I had never really thought about it.

"You have the visionary, the charismatic boss who comes and makes changes. But the institution doesn't change with the leader; the institution is run by the middle management, down to the secretaries and the guys collecting the garbage. There are the rules and regulations, and then there is the way things have always been done. We are functionaries who have realized their power. The boss decides the color of the car, we decide the make and how much to spend. IDESC is the most powerful organization in the world, because we control the men and women who control the world," he went on.

"Your powerful people, do they know what's going on?" Muddy asked.

"No. Isn't that the whole point? We need their honesty. In Kenya, after creating a vacuum, our fronts are going to be called in to help guide and stabilize the government.

"Look here, my friends, we have disaster prevention programs for just about everything—epidemics, floods and hurricanes, wildfires—but not for political disasters. People die from hunger because of bad politics, malaria has not been eradicated because of bad governance, and then there is war. This is where we come in. We manage political disasters before they happen," he said, banging his hand on the table excitedly.

He paused. "May I refresh your glasses?" he asked, standing up and walking to the mini-bar. We declined and he fixed himself several double shots.

"Kenya is our coming-out party. We are going to take Kenya, bring it to its knees, and then rebuild it," he said.

"Why not start with Somalia?" I asked.

"Are you listening to anything I'm saying? You have to have institutions; cut off the head, replace the organs, transfuse blood, and something new and beautiful grows. Somalia is a Frankenstein of a state," he continued, explaining patiently.

"IDESC—Kimani, let's get back to that," O said, and looked at his watch.

"Let IDESC take Kenya and see what we do with it. If you don't like the results in five years, come for me, come for all of us," he said, sounding like he expected us to join him in the end, like we were bound to see things his way in time.

"Why the meeting? What did you discuss?"

"Delaware called the meeting—to give us an update and to suggest we take countermeasures in case we had been exposed."

"What countermeasures?" O asked.

"Disband—and walk away—and start afresh. We are the organization," he answered. "Our plan was working. If you hadn't interfered, we would be in control by now."

"Delaware—what else does he have planned? More bombs?" O asked.

He sipped his drink and winced in pain, but he didn't respond.

"You're running out of time. Tell us what you planned at the meeting and we will let you live," O said, sounding a bit tired.

Kimani looked at his watch and smiled painfully. Somewhere in the back of my head I heard Sahara's plane lifting off. We had been filibustered.

O hadn't broken him—he had scared him into taking us seriously, but the sudden show of violence and the humiliation hadn't really made a difference. The information he was giving us was already old news. Helpful, in that we now knew things we didn't know before, but it was all yesterday's news. This is why we had found nothing in Sahara's office, and why he had blown up the IDESC offices, and why, in this room, a man who had come to a business meeting had no useful papers, no laptop, not even a briefcase.

Once we entered the room, Kimani's strategy had been to try and win us over, because at that moment there were only two possible outcomes—we converted or we killed him—what middle ground could there be? And when that failed, to keep us in the room as long as he could, to buy time for Sahara.

I wanted to get at least one concrete detail that we could use. By this time tomorrow there would be nothing linking IDESC to the Norfolk bombing, and it would reconstitute itself into something else—change location, move personnel around. We weren't going to get them all, but we sure as hell could take out Sahara. With their military arm cut off, it would take longer to regroup.

O also knew the interview was over—in the same way that Kimani knew he had taken it as far as it could go. O turned up the volume and he started walking toward Kimani, but then I motioned for him and Muddy to leave.

Kimani's eyes opened wide in disbelief, trying to beg for his life, as he saw me walking back toward him, holding a pillow. I placed it on the back of his head and pressed it down with my Glock. In spite of himself, he was shaking.

"One last chance … you think you don't have a choice. Tell us what we need to know, and I will walk out," I said to him.

"How do I know you won't kill me after I am of no use to you?"

"Because I give you my word between two men—you understand that language," I said. He didn't respond.

"You knew Jack Mpande was at the hotel, yes?"

"Yes—we knew," he answered.

"Why did you want to kill him?" I asked.

"You know why," he countered.

"Are there more bombs?"

"I am a believer, Mr. Ishmael. I am a believer in what we do. How can I betray my faith?"

"Kimani, you might not think so, but you're done. It was over the moment the bomb went off, when your organization killed O's wife, when you cornered us … but tonight we can all walk out of here, for now …" I reasoned with him. I guess that in the same way he had wanted us to take his offer, I now wanted him to take mine.

He sighed.

"I'm very sorry this is the choice you've made," I said.

"Son, I too am sorry that this is the choice you have made," he said to me. He started whispering a quick prayer.

Suddenly, the phone rang. He stopped his prayers and looked at it.

I shot him.

CHAPTER 16

AMOS'S FATHER

There was one last thing we had to do before leaving the U.S. Amos—we had to go see his parents, explain what had happened, give them closure, and, with a little bit of luck, learn exactly what it was that got him killed. We had to do it—it was the reason we were in the States.

Our cover had been blown and we were risking being thrown into Guantánamo or some other hellhole, or simply being tried for murder in the U.S.—it was stupid not to just leave, but that ever-blurry line between us and the criminals had to be maintained. That's how I explained it to myself, yet I also knew I wanted to claim back a bit of my conscience from this thing I had become.

Amos's father lived in an apartment complex in Compton, and I drove us there in a nondescript white Hyundai that Julio had managed to "rent" for us.

Kimani was still on my conscience—O, Muddy, and I had yet to talk about it—not even after we got back to Michael's for a sleepless night. And now that Mo was with us, on our mission to see Amos's father, it gave us more time to bury what had happened with silence.

For all the barbed wire wrapped around sharp metal stakes on the concrete walls, there was no gate and so we just walked in. We didn't attract any curiosity; our look of desperation ensured that we fit right into this hard world of poverty, drugs, violence, and most of all hopelessness. That was the difference between the projects and Julio's slum—hopelessness. In Julio's slum, there was still fight left in the residents.

There was a black cop, alert and ready to prove himself, doing his beat. He glared at us and smacked his lips, daring us to make one wrong move. It wasn't because he recognized us from anywhere; it's just what you're supposed to do when you make eye contact in the projects—you convey violence. I looked back at him casually, because to look away would suggest that we were doing something wrong. With his nightstick, he pointed to the door. He had to have the last word and that was okay by us.

We walked up steps that smelled of stale urine. Eventually we got to the apartment and I knocked. An old man, dressed in faded, blue-striped pajamas in spite of the time of day, opened the door without even looking through the dusty peephole. He was holding a bottle of Hennessey in one hand and a joint in the other. He waved us in.

"Sir, ain't you gonna ask who we are?" I asked him, trying to sound like I still belonged.

He looked at us and laughed.

"You planning on telling—ain't yah?"

He didn't wait for an answer, just shrugged his shoulders, and so we walked in. He cleared an old black leather couch for us and asked us to sit down.

I introduced myself, then O and Muddy, giving him our real names and professions. I explained that Mo was a reporter from the *Madison Times* and she was writing a story about the case we were working on.

"That's a name you got on you there, son. But you ain't from Africa ..." he said to me after I was done.

"I'm from Madison, Wisconsin," I said.

"What is a country boy doing living all the way up in Africa?"
I explained as best and as fast as I could.

"Now, what I can do for you?" he asked. He passed the bottle
and the weed over to me. I took a small sip and passed both to O.
For a moment, I was young again and back in Madison with my
boys, being all tough in an empty Wal-Mart parking lot, drinking and smoking cigarettes.

"Sir, I'm afraid I might have some bad news," I said.

"Of course you do, son, of course you do. Why else would
you 'sir' me? Out with it … time is no longer on my side," he said,
tapping at his wrist.

"You have a son by the name of Amos Apara?" I asked.

"Yes, that's my boy," he said, standing up and walking to the
mantel. He took down a photograph and gave it to me. It was
a photo of Amos at KICC, posing with the magnificent Jomo
Kenyatta statue.

"He got bit by the Africa bug, just like you—you dig? And
Africa has taken his life. I know coz, you see, son, my wife, she
saw it before she passed on a year ago. She tells me … don't wait
for our boy, he ain't coming back." He motioned to us to walk
with him.

We followed him to Amos's room—the only room that
didn't have the stale smell of whiskey and weed in it. It was
clean and recently painted. There were even fresh flowers beside
a well-made bunk bed.

We looked at him in confusion. If he knew his son was dead,
what was all this?

"No graveyard for my boy, this is where I come," he answered
our unasked question. "At least with my wife and our girl, I have
some place I can go talk to 'em." He excused himself and left
the room.

Hanging on the wall, there were photos, arranged chronologically, of Amos in various countries. The last ones were all from Kenya and they had something in common. Counting the one downstairs where he was standing in front of the Kenyatta statue, they were all taken at the sites IDESC had been scouting. Was he trying to tell his parents, and now us, something? Or was it because his tourist sensibilities kicked in every so often? We had, after all, scoured the sites from top to bottom and found nothing. But it seemed like something bad was going to happen in all these places. We just had to find out what, and how far along Sahara was with his plans.

Mo called to us. She was taking a photograph of a short handwritten letter from Amos to his parents, dated four years ago. Muddy started reading it aloud.

"Popsicle and Momsicle," the letter started, and in spite of the solemnity of the "graveyard room," we had to laugh.

> *If you had a chance to kill Hitler before he became Hitler, wouldn't you? Not exactly my work, but we have a chance to do a lot of good by preventing a lot of bad. I can't say more but just know I am out here doing the "Lord's work" as Popsicle would say.*
>
> > *Your Sonsicle,*
> > *Amos*

It made sense in the context of what Kimani had told us … they wanted to prevent political disasters before they happened. We still didn't have a clear picture … until we spoke with Mpande and Sahara we wouldn't know exactly what was going on. But that they were on some kind of preemptive agenda gone bad was clear.

Next to the letter, there was a cryptic postcard, posted a few days before the bombing: *"Resigning. Coming home soon. Almost done!"*

He had drawn an arrow pointing to the face of the postcard. On the front of the card there was an ostrich burying its head in the sand. Amos had died fighting Sahara and his men, after he stopped pretending that he didn't know what was going on.

Amos's father walked back into the room, dressed in a heavily decorated Vietnam War–era soldier's uniform. He holstered a pistol before standing at attention, then falling back at ease.

"Now, in this room, tell me what happened to my only son," he said. He could sense from the moment we walked in that we were here to confirm what he already knew. He had been in mourning for so long that he could afford to delay the moment of truly knowing until he was ready. I explained all we knew, with Muddy and O filling in bits here and there. All the while, he was listening, sometimes asking a question, other times just nodding.

"I want to shed blood for my son, not my tears. I want the men you say did this," he said, his voice heavy, trembling in anger and determination.

"You cannot come back with us," Muddy said gently. "But I promise you we will get the men who killed him. But first bury your son ... properly."

"No, let him rest in Kenya—his ancestors are from Africa. He is home. I want blood—you have names. Give them to me," he half-pleaded and half-commanded.

I started to say no, but he walked over to O.

"Your wife, my son ..." he said fiercely.

O asked me for my phone and copied the names and addresses of the five IDESC men residing in California onto a piece of paper.

"I've been holding my peace too long—what good is it? Peace fed my family to the dogs—picked off one by one by thugs, police, and by life itself—don't make the same mistake," he said as Muddy looked at me.

"We're leaving for Kenya. You are on your own, old man," I said, not sure why I was angry with him.

"Ain't that the truth, son … ain't that the truth," he said, reminding me of Mary's mother.

"It's suicide—you get one or two—then what? Let us do our jobs?" I said, half-heartedly trying to talk him out of it.

What did it matter anyway? We were never going to get them all. The most Mo's story would do was embarrass them into resigning—they would regroup. Their brand of evil—patient, cold, methodical, and impersonal—would survive anything human. They would be at it until we won or they were all killed off, every last one of them.

"My boy, he thought history was more important than family—and he wanted to change the world—things he saw down in South Africa, things I seen in Georgia …" he began, as if giving the eulogy that he had been practicing for years. Like mourners in a funeral, we had to let him finish, no matter how long it took.

I wanted to pull the old man to the side and talk to him—I wanted to tell him just how exhausted I was, how for days I hadn't slept more than a few hours. And then he would ask why, and I would say that the life I had been living and the one that I wanted to live were pulling me apart. I would point at Muddy and say "because I love her" and say "there is O, my best friend and best man." I would tell him that was real but so was all the wrong behind us. And what did I want him to say? If he were a wasted old man at Broadway's, what would he say? That you cannot live two lives? I silently promised myself that if Muddy and I survived Sahara and his madness, I would take her to meet my parents. It had been years since I had felt that I was a son with responsibilities to those who called me "son." If a father's duty didn't end, even after the death of his son, how could mine to my parents, who were still living?

I still had the Glock and the extra clips from the cop back in Berkeley. I placed the one I had used to kill Martin Kimani on the table.

"Look, old man, that is the gun I used to kill one of the men responsible for your son's death. If you ain't planning on coming back, take it," I said.

He took it.

"A one-way ticket to hell," he said absentmindedly, as he removed his World War–something pistol from his holster and replaced it with the Glock, which fit awkwardly.

Muddy pulled me away and took his hand, then hugged him. "Kill as many of them as you can," she said. I imagined that he had held on to life just long enough for us to walk through that door and make his revenge mission possible, to kill one enemy for all the other wrongs that had been done to him and those he loved.

"This shit is getting way too crazy—I can't be a part of it," Mo said, looking angrily at me. She was right, I should have kept her at a protective distance, but I had been in Kenya too long.

"We're a long way from Wisconsin. You can walk away, go to the police, or you can stay with the old man and hear his whole story," I said to her.

"Think of yourself as embedded—a covert front line," Muddy said humorously.

The old man took Mo's hand and led her toward the kitchen.

"I got a lot speaking to do. I got another bottle of something sweet stashed somewhere," he said.

"Shit, old man, I might as well drink my damn career down the drain," Mo said as she followed him.

If Christ had rejected the idea of a messiah, the trappings and cultishness, and yet believed he was the messiah—that would be Sahara. He worked well with others; he hated anything that got in the way of the mission. He was efficient, ruthless, but always for a reason. Imagine Jesus with all that power, now imagine if all he had was the clarity of his mission—that was Sahara. It didn't stop others from believing in him—and doubting him: that was the paradox. The more he shunned the messiah complex, the more people believed in him. But Amos had doubted, and he had died.

O and I shook Amos's father's hand, and the three of us left, knowing one thing: it was going to get messier.

We left two thousand dollars on Michael's kitchen table with a note—*For your Tuskers*. We walked to a supermarket and hailed a cab. It was a Mexican driver, and Julio negotiated the price for what was going to be a long ride. They came to an agreement, we napped as the cab traveled down the length of California, and after the driver dropped us off a few miles from the border house, one of Julio's men picked us up. Not long after that, we crawled through the tunnel back into Mexico and made our way straight to the airport. There were no surprises. I guessed we had drained Sahara enough so that soon it would be just him and us.

CHAPTER 17

JESUS ON STEROIDS

With our adrenaline always pumping, we had been running on very little sleep. We were a mess, and so the two connecting flights were a blessing. When the Kenyan Airways flight attendant finally announced that we were about to land, we woke up still tired, but rested and determined.

When we arrived at the immigration kiosk and the official, dressed in a faded blue cardigan, took us to his superior's office after glancing at our passports, we weren't worried. It meant that Hassan had come through for us. In the office, the man gave us a large duffel bag. O smiled as he pulled his trusty .45 from the bag. I retrieved my Glock and Muddy an AK-47 and an overcoat under which she was to hide it. Then we put on bulletproof vests and took some extra ammo. There were also cell phones and SIM cards in the bag, and I called Helen as the supervisor walked us through customs to where O's Land Rover was parked—gassed, serviced, and ready to go. Helen had good news: she was about to break through the encryption.

We entered the country, which was still trying to claw its way out of hell, as quietly as we had left it. On the whole, things had calmed down, except for some riots, which seemed liked a wedding celebration compared to the violence from just a few days ago. Reconciliation was looking possible, and the government and the opposition party had started talks about sharing power.

What this meant was that, with enough care, we could move around and work on our case, which now hinged on finding Mpande and Sahara. It meant that, without the threat of a mob descending on us by surprise, we now stood a fighting chance against anybody trying to collect brownie points by killing us for our supposed terrorist affiliations. We had the terrain—the odds were almost even—and with O and Muddy by my side, I'd say the odds had even tipped in my general direction.

We couldn't go to O's or to Muddy's. We were too recognizable to slip quietly back into our old lives. Broadway's was out as a safe haven—that was a place you went to when all bad and good things were equal, not when you were a cop in trouble. The delicate balance could not accommodate weakness. Our best bet was to find a discreet bar and some lodging in Kiambu. The Red Nova, the bar Joe Sherry ran, was close enough to Limuru, in case we needed to get to Muddy's, and to Nairobi. Even though Joe Sherry had dated Mary long ago, they had maintained the kind of friendship that was strong enough not to need constant upkeep through birthday cards and the like—the kind where even though you might not see each other for years, the trust remains. Rare enough friendships—like Mo's and mine. Joe Sherry and Mary had had that kind of friendship, and now we needed his help.

In the United States, we had operated without the usual resources of a government behind us. In Kenya, we had had the run of the place until just a few weeks ago. Now we didn't know who to trust, who the next police commissioner would be once the deals for the new government were reached, or if we would have a government, let alone one that might back us up when the accusations came and calls for extradition were tied to foreign aid. But we knew our way around the "black roads," as O had jokingly called the underground Kenyan criminal life.

Joe Sherry didn't ask any questions. He gave us rooms and we went to bed.

Helen and her timing—I hadn't slept for more than an hour when my cell rang. She had broken through the encryption. She texted me a Web address and a password so I could access the file. Muddy and I woke O up, and we went to Joe Sherry's office. After trying to connect a couple of times, we finally opened the file, which turned out to be an IDESC Project Assessment File put together by the New York–based African Open Society.

It was a study of the military coups that had assassinated political leaders of all stripes, and the counter-coups that had in turn killed off the military leaders. It looked at revolutions in Africa, Asia, and Latin America where sitting leadership had been tried, jailed, or simply killed off. It factored in the inter-ference of U.S. and Russian governments in these coups and revolutions and the conclusion was always the same—the body cannot survive without its head, no matter how rotten. But even with successful operations, hundreds if not thousands of people would die before a new non-corrupt leadership could be formed and installed.

The bottom line was that the study gave the IDESC Af-rica project a 25 percent chance of success. In the end, the good people at the African Open Society were asking whether that 25 percent chance was worth the risk of destroying a country and the loss of thousands of lives.

Sahara and IDESC had answered yes; the future was worth

a little blood-letting in the present. We looked over and over the document, trying to understand it—figures and percentages about human life. People playing the gods of change, life measured against life.

Yet if I had been reading this document in the comfort of a classroom or bureaucratic office, I would have argued against it, but only to look for ways to improve the plan. It made sense, but only on paper. I had seen the idea in practice in the Norfolk bombing and the tea plantations of Limuru.

Sahara and IDESC had to be stopped, if only so that we could continue living on in our undemocratic and corrupt societies, hanging out with thieves at Broadway's by night and tracking them down by day. If only so that we could elect a black president every now and then, buying time until someone came up with a better plan. I printed out the ten-page document to show to Mpande.

Hassan, as we had requested, had picked up Mpande but couldn't officially take him into police custody. He also couldn't hand him over to the Americans, because we didn't know how deep his connections ran, or worse, now that Hassan was out of favor, how deep his enemies could reach. Therefore, after providing Mpande with a cover story so that his wife wouldn't worry—the Kenyan government had asked him to help set up a truth-and-reconciliation program, South Africa–style—Hassan had stashed him in a safe house out in Runda Estate.

"Like the aristocrats in fucking England—holding other nobles as prisoners of war in castles, with servants and everything," Muddy exclaimed as we wound through an island of wealth and calm—the violence hadn't touched Runda.

Dandora slum, en route to Runda, was still smoking from the fires of a few days ago. The debris and trash along the road to Runda was much worse than it had ever been before, and hundreds of people now stood there despondently, looking at the passing cars. Runda was clean—clean security company cars parked by the gates manned by armed guards in clean blue uniforms. In Dandora there was no vegetation—Runda was like being in another climate, where manicured green hedges sprouted from the ground.

"This is the no-in-between country," O said philosophically, making me suspect he had sneaked in a puff or two.

The cop at the gate let us in after we showed him our badges. We were led to the back of the house by a maid dressed in a blue-checkered uniform, where we found Mpande in a white T-shirt and shorts, drinking orange juice and reading the paper. There was an extra tennis racket on the table and it made me wonder with whom he was playing. He didn't look surprised to see us—he offered us chairs like he'd been expecting us all along, and called to the house. Before we had even sat down, an old man dressed in a chef's uniform shuffled over to us.

"Breakfast?" he asked.

We were okay—Joe Sherry had allowed O into the restaurant kitchen and he had stuffed us full with his yet-to-be-perfected omelette, but we asked for coffee. We sat around for a bit talking about the weather, the violence, how Kenya compared to South Africa, how his family was, and how he was coping with being Kenya's most famous Norfolk survivor. We had the kind of bond that comes from having gone through an extreme situation together—like two soldiers from the same violent campaign who, years later, find themselves on opposing sides.

"Listen, guys. Even without Hassan's kind intervention, I

would have contacted you," he finally said, after the general conversation had petered out. He started to explain.

Two years ago, Amos Apara had come to him with some disturbing news. IDESC was planning to set off bombs in Kenya. The purpose: to destabilize the government by targeting leaders from all the political parties. In the absence of the leadership class, IDESC would take over stewardship of the country and cultivate a new leadership recruited from the youth who respected democracy—a second independence, Mpande explained.

"Like things in Afghanistan and Iraq have worked so well," Muddy said.

"That's not our work—it was a stupid and foolhardy move. In Iraq, Afghanistan, the policy is: invade, destroy the sitting government, then try to build an opposition, or a new government from the opposition and the leftovers. It is like trying to cure cancer with cancer. No, our goal was to eradicate all of them, the sitting government, the opposition—leave the country without leadership, scoop out the cancer, and then let a new leadership emerge from the people themselves ... with a gentle guiding hand from IDESC."

"Obviously things aren't working out ..." I started to say but he interrupted me.

"Ours was not to create the circumstances; it was to take advantage of them. At the right time, take out the opposition and the ruling party and then offer interim stewardship that comes with economic assistance, security, and nurturing of leadership by forward-looking youth ... As you can see, we weren't wrong about Kenya. All the signs were there—I don't need to tell you that ..." he said as he pointed in the direction of Dandora.

"Look, Bush was right about one thing, the principle of preemptive strikes—take them out hard and take them out early—but he didn't have the intelligence or vision. He didn't have the heart for it—the conscience, the love for balance and democracy. We would have taken him out if we could," Mpande said with conviction. It was hard to tell whether he was out of IDESC or still in it—a man waiting for an opening, waiting for us to eliminate his enemies in an organization whose goals he still believed in.

"What is Delaware's next move?" I asked him.

"I don't know where, or how—but Delaware is a believer. He will carry on. You can be sure he is after the political leadership now."

Martin Kimani too had said that Sahara was a believer, and he hadn't lied about the political wing not knowing what the armed wing was doing.

"What happened after Amos came to you?" O asked him.

"I agreed that we needed to rein in the armed wing and the radical elements. They were supposed to follow our lead and not us theirs. We wanted to call the whole thing off, but you don't just call off something put in motion by the most powerful organization in the world," he said, trying not to sound proud.

"I didn't think Delaware suspected that Amos had come to me. It had been business as usual, when out of the blue Delaware called an emergency meeting in Nairobi. He said the political and armed wings needed to synchronize, because things were deteriorating fast in Nairobi and we needed to make a move. I thought the rest of IDESC was booked at the hotel. If I suspected anything, I wouldn't have brought my family with me."

"Do you know what 'capture the king and kill the queen' means? Some sort of code?" I asked Mpande.

"No, why?" he asked.

"Something Sahara ... Delaware said," I answered.

"Listen, O, I'm very sorry about your wife—and Amos, I was too late," Mpande said. O didn't respond. I produced the document and let Mpande peruse it. When he was done, he handed it back to me.

"That, we never saw—we didn't know it existed. But I doubt it would have changed my mind—I am as guilty now as I was then. Last year there were over half a million deaths from malaria. Half a million! Do the math," he said with a sigh. He leaned back in his chair and looked up to the sky as if searching for some sign. His disagreement was not with the principle, but how to implement it.

"Can I ask you something?" Muddy said, and he looked at her in surprise.

"Yes, of course," he said.

"Why did you stay?"

"I wanted to bring them down quietly—from the inside," he explained, sounding like he was trying to convince himself as well. Judging from the postcards we found in his room, Amos had been ready to bring down the organization from the outside and it had earned him a spot in Ngong Forest. And Mpande had barely escaped with his life. If they hadn't made the mistake of coming after us, their plan would have been almost foolproof.

"The road to hell is paved with idiots like you," Muddy said angrily. Mpande looked at her, then away, but he didn't say anything.

Needed to make a move, move fast, business as usual—ordinary language to explain the planning of terror and death, I thought to myself. I had a fuller picture now—imagine all you want to do in this world is some good. You go from trouble spot to trouble spot and do your best to make a difference. You start in the Peace Corps in some village somewhere, drilling wells and building makeshift schools. When you leave, in spite of your efforts, the well dries up and the school decides to stop admitting girls because a local fat cat angling for political office has decided it is against African culture. You get another job where you have more power and you continue up the do-gooder ladder until you land in some of the most powerful offices in the world—of former U.S. presidents, world monetary organizations, the United Nations—and still nothing is changing.

You start dreaming of taking over one of these countries one day and showing the world how it can be done right. You realize that, with others like you, other people in the powerful offices who are in it not for money or glory, just to do some good, that you can in fact change the world, not one person at a time, but country by country.

Because you can, you decide to do it. If the cancer could be gutted out and replaced with Kenyans who really cared for their country, would that be so bad? It would be a revolution.

In my line of work you come across many things—murders committed for money, sex, drugs, and just as often for power—but to take out not just a single politician, not just the president but also the opposing candidate, to wipe out the leadership of all the political parties regardless of where they stood was something new.

The deadly and efficient Sahara was stalking Kenya's corrupt leadership to create a vacuum. With the ethnic tensions still high, his move wouldn't leave a Kenya open for reconstruction. It would only lead to a Somalia-like implosion. We had to find him.

It was close to midday when we left a deflated Mpande. As we drove back to Nairobi, debating about where to look for Sahara, the news filtered in: a crazy old Vietnam vet, in what appeared to be a random shooting spree, had stormed two separate offices in Oakland, California, killing two mid-level managers. At a third office, armed guards had shot him down as he drew his weapon. He was also being blamed for the shooting of a Kenyan national at the Hilton—one Martin Kimani. It wasn't difficult for us to surmise what had happened. The remaining members of IDESC knew the shootings weren't random, and they took him out at the first opportunity. But the pundits had already diagnosed him as suffering from latent post-traumatic stress disorder.

"We should have taken care of Mpande—we really should have," Muddy said, bringing me back to the journey into Nairobi.

"But we saved him," I said, not sure how that made sense. But it did.

"These motherfuckers are like Jesus on steroids," O said.

As we drove back into town, we kept trying to figure out what to do next. We hadn't contacted Jason or Paul yet—one of them had sold us out back in Mexico and the U.S. But we were desperate, so in the end we decided that I should call Jason. In any case, Julio would have told him we had returned and he didn't pretend otherwise.

"Have you found him?" he asked, on hearing my voice.

"No, that's why I am calling," I said.

"I've got nothing here. My hands have been tied—pressure, trying to find the next targets in Somalia," he said, sounding frustrated.

We heard a news alert come on over the radio: the president and the prime minister, their ministers, and their key supporters had agreed to meet today at the Kenyatta International Conference Center to discuss forming a unity government.

"That's Sahara's target," Muddy called it as I hung up on Jason.

The whole leadership, opposition and incumbents, were meeting there to build what the Kenyan media now dubbed a "road map to peace." There would be no other opportunity like this to scoop out the cancerous cells and graft in what remained of IDESC. Sahara was going to go for it. And I wasn't so sure I wanted to stop him. I remembered the letter from Amos to his parents—this was not abstract preemption. This meeting—it was a meeting of the worst of Kenya.

"Jomo Kenyatta is the bomb," O announced. Muddy and I looked at him.

"You mean he is phat? The coolest cat?" Muddy asked, breaking into laughter, as I thought how irritating O and his Americanisms could be at times.

"No, I mean his statue at the KICC—it's the bomb," he said animatedly.

It was so simple, the kind of simple that you have to go through hell to get to: the bomb was concealed in the massive statue of Jomo Kenyatta in the convention center.

We had an hour before the meeting started. We thought over all the hotels that would give Sahara the cover of whiteness and at the same give him access to the KICC. There were several hotels around the KICC like that—we needed to narrow them down to one.

The Visitor Hotel made the most sense to all of us. A few hundred meters from KICC, it was close enough to see who was going in and coming out. He could detonate the bomb and watch the collapse, and it was a tourist hotel so his presence wouldn't raise eyebrows. I called Hassan to see if he had anyone close to the hotel, but all the cops and detectives were dealing with the remaining pockets of violence.

We stepped out of the Land Rover, checked our weapons, and put on our vests. I called Jason and explained what was up. He said that he and some of his people would be at the KICC in a few minutes. With the danger so immediate, he could now divert resources from the Al Qaeda manhunt.

Nairobi traffic! Unlike in the U.S., where cops have the run of the road and where, on the highways, the shoulders are reserved for them, in Kenya there are no shoulders to speak of. Everyone drove where they could, so that even the bare muddy paths that pedestrians used were full of cars. We weaved in and out of traffic slowly, knocking a car out of the way here and there, pleading for a truck to let us through, until we got to within a mile or so the Visitor Hotel and could make a run for it. There were five minutes on the clock before the conference was supposed to start by the time we got to the hotel.

We rushed into the lobby with our weapons drawn. The two or three tourists who hadn't listened to the travel advisories from their respective countries scampered out of the lounge. O quickly described Sahara: ordinarily, finding him would have taken a long time, but with only a few guests, further narrowed down by ones who might have insisted on having a room that looked in the direction of the KICC, he was easy to find.

He was on the twentieth floor. There was no way we were going to make it. I called Jason to see if he had gotten to the KICC, but he was stuck in traffic, together with his team.

Any minute now, the bomb would go off. We made it to his door one minute past zero hour and I started to wonder if we'd had it all wrong.

Muddy sprayed the door with her AK-47, and O and I burst through. Jim Delaware, the man we knew as Sahara, reached for his gun as he spun around from the window. O fired two disciplined shots into his chest and the cell phone he had been clutching fell to the floor. Sahara sank to the ground—dead, I thought, until he coughed and tore into his shirt to reveal a bulletproof vest. O had aimed for the heart, the grouping not more than an inch apart.

"Your name!" O demanded.

"You know who I am," Sahara answered.

"Where are the rest of the bombs?" I asked, my Glock still trained on him.

He gestured painfully toward the KICC as he eyed the TV. I looked too. The politicians from the various political parties were just arriving—they were expecting the prime minister and president in fifteen minutes. They were running late. Had they been on time, we would have gotten to Sahara, but it would have been too late, his plan would have been in play.

"Fucking African time," he said as he coughed again.

"Good thing the fuckers are not really trying for peace," Muddy said.

Sahara's chest heaved up and down rapidly. I knew something about him that he didn't know about himself; he had never been the one on the other side of power and he didn't know why he was afraid. Now he was all alone, staring into the eyes of the man whose wife he had murdered.

Seeing O standing over Sahara reminded me of seeing him standing in his apartment, Mary's blood still dripping from his hands, his eyes alive, burning, looking hungry. I felt chills. Sahara wasn't going to survive this encounter and he knew it—like Kimani at the Hilton.

"I have a request—man to man—soldier to soldier," he said to O. O smiled and signaled for him to continue.

"I am going to reach into my back pocket," he said.

"It's too late," O said, as Sahara produced a checkbook. Sahara asked me for a wet cloth and I went to the hotel bathroom and ran a towel under the faucet for him. He wiped his hands, now sweating profusely from fear and pain. He asked me for a pen and I gave him one from the hotel desk. He calmed himself down by taking a few shallow breaths in quick succession.

"Have to get the signature right," he said to us as he finished writing two checks.

I found two envelopes for him to address. He addressed one

of the checks to Amos's father and the other to his favorite football team, ten thousand and some loose change each.

"It's all I have," he said, as he read the look on my face.

It was true all along—that thing I had seen in them before they killed Mary. These guys weren't mercenaries; they weren't in it for money or glory—for the power, yes, but without personal gain. O's summation was right—Jesus on steroids.

"Amos ... All his people are dead," I told him. There was no forgiveness for him to buy.

"Yes, his father ... I heard the news. I thought the mother ..." he said, as he wrote another check. It was to the Peace Corps.

"Capture the king and kill the queen—what did you mean by that?" I asked.

He looked puzzled.

"Something Jamal overheard you say," I clarified. He smiled, as if the thought crossing his mind gave him some comfort.

"My nephew, he is learning to play chess. Some things are as they seem," he said. This was the guy who, just a few weeks ago, had set off the bomb in the Norfolk and killed O's wife? And tried to plunge a country already at war into a leaderless nightmare?

"Why?" I asked him, wanting to understand.

"You don't know what you are doing. I forgive you for that. If you could open your eyes for a minute, if you could see what I see, you would be helping me create new men and women, a new country, one that is not tied to the past. A society past the point of singularity, a people so far into a new and better future that there would be no going back," he answered, waiting for the inevitable question—*what the fuck are you talking about?*

"Point of singularity, that peaceful place where the laws of the past no longer affect the present. Call it a clean slate, a new beginning. Genesis … only there is no God. Only man. And only man can give man a new beginning—we are our own saviors. What is it that Obama likes to say? We are the ones we have been waiting for. That waiting, for Kenya, it can end today, if you just let me … if you look outside yourselves … this is your moment," he said, sounding like a general about to lead a charge.

"Do you hear yourself? Why you and not somebody else?" Muddy asked him. She had been quiet, observing all along—perhaps wondering what made Sahara possible.

"You see, that is the problem, if I had cancer, I would be asking why me and not someone else. Well, damn it, why not me? Why not me to bring in the new day? Why not you? Or O? Or Ishmael? Why not all of us?" Sahara asked, looking at each of us. "I am not a megalomaniac, or a savior. I just happen to have taken responsibility for the world I live in. My conscience is clean. Can you say the same?"

I could see it; if I had been younger and had just witnessed the brutality of apartheid South Africa, like Amos and the other young men, I would have joined him.

"I am going to kill you now. This is not for my wife—she would want me to forgive, not to kill in her name. But you have no place in this world. There is no place here for men like you," O said without emotion, raising his gun to Sahara's head.

I had seen O kill people without so much as second-guessing himself, and all the talking he was doing now—Sahara must have got to him somehow.

"Let the bomb go off, damn it, let the country be born again. Let the bomb go off, these people need …" Sahara pleaded.

O shot him once in the head.

I was surprised, even though I wasn't expecting any other outcome. It was just that I hadn't expected Sahara to die so easily.

O picked up the phone, pointed to the SEND button, and looked at Muddy and me. I felt a fresh rush of adrenaline.

"Blow them up—they are the fucking problem. We let them die and the country can piece itself together," I said, thinking back to the young men at the roadblock, dying and killing for the men meeting at the KICC, chauffeur-driven from their safe houses in Runda.

"O, we can do a lot of good all at once. More corruption, more famines because maize has been sold off, more and more of everything. Let's end it here. We let them die …" Muddy said.

"Over one thousand people dead because of these mother-fuckers …" O said, his thumb hovering over the SEND button.

It was like we had just entered a world where anything was possible, where instead of solving a murder here and there, we could impact forty-two million lives with the simple push of a button. We had gone insane and entered a universe of calculation and logic.

"Let them all die … this country will be better off without them. In Rwanda, I would have killed for an opportunity like this—we could have ended it all. Let them all die. Nobody wins by letting them live. Everyone loses—let's end it now, once and for all. Not for a new beginning, just a chance, a breathing space, a chance to grow something real," Muddy argued.

"What if we're wrong? What if all that could go wrong goes wrong?" I asked Muddy, wanting her to give me a compelling reason as to why the motherfuckers should die.

"Then one million people die, like in Rwanda," she answered without hesitation.

I looked at O.

"Let's do it," I said with a trembling voice as I went to stand by the window, where I could see the last of the VIPs being ushered in. "Look, we have Sahara, we can blame him, say we got here a second too late."

"Jesus, so this is what power feels like. So this is what it feels like to be a general," O said to himself, as if in a trance. Everything was moving slowly now—as if time itself was waiting for us to make a decision. He looked at Sahara, dead and still bleeding on the floor.

"We let these bad people die and he wins. Let's vote—and this time we count the votes right," O said, finally piercing through the madness that was consuming us.

Ultimately, power, like any force, simply existed. For Sahara, power was becoming a force of nature, rare, ruthless, and to the point. I wasn't like Sahara and the rest of IDESC—I didn't want to be a force of nature. I didn't want to impact forty-two million lives for better or worse all at once—I just wanted to see justice for Amos and Mary. All this other shit was way beyond me—I could live with that. IDESC was going to reconstitute itself. If Mpande was telling the truth, the organization existed in the memories of those involved. They would find another body, another organization. But for now, we had done our little bit.

"It's messy, very messy, but it's over—we walk away," I said.

"This, what we have here, this moment, we shall never have it ever again. You both know I am right," Muddy said as she sat down and put her AK on the floor.

"Muddy, it's two against one," O concluded, after looking at me to make sure Muddy hadn't changed my mind.

"You are a bunch of pussies," Muddy said, and she stood up and forcefully shoved me in the chest. She too had come to her senses—we had all broken out of the trance.

We didn't know what to do with the cell phone detonator, so we took it down in the elevator with us. We made it to the lobby as Jason rushed in. O gave him the phone. Jason hit SEND and covered his ears.

"Just wanted to make sure my boys did the job right," he said, laughing, pointing at our faces.

Sahara had claimed that there was only one bomb. But that map I had retrieved from the Range Rover, the map with all the landmarks ... I was sure that there were bombs in every location, designed specifically for each place. Jason and his team had their work cut out for them.

I gave the envelopes from Sahara to the hotel manager.

"Make sure you use DHL," I said to him.

The manager hesitated for a minute.

"Who is going to pay?" he asked.

O found his wallet and gave the man a hundred dollars from the money Jason had given us to use in the U.S.

O and I didn't ask each other why it mattered, because we knew, as much as we wouldn't admit it, that someday it could be him or me asking someone with a gun to our heads for a last favor.

"I need to seriously get high," O said as we walked out of the hotel. The Nairobi sun was treacherous, but it felt welcome.

"Maybe now you guys can actually do some good?" Muddy said, as she pointed to a mob gathering around a young man who they were accusing of being a thief.

We went over and broke up the crowd, and the young man ran off.

Then we sat on the pavement and laughed for a long time. I didn't know why I was laughing. Perhaps it was at the idea of letting a conference center full of thug politicians live to kill thousands tomorrow, only to save a pickpocket.

CHAPTER 19

AND THEN IT RAINED

O, Paul, Muddy, Jason, and I were sitting with Hassan in his office, talking about Mo's story, which had broken the day after Amos's father was killed by the remaining IDESC members. There had been immediate questions about her sources, how much prior information she had, since she seemed to know so much about the case. The thing about Mo, though, was that the more you came after her, the harder she pushed back. She was an investigative journalist on assignment—she would never reveal her sources. But she did have some questions of her own: Why were two respected detectives on the terrorist watch list? Why was the U.S. government bombing the hell out of Somalia when the perpetrators of the Norfolk bombing were Americans? Mo had thrown the closing salvo out to the public and it was best to let it lie there—anyone who claimed it would have to own it. And, sure enough, just as mysteriously as our names had appeared on the list, they were removed.

As we expected, nothing came out of her story: no grand juries, no evocative pronouncements from a barely formed Kenyan unity government about foreigners planting bombs, no major speeches by Obama on the importance of international law. It was all going to be as it had been before, a cat-and-bomb game between the U.S. and Al Qaeda. Thanks to us, the official story ran, an international Al Qaeda wing had been brought to justice.

There was nothing more to be done for now, except to go find some beer and good *nyama choma*.

I was the last at the door when Hassan seemed to remember something and called me back.

"By the way, not that it matters now, but a guy from Mexico— the teacher?—has been calling for you," he said. He gave me a number and pointed to his office desk phone.

"Teacher, Ishmael here," I said as soon as he picked up.

"Listen, my friend, things have changed here. My *jefe* is gone—a lot of cleaning, you know. And hidden under the carpet was something of interest: your friend Jason, he and Julio have been trafficking drugs into your country. Then those drugs are shipped all over Africa," he said.

"You're sure about this, teacher?" I asked, knowing there had to be some truth to it.

"This is for saving my life—and now I risk it to tell you this. If Julio finds out, I am dead. Yes, I am sure," he said.

This nightmare would never end. It would keep going and going, taking more lives until we all were dead.

"Ishmael, are you still there?" the teacher asked.

"Yes, just thinking … does this shit ever end?" I asked him.

"No, my friend, not as long as there are human beings. It is our nature to eat and produce shit. I wish you all the best. And pass my greetings to Muddy and O," he said, as we both laughed at the much-needed joke.

By the time I caught up with them, Muddy, O, Paul, and Jason had settled on going straight to Kariokor for the *nyama choma* and Tuskers. Paul and Jason would drive there together. And O, Muddy, and I would pick up Janet from the university for some "normal" time.

As soon as we got in the Land Rover, I told Muddy and O about my conversation with the teacher. It seemed both Jason and Paul were dirty, but for different reasons. Jason had every incentive to see IDESC out of the democracy business. The threat of anarchy in Nairobi would have turned Nairobi into a CIA and Interpol hub; it would have meant closely watched ports, airports, and borders—bad for business. Paul, on the other hand, wanted to put pressure on Al Qaeda and not on IDESC. But what would he gain from an IDESC-run Kenya, unless he too was a believer?

I made a call to Mpande.

"You owe me," I said.

"Yes."

"One question—and we're even. Jason or Paul?"

"Paul," he said. "Paul is one of us." He hung up.

We now knew what we knew, but did it really matter? What were we going to do? Kill the U.S. Embassy spokesperson because he fed information to Sahara and his army? And kill Jason because he wanted to stop terrorists from entering Kenya so that he could traffic drugs? Kill Paul for Mary's death? If we went after Jason and Paul, why stop there and not go after the surviving IDESC members like Mpande?

"We have to stop somewhere," I said to Muddy and O. They didn't respond. As we waited for Janet, I looked at all the young people walking about, laughing, others holding hands, and some too young to look so serious. Janet skipped to the Land Rover, hopped in, and we drove off to the market to wait for Jason and Paul.

At the market, I drifted off, staring into the Nairobi sun, wondering what my parents would think of being grandparents. Muddy had once told me that if you can still dream, then you are still alive. It was dreaming that had kept her alive in Rwanda.

I let myself soak in the sun, the stale smell of old malt beer that turned the naked ground muddy, the humming voices, the hot sticky touch of Muddy's hand on mine as she talked and laughed, Janet's college-girl giggles, and O's voice, sounding rambling and relaxed now.

"You know what they call cocaine in Nairobi?" O was asking us. "*Unga ya wazungu* ... the white people's maize flour," he said, laughing.

People were milling all around us and you could have sworn the whole of Nairobi had descended on the market.

The Tuskers, for an extra shilling, were extra chilled, and O ordered a round. He looked at the time and said he needed the bathroom and we made fun of him, saying that he was getting old and peed by the hour. He wandered off and I leaned back into the chair, watching Muddy and Janet talk animatedly about campus life and boys.

The sound of a single gunshot froze the whole market, bodies tense, waiting for a second report. Nothing pierced the silence and soon everyone resumed tearing into their *nyama choma* and Tuskers.

I asked Muddy, who by now was holding a gun under the flimsy plastic table, to stay with Janet, and I ran after the sound, thinking it was far from over—and that O had been shot. A few hundred feet from the bathroom, I saw Paul, bleeding, gun in hand, staggering away. I followed him carefully. He got into his Pajero and drove ten or so feet before releasing the clutch so that the engine stalled.

I yelled at him to step out of the vehicle. He put up his hands through the driver's window for a few seconds before they came flopping down. I edged closer to the car. He managed to open the door halfway and fell out into the dust and mud. He reached for my hand, I edged closer to him and took it. His body went into spasms and then he died.

Some young men in the crowd yelled at me and moved in closer. Their leader had what appeared to be a homemade pistol. They wanted the car. I holstered my Glock and turned to look at them, wanting to find relief, for it all to end.

"Are you crazy? He is the American, the one who works with O," someone warned them. They stepped back. I came to my senses.

"If you take the car, then he is yours," I said, pointing at Paul's body.

"Thank you, sir," their leader said as they bundled Paul into the car. If O had killed him, at least for now it would appear to be a random car-jacking gone bad. Paul was dirty enough that no one was going to dig deep to find whoever had killed him.

"Are you trying to get yourself killed?" the same person who had warned the mob about O asked me as he stepped out of the crowd. I noticed the golden MC Hammer pants.

"Did she agree to marry you?" MC Hammer asked.

I smiled and hugged him.

I walked back to our table to find everyone except Janet tipsier and higher. Jason had arrived and he was passing O a joint to light. O laughed and passed it on to me. For the first time in many years, I lit up. It had to be O who had killed Paul, but then again it could have been Jason.

"Paul? What was the point?" I asked O. He didn't answer or show any surprise. He pointed to the *nyama choma* guy standing at our table with a kettle of warm water and soap. We each washed our hands. No one asked me why my hands were bloody.

"And you, Jason? Did you kill Paul?" I asked him. Janet, Muddy, and O continued on talking and drying their hands.

"Paul? Why? No," he said casually, in a tone that suggested his denial was for protocol purposes only.

"We know all about you and Julio," I said. He looked serious for a moment.

"I know you do. Yet, here we are having brewskylunch," he said, laughing.

"What the fuck, motherfuckers—we police!" O said suddenly, slapping his knee and passing me the joint.

"Shiznit, motherfuckers—we CIA," Jason said, mimicking O.

It was the funniest thing I had heard in a long time, and in spite of myself, I broke into high laughter that, in its wake, left me with some clarity. I doubted. I no longer believed that we were serving justice, because the price was justice itself. I had nowhere to go.

A guy was walking by with a *nyatiti*. Muddy waved him over and asked him to play something. She stood up on the wobbly table and balanced herself. The people around us stopped tearing into their meat to look at the beautiful tall woman. As the *nyatiti* picked up speed, the market became quieter and the outer rings strained to hear the music.

A man selling conga drums laid his load by her feet, pulled one from his pile of wares, and joined both of them. Muddy was syncopating her cadence so that the words and her voice became an instrument—so that it was no longer her words that mattered but her voice. It went on like that, merchant after merchant of different instruments coming to join in until we had a fucking orchestra of voices and African instruments. And in the middle of them, Muddy, arms raised, palms curled inward, her voice rising up and down like a bird gliding over a stormy ocean.

I thought I had heard it all—but not the sound of a voice, a tongue, the sound of Muddy's voice wrapped around the four-stringed *nyatiti* that had now taken the lead, improvising above the rest of the instruments. The music, the single notes held together by Muddy's voice were like a hand guiding me through a nightmare. I wanted to pray.

I listened closely—there was a clash of instruments and voices. But there was also some tense harmony in there—like a dinner with quarreling lovers. There was a tug of war but the more each of them pulled, the more it brought them closer. They were fighting but not to destroy each other, they were fighting to build—their fighting, their calling out to each other, their competing, it was all to build something they felt we could all use. Something they were offering, for us to take, or leave behind. And once we took it with us, this rage that was love, this violence that claimed to build, what was to become of it? Would it not justify a machete or a Glock? But the musicians were building.

I, on the other hand, did not build. Mary had died and to bury her we had killed many more, and to get Sahara for killing Amos, we had killed many more again. It struck me—I was part of the problem. I was just several rungs above the Saharas of this world. So were O and my wife-to-be, Muddy.

I listened closely to the voices, the drums, and the strings. The refrain was asking a simple question, over and over again.

Why?

ACKNOWLEDGMENTS

A writer needs a community of readers and critics. I have been lucky to have two such communities. A family full of readers and writers who love wielding the red pen—Ngugi, Njeri, Tee, Kimunya, Nducu, Ngina, Wanjiku, Njoki, Bjorn, Mumbi, and Thiong'o. Thanks to you, I have concluded coming from a family of writers is, for better or worse, like being in a creative writing workshop for life. And a community of the diverse bloggers (Eve from Striped Armchair and Robert Carraher from the Dirty Lowdown immediately come to mind) who read, commented, and lovingly savaged *Nairobi Heat*. I hope you will find *Black Star Nairobi* equally compelling but without some of the issues you took umbrage with (or at the very least a new set). You are my most honest readers.

Also thanks to my publishers, Dennis Johnson and Valerie Merians at Melville House, for their belief in the continuing adventures of Ishmael, O, and Muddy and to my editor, Sal Robinson, for edits that turned out to be a conversation about the novel.

Finally, thanks to my agents, Gloria Loomis and Julia Masnik over at Loomis and Watkins agency, for fending for me as well as giving me useful feedback on the novel.

MUKOMA WA NGUGI is the author of *Nairobi Heat*, which introduces the detectives Ishmael and O. His fiction has been short-listed for the 2009 Caine Prize and the 2010 Penguin Prize for African Writing. His columns have appeared in *The Guardian*, *International Herald Tribune*, and the *Los Angeles Times*, and he has been a guest on *Democracy Now*, *Al Jazeera*, and the BBC World Service. His essays and poetry have been included in a number of anthologies, as well as in his own poetry collection, *Hurling Words at Consciousness*. Ngugi was born in 1971 in Evanston, Illinois, the son of the world-renowned African writer Ngugi wa Thiong'o, and grew up in Kenya before returning to the United States for his undergraduate and graduate education. He is currently a professor of English at Cornell University.

READ THE FIRST BOOK IN THE SERIES

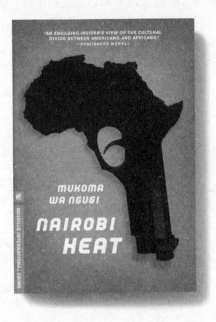

In Madison, Wisconsin, when a body is found on the doorstep of an African peace activist who saved hundreds of people from the Rwandan genocide, local cop Ishmael Fofona is summoned to investigate. But then he gets a mysterious phone call: "If you want the truth, you must go to its source. The truth is in the past. Come to Nairobi." It's the beginning of a journey that will change Ishmael's life forever, to a place still reeling from the aftereffects of the genocide around its borders, where big-oil money rules, where the cops shoot first and ask questions later—a place, in short, where knowing the truth about history can get you killed.

978-1-935554-64-6 $14.95 U.S./$16.95 CAN.

Ⓜ MELVILLE INTERNATIONAL CRIME